Colors of Magic

NOVELS BY **LIZ SAUCO**
available from Dark Waters Publishing:

BLADES OF THE GODDESS
LOST BLADES
BROKEN BLADES
BLADES REFORGED

COLORS OF MAGIC

Colors of Magic

A Blades of the Goddess Anthology

Liz Sauco

Dark Waters Publishing

Colors of Magic
Hardcover ISBN: 978-1-960723-10-9
Paperback ISBN: 978-1-960723-09-3
E-book ISBN: 978-1-960723-08-6
Audiobook ISBN: 978-1-960723-11-6

Published by Dark Waters Publishing
5600 Post Rd
Suite 114-PMB#307
East Greenwich RI 02818

First edition: May 2024
10 9 8 7 6 5 4 3 2 1

Cover design by Liz Sauco

lizsauco.com

To Lydia.
And coffee.

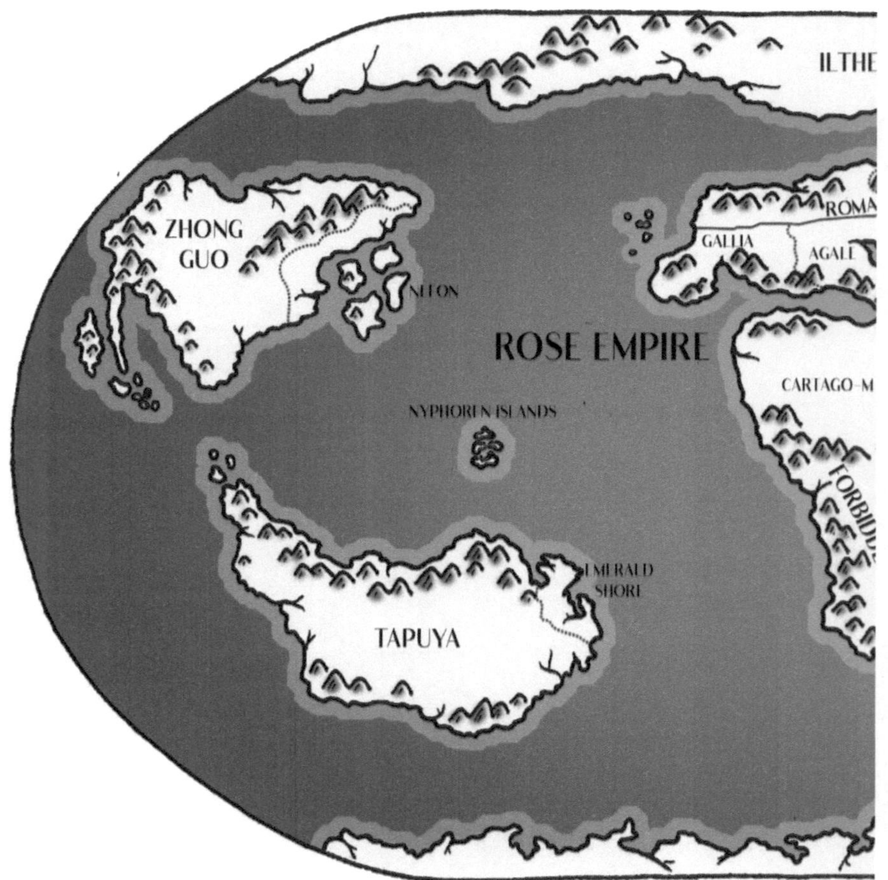

WORLD MAP
GAIA
COUNTRIES - 2026 AG
ILTHE
ROMA
GALLIA
AGALE
ZHONG
GUO
NEON
ROSE EMPIRE
CARTAGO-M
NYPHOREN ISLANDS
FORBIDD
EMERALD
SHORE
TAPUYA

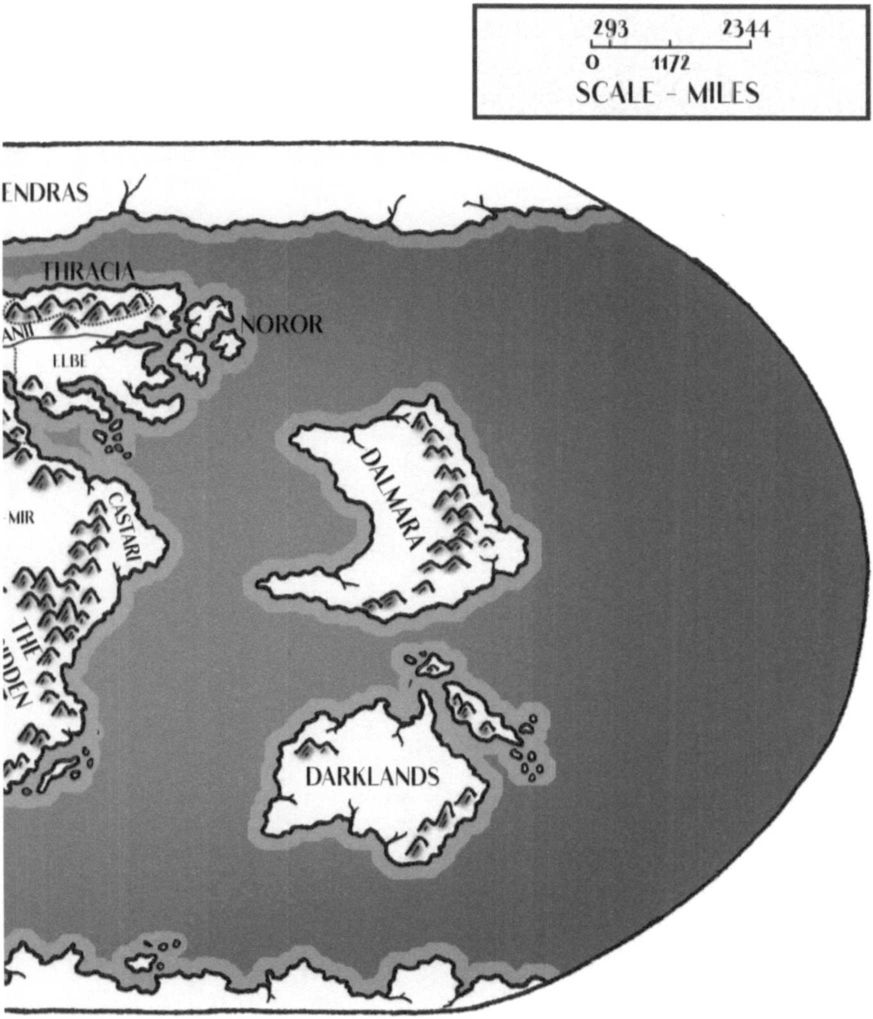

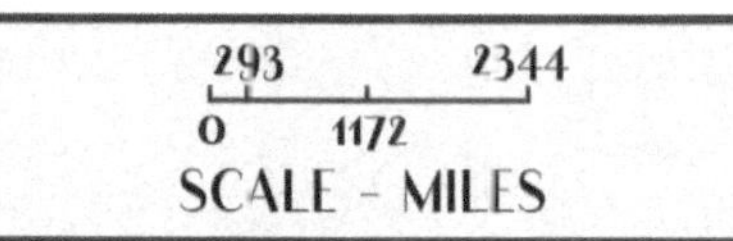

293
2344
O
1172
SCALE - MILES

ENDRAS
THRACIA
NIT
NOROR
ELBE
DALMARA
MIR
CASTARI
THE
DEN
DARKLANDS

History of Gaia: Colors of Magic
9 DY
Black
2004 AG
Blue
1023 AG
Yellow
2024 AG
• Lavender
• Silver
570 years
1513 years
698 years
2001 years
Dark Years
Age of Monsters
Age of Romanus
Era of War
Age of the Gods
6812 YEARS OF HISTORY
1013 AG
Scarlet
2025 AG
White
0
Cataclysm
Violet
1689-1717 AG
Green

Violet

The Beginning of the End

As soon as they succeeded, Alexia knew they'd failed.

It stared at them curiously from within its new prison, form flickering rapidly as though it couldn't decide what kind of person it wanted to be, but its eyes... those violet eyes remained the same. Oh, the entity was here all right, and it didn't seem to be able to leave if the flicks of energy exploring the new space were any indication, but...

"Something's not right," she heard herself say over the cheers of some of her more exuberant colleagues.

There was a pause in the celebration, deference afforded her based on her status. "Everything looks good here. All blue," the tech at the monitor panel reported. "The electromagnetism is holding."

"What is it doing, exactly?" The general assigned to the project strode forward to tap on the glass, narrowing his eyes as the energy tapped back. "Looking for weaknesses? A way out?"

"That's likely," one of the senior scientists agreed. "Chances are it's never been confined this way."

"But the tests all show that the magnetism should hold it," another scientist stated.

The general frowned. "'Should'?"

Alexia remained silent, watching those violet eyes as they studied the humans around it, not even glancing at the large window showing the perfect globe of the Earth far below. Perfect, save for the Rot ravaging her and her people. Even animals, plants... nothing was safe from it. This was their best chance of, if not fighting it directly, then buying more time to find a solution.

"This has never been attempted before," the first scientist pointed out. "Or perhaps it has, if some of the old mythology is to be believed, but certainly not to this level of success. It would have freed itself by now, if it could."

"And we'd all be dead," a tech near Alexia muttered under his breath.

She chose to ignore him. Some part of her just knew that this hadn't worked. But if that were the case, why was it still here? She brushed her long black braid over her shoulder, trying to ignore the feeling twisting in her stomach. "You are sure all of the aligned energy was collected? There isn't any being picked up by the sensors anywhere around either the planet or relevant bodies?" she asked instead.

The man's eyes flickered over the projections, hands flicking from panel to panel as he searched the reports. "All the aligned energy is here. No readings of it anywhere else."

"Then we've succeeded," the general murmured. Despite the positive sentiment, his brow was furrowed. "We've... trapped the 'god' of death."

"We've trapped the metaphysical energy associated with the ending of life," Alexia corrected absently, ignoring his use of "we." As though the military had actually done anything other than babysit the project. They hadn't even supplied any funding. "Though, the theory is entities like this could have posed as such to our ancestors." Which explained why it appeared to be mimicking human form, even if it couldn't decide on a specific one. Even as Alexia watched, first a red-haired Irish woman, followed by a small blond boy, then a grizzled old man of some Asian descent housed those unnatural eyes.

Those violet eyes that turned in her direction.

The general shook his head. "Whatever you want to call it. So then, no one can die?"

Alexia's stomach twisted again, though her mind told her she should be celebrating. "I'm not sure how they could, with the relevant energy trapped." Detecting the energy present at the moment of death had been a huge breakthrough in their understanding of it. No matter the cause – sickness, injury, old age – this energy gathered at that final moment, named "Omega energy" by her team, and this massive spike had been proven to be what actually ended life at the cellular level. They'd already had some success with mice; shielding them from the buildup of Omega energy allowed them to survive violent trauma that otherwise would have killed them instantly.

The general nodded.

Alexia was not the only one to scream as he pulled his gun and shot the tech watching the monitors.

"Looks like there's a flaw somewhere, though I'll admit that whatever you've got in there looks promising," he said dispassionately as he toed the tech's lifeless body, blood pooling on the floor, matting the tech's blond hair. "Keep me updated on your progress. I'll send in some of the boys to clean this up." He turned and left the room.

Alexia's hands were plastered in front of her mouth as she fought through the shock and nausea, her heart hammering like a jackrabbit's. Her mind raced without her permission. The tech had been... he'd just been... where had they gone wrong? He shouldn't be dead, even with a bullet in the head. The energy buildup could not have occurred, as it was contained in the electromagnetic sphere, sealed with mercury and iron. Injured, yes; dead, no. Cold iron, there were legends that said cold iron was necessary, and there were reasons for legends, truth hidden in stories, but what was colder than the dead of space? How could Tr– how could the tech be dead?

She sharply pushed back against the building rage and fear. The general had no right. There was a process to follow. There were other ways to test the theory.

Someone was vomiting into a trash bin. Several members of her team were crying. Where had they gone wrong? She glanced towards the containment field again.

Those violet eyes were filled with pity as they met her own dark ones, the entity's form finally settling into that of a pale man with short black hair, long bangs swept to the side, though the clothing continued to change. Very, very slightly, it shook its head.

Yes, she reflected bitterly. They certainly had failed.

The Middle of the End

Alexia gazed through space at the planet below. By this point it was very clear the tech's death had not been a fluke. People were still dying. The planet itself was still dying.

She caught a glimpse of herself in the ghostly reflection offered by the glass. Bags hung under dark eyes, lines beyond her years crossed her face. Her black hair was streaked with white, a result of the stress and the pressure of the last four years. She looked older than thirty-six. Some thought she was too young, had gotten the job because of who her father was, but they didn't realize she was all too aware of the burden that had been placed on her. This job wasn't a reward; it was a desperate attempt to save life.

"Why didn't it work?" she whispered to the empty room. She should have been asleep like the others, but how could she? She'd been over the data a thousand times since... since, but nothing made sense. It should have worked. There had been no buildup of Omega energy, and still...

She wrenched her mind away from it. She didn't have time to dwell on it. They had larger problems.

"Why would it?"

Alexia's mind stuttered to a halt. She turned to look at the electromagnetic prison and the entity contained within. It had decided on black slacks and a turtleneck sweater. "You speak English?" she demanded. They had considered the possibility it would try to communicate, but she hadn't thought it would know a modern language. Religion had died out a long time ago. Who would it have communicated with? What use did the metaphysical even have for language like theirs?

Those unnatural eyes were studying her closely. "Yes. What is it you think I am?"

"I don't think you're a god, if that's what you are getting at," she snapped, eyes narrowing. Was this partly how it had convinced ancient humans to worship it? "Humanity cast off its belief in gods long ago."

It blinked at her. "'God' is a term given to me and my siblings by others of your kind. I need not claim it. What would you call me?"

She stared at it, thrown by the complete lack of argument. She rallied, pulling off the tie of her braid and combing her fingers through her hair, the familiar motion steadying her. "You are just... sapient energy. Metaphysical, able to manipulate yourself to have a physical form."

"As you wish," it stated placidly.

That made her pause. "Don't you have a term for yourself, then?"

It shrugged. "I am. I do not think it is so complicated."

She shook her head. Classifying things was practically in her blood. She was a scientist. Omega energy it was. "Everything is complicated." She returned her gaze to the planet. "Otherwise, it would have worked."

This time, the entity said nothing.

It never spoke when there were others around, only ever watching, quiet.

Silent as the grave.

But late at night, when the rest of the station powered down and its crew slept while Alexia continued to try to find the solution...

It almost couldn't *stop*.

"What about... your favorite color?" it asked, yet another inane question she was certain was meant to prevent her from succeeding. It still wore the face of the dark-haired man, violet eyes glued to Alexia.

She ignored this question as well, marking a passage for cross reference with report 9.21.b. If she couldn't sleep, she might as well try to make some progress.

She fought back a sigh. It was like they were going in circles. Everything said that all of the Omega energy was trapped, yet people continued to die. Interestingly, there was no longer a gathering of Omega energy at the moment of death, but there was something... else. Had the Omega energy been hiding it? How?

Why did she feel so unsettled now whenever something died? Like nature itself was rebelling against it?

(If she was being honest, she'd felt that unease for a long time before they'd trapped the entity. Anytime she'd been near something affected by the Rot.)

The entity was humming now, an old song she remembered her parents listening to when she was little. Her lips pressed together. Her father was one of the many dying, though his position gave him access to the best care available. Her mother had been among the first to succumb. "The best care available" hadn't saved her.

Alexia tuned it out.

"Did you really hope to stop death from occurring by imprisoning me?" it asked her another night. Those violet eyes briefly flickered to the planet below before returning to her. "That which brings about this end... it is not me. I cannot stop it, either. I would have to give up... something I do not have."

"It should have worked," she snapped, still bitter over the failure. They had run all the tests over and over, but the outcome never changed.

She preferred the bitterness to the grief.

It shook its head, but the eyes were kind. "It is not within the power of humanity to stop such a primal thing, even if your understanding of the world has grown far past what it once was. Chaining me here does nothing. It imprisons me, but the 'energy' as you call it will not be confined by such things."

She sent it a sharp look before returning her attention to the reports. "You just want me to free you."

"No," came the gentle answer. "I will remain here, until the end."

She considered that for a moment before something clicked. She thought briefly to all the people on the surface dying of whatever it was that rotted them from the inside out, of the planet itself theorized to meet the same fate in less than five years if the nations didn't descend into war and wipe everything out before that point. "It affects you, too. Or it can." She eyed it warily, but it didn't show any of the symptoms of the Rot. Her heart was sinking. If even these entities could not stop the Rot, then what could? They'd put all their hopes in this project. Without it, they were back to square one. They didn't have time to be at square one!

"Oh, yes," it agreed. "It hasn't begun to affect me yet, but I can only assume it will begin in due time at its current acceleration. As for my siblings... well." It glanced towards the planet again and winced. "I suppose it won't matter soon, anyway. Maybe it should all end, and put us out of our misery." Its tone was thoughtful.

She blanched. "The other entities like you... they already...?"

It hummed. "Not all of them, not yet. Some of us are more distant by nature." It looked back at her. "It is the nature of things to end, even us."

"There's no way forward? No way at all?" She sounded desperate even to herself.

It shrugged. "I prefer to let my older sibling be the one to look forward to the future... I suppose I could do it too, it is within my composition, but that one doesn't need any more reasons to hate me."

"No," she declared. "It won't end this way. I won't let it."

It watched her, still and silent once again. She refused to acknowledge the pity in those violet eyes.

Two of her team had begun to show signs of the Rot and had to be sent back to the planet. If it was able to reach them up here, on a space station, then time was running out.

Her team continued to study the entity and the phenomenon surrounding the Omega energy. They were now speculating that the new energy was somehow related to the Omega energy, and had named it Omega type B. It functioned almost exactly the same as Omega energy, but on a much weaker scale. Another entity, perhaps?

The other researchers didn't like the thing they had trapped. Most reported feeling chills down their spine if it looked at them too long, unease spiraling into anxiety. Alexia wasn't quite sure why; the entity didn't seem to hold a grudge or any sort of malice towards them, and never acted aggressively or even annoyed. In fact, it was taking its imprisonment almost too much in stride for her liking. Like it was on a vacation, instead of trapped.

A few times, they tried to talk to it. Members of her team found it impossible to get the words out, breaking into a cold sweat after just a few minutes of trying, before fear forced them to flee. Only Alexia could approach it without negative side effects, but it continued to refuse to speak while others were in the room.

It was all some sort of puzzle, and Alexia was struggling to make the pieces fit.

She didn't have time to make the pieces fit. She needed to focus on the Rot.

Yet despite herself, she continued to visit it late at night.

"They sense what is coming for them," it informed her when she asked about its effect on the others. "Humans don't like to listen to their instincts, but being near my presence lets their hearts know the end is near, even if their minds will not acknowledge it. My siblings fear it, too."

She considered that. "Omega energy spikes at the moment of death. Are you saying you put the fear of death into my researchers just by existing?"

It shrugged. "Not quite, but close."

She shook her head at the ridiculousness of it. They were as safe as could be up here, and the entity was trapped with no way to harm them. "Then why wouldn't I be affected?"

It pursed its lips. "There are a few possibilities."

She shook her head. While it liked to talk, it also liked being vague. Though, on that note... "Why won't you talk to any of the other researchers?"

The entity snorted. "If simply standing within a few feet of me disturbs them so, what do you think the effect of my voice would be?"

Alexia didn't have an answer.

Omega type B was proving much harder to pin down than Omega energy. Alexia ran her hands through her long black hair as she tried to make sense of the day's reports.

"There are too many of them," the entity offered gently. "Even if you tried to trap them as you trapped me, you could never hold them all."

"So it is other beings like you," she hummed. Many smaller entities then, compared to the one they already had trapped.

But it shook its dark head. "Like me, but not. I created them once long ago to help me. Fractures of a whole, but they do what must be done when I cannot."

"If they are like you, then they can be trapped," she declared, pleased to have a direction. "So there was no way to detect them before we contained you, because they weren't doing anything. You built a failsafe. Impressive."

Those violet eyes were sad. "No, that's not why I made them. You misunderstand what they– ah, I suppose it doesn't matter. You may try to trap them if you wish. What else to do, but find ways to occupy our time so close to the end?"

That, more than anything else it had said so far, disturbed her in a way she couldn't quite pinpoint.

Another tech had been sent back to the planet's surface. Alexia felt her throat close when she thought about it, so she pushed it from her mind. She needed to focus on finding a solution. She'd always been good at compartmentalizing. Some people found it off-putting, but it made her good at her job.

The entity had been more correct than she wanted to admit. Theoretically, it should have been easier to contain the Omega type B entities after having successfully done so to the parent entity, but so far they hadn't managed to trap even one. Why? What was the difference? The two energies had proven to be remarkably similar. Maybe it was a matter of scale?

She frowned, turning to look at it. It was watching her, as always. "Why do you look like that?" she asked abruptly.

Its head tilted to the side. "What do you mean?"

"When you first came here you kept changing between all manner of appearances. Why did you choose that form?"

It blinked at her, as though perplexed by the question. "It's what you think of, what you expected."

"What do you mean?" It was her turn to be confused. "I had no idea what you would look like."

"You didn't know what the creature you were capturing would look like, no," it agreed. "But most people have at least a hazy concept of what a... um... 'god of death' would look like, if you'll excuse the verbiage. This was yours."

"How would you know that?" she asked, disturbed even as she considered the point. Was this what she had thought of when she pictured a "god of death"? A regular guy in a turtleneck sweater? Where was the hood, the scythe? The creepy atmosphere?

"You think of that, too." Its voice was wry. "But have there not been many 'gods of death' you have learned about, through all sorts of mythologies? Very few people believe the Halloween monster is what will come for them. As for how I know – I just do. I always know." It shrugged.

She took a step back. Though the explanation made sense, she didn't like that it appeared to somehow be reading her thoughts.

The entity just stared at her placidly.

Alexia pulled herself together. This creature, and others like it, had posed as gods to a young human race. It was sapient metaphysical energy. It made sense that they were able to do things humans didn't understand. That was how they had convinced the humans they were gods in the first place.

She knew better.

Still, perhaps... "Do you have a name, then? One you prefer out of the hundreds you've given to humans in the past?"

The handsome face it wore smiled. "My siblings and I have no need for such address. All of my names have been given to me by your kind. You may choose one that strikes your fancy, or give me a new one entirely if that is what you would like."

She turned to the large window and the dying planet far below. She'd always been fond of the ancient Greek stories.

"Hades."

She paused before entering the central research room, giving herself another moment to push the news she'd gotten that morning and the grief it caused into a little box at the back of her mind. It was harder than she would have liked. She wasn't sure why; she *had* known this was coming.

It still ached, in her heart and in her throat, and behind her eyes.

Willing the tears away and steeling herself for a long, productive day at work, she strode through the doors as they slid open.

"I'm sorry."

They were the first words she had ever heard it utter around other people. She could see her colleagues flinch back from the containment unit as though struck.

Alexia turned around and walked back out. She didn't bother to ask how it knew.

It had been three months since they had contained the Omega energy, but Alexia felt they were even further from a solution than before.

Still, people died. Still, the Omega type B refused to be contained. Still, sections of the planet down below were being wiped out by Rot. Even if they could stop it now, projections were showing that the ecosystems might not be able to recover. Their world was changing, and not for the better.

The general had been returned to the surface. There was a feeling of vindictive relief, but it was a hollow, distant thing.

She could feel their chances of success slipping away, and no matter what she did she couldn't stop it.

They had accomplished so much as a species. Was this really how it would end?

Hades watched her quietly. There was nothing but understanding in those violet eyes.

The Dawn of the Beginning

Her staff was decimated. Of all the groups trying to find a solution, hers had been one of the last as avenue after avenue closed. In the end, she made the decision to send those that remained back to the surface to be with their loved ones. It wasn't as though there was a military presence on the space station to stop her anymore. The Rot didn't discriminate.

She alone stayed. It wasn't as though she had anyone left to go back to.

Alexia walked through the empty corridors. All that was left was a bone-deep feeling of exhaustion and the bitter taste of defeat. And the entity. Hades.

"Why did you stay?" it asked in lieu of a greeting.

She walked past it to stand in front of the large windows, gazing at the doomed planet below. She could see the Rot staining sections of it even from up here. Even though there was no longer a path to survival, some part of her still hoped for a miracle. And she'd spent long hours going over everything it had said. One thing stood out.

Her whole life, given to science. And in the end it was mythology she turned to.

She swallowed past the lump in her throat. "You told me once that in order to stop this, you would have to give up something you don't have. What did you mean?" She looked at its reflection in the glass.

Hades was silent for some time, eyes never leaving hers through the hazy reflection. Finally, it sighed. "You won't like it."

"Tell me anyway."

"My kind draw power from the belief of yours. As you have pointed out on multiple occasions, that belief in us as individuals has waned considerably in recent centuries, leaving us... weakened. The relationship between us and you is supposed to be symbiotic. Technically, all of us gave part of ourselves to–"

"What would you have to give up?" she interrupted, not interested in a tangent.

Hades sighed again. "I would need a living vessel to work through, one that shares a significant amount of my own composition, able to resonate with me. That vessel would need to be willing, since I would need to... reabsorb that which is me from within them, and that would cause the vessel to cease existing. This thing that comes for us all... it is not of this world. It is sin. Abomination. And it has been rampant for too long; drastic measures need to be taken."

Alexia turned around to stare at it. "Are you telling me you need a *sacrifice*?"

It looked thoughtful for a moment, then shrugged with a bit of a nod.

She was flabbergasted. "Billions have already died. Is that not enough? Not a single one meets the necessary qualifications?"

"None that have died, no." For the first time, its eyes slid away from hers.

Alexia felt a chill run down her spine. She felt like she was on the cusp of understanding something important, something that would turn the puzzle into a picture.

"I would never ask it of you," it rushed to reassure her. "I am glad to spend this last bit of time at the end with you. I didn't think it was possible for one such as you to exist at all, until I heard your Call. As many millennia as I have existed, and even still – something new, right at the end."

"My call?" She felt like she was grasping at straws.

Her. It needed her.

"Your desire, your need to trap me, yes."

She stared at it. "And you came? Knowing that?" It had *known* it would be caught? No wonder they'd had no success with Omega type B.

"Of course." As though it were the most natural thing in the world.

It had chosen a form to her specifications.

It was her. Something about her called to the entity. "I don't understand."

It winced slightly. "Your ancestors would have called you a priest, or perhaps an avatar. I know you don't care for that terminology, but maybe the context helps?"

She felt a hysterical laugh bubble up. "You've had hundreds of thousands of priests!"

But Hades shook its head. "Not real ones. None whose being spoke to mine, and who mine spoke to in turn. There is resonance between us, one my siblings have spoken to me of before, but it has been so long since the beginning... I did not think I would ever experience it. I am glad to have met you, Alexia."

"And you need to sacrifice a priest," she murmured faintly.

"No," it disagreed. "You are the only one I've ever had. The kind of sacrifice that is needed... it is not death. I would have to use you, recreate you into something else. No part of you, what makes you Alexia, would remain. I will not do it. Best to stay here with me, and in the end, there will be Silence."

"Stay here? With you?"

"Would that be so bad? It will come for us, too, eventually. I desire nothing more than to await the end with you."

How was she supposed to respond to that? To any of it? She turned back to the window and its view of the dying world beneath them to give herself a moment.

Compartmentalize. Put things in boxes, shove the unimportant ones away. Keep only the relevant info. If nothing else, Hades was correct – most of this information would be irrelevant soon anyway.

She took a deep breath, making sure to shove the fear as far away as she could, allowing the exhaustion to take over. After years of searching, she finally had the information she required. There was still a way forward.

What was one life in exchange for billions?

Perhaps Hades was more correct than it thought.

Let it all end – but just for her.

"If you've never had a priest before, then maybe... maybe that's the point. I'm here now because you needed something to give up," she heard herself say.

It frowned. "That would indicate the presence of some sort of higher architect, would it not? I thought you were wholly against the concept."

That was a moot point in her opinion. "If we did this, you could save them?" She lifted a hand to rest it against the glass. "End the threat of the Rot?"

Hades was silent for a long time. "There is no true end to Abomination, but this expression of it I could put a stop to, yes." It did not sound happy.

Too bad. "What about the damage it's caused? To the planet itself?"

"I do not want to do this."

Neither did she, but this was the only possible solution to have presented itself. She'd gone too far, lost too much to back down now. "Answer the question."

It heaved a sigh. "Abomination has already begun to infect my siblings, but it is in our nature to rebound. The planet would be able to heal in time, though it would not be the same. In order to wipe out the Rot, I would have to destroy... much."

Her heart sank. "Would there be anyone left?"

"My siblings would do their best to protect those they could." The words sounded like they were being dragged out unwillingly. "Those humans and other life forms may or may not be the same, when all is said and done."

"But they would be alive? Free of Rot?" Hope rose again.

Grudgingly, it nodded.

She paused as a thought struck her. "How do I know you are telling the truth?"

"I can't lie," it admitted. "If I could, I would be doing so to convince you not to offer yourself thusly."

There were literally no other options, so it didn't matter. She pushed the thought away. The more she delayed, the more people died. "How do we go about this then?" she asked, steeling her nerves and trying not to think too much about what she was offering. Her mind refused to cooperate. What would it mean to not exist anymore?

"Why?" it asked, sounding petulant.

"Because." Two could play at that game. She needed it to agree. This needed to end.

"I'd rather have you for this short time, than to continue on throughout the centuries without you."

That was when she realized – Hades was *lonely*. She hadn't thought energy could feel lonely. "What about your siblings?"

"They are not the same." Its voice was sad. "And I am not often welcome."

"So you will let them die?" she asked. "Them, and every other living thing on that planet?"

It made a pained sound.

"You've already said that the Rot will find us here anyway," she continued, trying to be gentle. She wasn't sure she was succeeding. "You will lose me either way."

"I'll lose you faster, if I do this," it snapped bitterly. "And I won't have to return to being alone if I meet my end with you."

"What if– what if there are supposed to be others?" she suggested, inspired by the thought. "What if by allowing all this to end, you miss out on meeting other... other true priests." She stumbled a bit over the words.

It eyed her warily. "I'm not quite sure you realize just how rare you are." It ran a hand through the short black hair, looking frazzled.

"Where there has been one, there is always a chance for more," she pointed out. "And maybe this world has only ever produced me, but you said life might not be the same. The conditions will have been changed. Maybe the world you create out of the wreckage of this one will be better suited to those you are looking for."

"Rebirth." It sounded tired. "Always, always I am bound to that which I am. There is no other fate for me, until the final Silence." There was anguish in those violet eyes. "You are committed to this path? There is no way to sway you?"

She laughed, though it lacked amusement. "I've dedicated the last four years of my life to solving this problem. If this solves it, then I've succeeded." She smiled wryly. "They'll never know it, will they?" She thought about that. "Maybe they shouldn't. Maybe... maybe it's better if the slate is wiped clean, and they can start fresh. No memory of the Rot."

For the first time since it had been captured, Hades' form began to shift. "I will know," it whispered softly as the body took on a feminine shape and the hair became longer. "And I will remember, always."

Alexia was looking at a near-perfect mirror of herself. The hair was longer and completely black, the face lacked the lines of exhaustion that had been etched into it, and those eyes were still the same unnatural violet, but it was her. As she might have been in a world not dominated by Rot.

"I will wear this form. When they look at me, they will see the face of their savior, even if they don't remember what they needed saving from."

"I thought you changed to reflect what people expect?" she asked.

"I will always change to reflect the species of those I collect," Hades admitted. "But the form will, at its core, be you."

An immortality of its own, she supposed. "Change the hair to white," she suggested, eyeing the white streaks in her own hair. "Let something remain of everything I went through."

Hades nodded, and the hair lightened. Lines of violet energy bloomed into existence along the electromagnetic field keeping the entity contained and gently began to dismantle it piece by piece.

"But... that's not how electromagnetic fields work!" Alexia exclaimed, watching with a sort of horrified fascination, struggling to understand what she was seeing.

Hades shrugged. "I've never really understood them. That does not affect me. I've been able to leave at any time, you see," it tried to reassure her. "It was smart to use the magnetic field – we've always had trouble with those; they seem to work on their own set of rules and weird things sometimes happen when we try to interact – but for something as old as me, it is not insurmountable." It stepped forward as the last few pieces were set on the ground. "You are believing in me very strongly right now, and it helps."

The remains of the container fizzled out and died.

Alexia reminded herself that if it wished to break the rules of reality, that was its own business, as she would not be part of it for much longer. Still, part of her longed to figure out how that had been achieved. Was there a way to duplicate it? What were the possible applications?

She turned back to the planet below, Rot visible on the surface. Hades came forward to stand next to her. Together, they stood in the silence of space for just a few moments.

Alexia found herself reaching out for the entity's hand, desiring just one last bit of physical contact. As much as she knew this was the only way, she was still scared. She'd never liked the unknown. She glanced at Hades' reflection in the glass and was surprised to see tears streaming down the mirror of her own face.

The hand squeezed her own, and Alexia found herself being pulled into the entity's embrace, and then all she could see were those violet eyes and everything shifted strangely around her, and then she was falling, and everything was a violet haze—

And then there was one woman standing alone, a black polearm with a wicked blade in her hands, sobbing even as she raised it up.

And the glaive swung down—

And everything ended.

And something new began.

Black

J ak truly gave up when he saw three people just dissolve into nothing right in front of his eyes. Three people who had been his friends, whom he'd known for years.

Three people who had been dying anyway, ravaged by the Rot.

Jak had known he would be next. The Rot struck without rhyme or reason, and while he'd been lucky, he doubted living with any number of others who had it was a good way to continue avoiding it. But... what was the point? The very planet itself was affected. Humanity's time was up. Prolonging the experience wasn't all that appealing, if he was being honest. So he'd stayed, tried to help. Tried to do some good with whatever time he had.

But now they were just... gone. Not even dust was left.

Wasn't there a passage in the Bible about something like that? Called the Rapture, or something? There'd been a book about it a long time ago. He'd never read it. That or the Bible. Jak wasn't a religious guy, but he was struggling to come up with any other sort of explanation.

So he stared at where they'd been a moment longer, then firmly put their memories away next to those of his wife and daughter.

Billions of dead across the globe; his dead weren't any more special than the rest. He'd be with them all soon; no point in dwelling on it. Then he went to get some of the whiskey stashed in the basement.

It was the end of the world anyway.

Perfect time to drink.

He drank for Lian, who'd been one of the funniest people he'd ever known, always ready with a quip at anything or anyone's expense. She'd still had hope that the Rot could be cured, and she tried to keep their spirits up.

He drank for Berke, always quiet and understanding. He'd tried the hardest to follow the various government and commercial plans to try to do something about the Rot, putting them in terms everyone else could understand.

He drank for Kris, whose anger at the situation never found a target it could aim at. Jak couldn't blame him; his family had been among the first victims. He hadn't always been like that though, a family man who did everything for his two kids.

He drank for Margaret, who'd left him years back after Rachel's death even though he'd tried to convince her to stay. He'd heard the Rot had claimed her last year. He still loved her.

He drank for Rachel, who at least had died long before everything else went completely to hell. Jak had never thought he'd be grateful for that, but here he was.

He drank for himself, the last one standing.

He drank until he blacked out.

The world was still there when he woke up.

Damn it.

What were you supposed to do after the end of the world?

There had never been any sort of manual for this, Jak reflected as he looked around the yard. Berke's cabin hadn't exactly been in the center of town before, but now there was nothing around that Jak recognized. The road trailed off into nothing after about twenty feet. There was still a forest, but some of the trees were different species. The sheer cliff overlooking the coast was new, too. There had definitely been no ocean anywhere near the entire state of Wyoming last he'd checked, never mind the near the cabin, which straddled the line between the woods and the suburbs. There were even mountains in the distance. When had that happened? *How?*

Wasn't there supposed to be, like, earthquakes or something when shit like this happened? There was no way he'd slept through *that*.

He sat outside on one of the lawn chairs for a bit, watching the waves as the sun set. Nothing seemed different outside of the scenery. His cursory glance around had not revealed any of the decay that signaled the Rot. The weather was pleasant. It was quiet, with the occasional call of a seagull in the distance.

It just seemed like everything was gone.

Should he do something for his team? Some kind of service or ritual? He was far from an expert on the topic, but it felt right to do... something. What, though? The only kind of service he'd ever been to seemed beyond his ability.

A small white coffin, descending into the ground on a bright, sunny day–

He wrenched his mind away from the unwelcome memory. Did it even matter? They'd disappeared on the wind, nothing left to bury.

The Rot didn't do that. What had?

How long ago had it been? He considered trying to figure out the date, then decided that probably didn't matter either.

It was too damn sunny out.

He went back inside to find more whiskey.

If he was now on a northern coastline, what did that mean for the northern half of the States? For Canada? Did they still exist? He had a good view now, and there was no land he could see when he looked out over the new ocean.

Was it a new ocean? Or had Berke's cabin somehow moved?

None of it made sense to Jak.

He remembered telling Rachel fairy tales where people found themselves in completely different worlds than the one they had started in. Maybe that's what had happened, and the world he'd lived in for the past forty-eight years was gone, and he'd been... transported? Teleported? ...to this other one.

The people in those stories didn't always make it out.

He kept a halfhearted eye on the woods while he sat by the cliff, but nothing appeared, human, animal, or otherwise.

Were the woods darker than before? The trees rustling just a bit more menacingly, the shadows more threatening? Was that why there were no animals other than the birds? Maybe the forest itself had consumed them in an attempt to stop the Rot. Life for life.

He looked down at the beer in his hand. Maybe he should stop drinking. He'd already run out of whiskey. His thoughts were going in weird places.

But then, why should he care?

Eventually he did run out of alcohol. Berke and Kris had stocked a fair amount, but it hadn't been a priority really, just something they'd liked to have on hand.

Jak found himself staring at the ocean again, trying to figure out what it was he was supposed to do. He still had food; they had made damn sure to stock up on that. But it wasn't infinite. If he wanted to keep eating, he'd have to figure out where to get more. He could hunt if it came to it, but he'd prefer not to. That felt like too much effort for the end of the world. And that would require going into the forest.

There was a stream dipping into the clearing he didn't remember. At least he'd have fresh water.

There hadn't been power in the house since... whatever it was had happened, so checking the TV for news was a no-go. There was a radio, but no matter how Jak tuned it he only picked up static. If there were any other survivors out there, Jak didn't have an easy way to know.

He supposed if it started to bother him enough, he'd have to go explore and find out.

Or maybe people would come to him. If there was anyone left.

He leaned back in his chair, listening to the gulls and the waves crashing on the shore far below.

Margaret had always loved the ocean.

Maybe this was supposed to be heaven. Or hell. It was hard to tell which when the days passed in a haze and nothing happened. Maybe it was purgatory?

No one came to Berke's cabin.

He spent a while watching the sky instead of the sea. No planes or aircraft. At night, the sky was different, constellations in the wrong places, but they *were* familiar constellations. He thought he still might be able to see one of the space stations twinkling among them.

What was going on? Was this the same place or not?

Perhaps he should try to find... something. Anything.

Thoughts of Rachel's fairy tales returned. It was never a good idea to go into the woods alone. And these woods didn't seem to want him in them, the shadows cast by their branches letting him know he was not welcome.

But luckily that wasn't reality. Trees didn't have opinions, and Jak was more than familiar with how to use a gun. He was beginning to miss proper coffee.

And whiskey.

He was considering trying to find a way down to the shore to attempt some fishing when he saw it.

At first he thought it was some sort of eel that had partially washed ashore, though it would be one monster of an eel if the distance wasn't playing tricks on him. Part of it lay dashed upon some of the rocks on the beach strewn with seaweed, and the black-scaled tail stretched across the sand into the water. At least the ocean creatures still seemed to exist, along with the birds.

A seagull landed on the rocks next to it, and one long, skeletal arm shot out and grabbed the poor bird. The seaweed moved, and Jak thought it was hiding a humanoid upper body as the gull was pulled out of sight.

He watched, eyes wide but refusing to move, secure in the fact he was over seven hundred feet above it.

Not ten minutes later it slid off the rocks, bony arms pulling the torso still hidden by seaweed across the sand into the water. It must have been over twenty feet long, black scales barely reflecting the dawn light as it finally disappeared beneath the waves, the gouges in the sand and the bit of red on the rocks the only proof it had been there. He never saw the end of the tail.

He watched the water for a long time after that, not completely sure his eyes hadn't been playing tricks on him. His mind once again helpfully reminded him of the fairy tales, especially the ones with monsters in them. He watched the woods for a little bit after that, too. He was far above the eel creature and it didn't seem like it would be able to climb, so unless he went down to the beach he'd be safe, but he knew nothing like that should exist – what if there were other new, horrifying monstrosities hiding in the shadows of the trees?

How else had the world been changed?

And by what? The Rot destroyed; it didn't create.

That night he locked the doors for the first time since he'd found himself alone, and slept with a gun in easy reach.

It wasn't the Rot, but *something* was wrong with this place.

Without the alcohol numbing everything, there was a weird current to the air that tingled over his skin. It was putting him on edge, making it difficult to relax.

He checked over the guns, making sure everything was in order and ammo was nearby, just in case. He pulled out his black tactical vest, but stopped short of putting it on.

Was he being paranoid? What had he really seen? Something far below on the beach had killed a seagull. That was just the circle of life. It wasn't a reason for him to jump at shadows.

But a chill still traveled down his spine when he thought about it. The longer he went without seeing anyone, the more he tried to enjoy the peaceful atmosphere, the more certain he became that something wasn't right.

The peaceful atmosphere felt like a lie he was telling himself. The shadows in the woods seemed darker with each passing day.

Why was he alone? Surely he wasn't the *only* person to survive? Jak found himself laughing at the irony. And if the laughter sounded a bit hysterical, well, he was the only one to hear it.

If only one person could survive the apocalypse, it definitely shouldn't be him.

He was relieved to see a deer come out of the forest later that day. A normal deer. Interested in eating some of the shrubs. Granted it was a red deer, which had been hunted to extinction in the States two hundred years ago and could now only be found in Europe and Asia, but he'd take it.

At least he had fresh meat for a while. He wouldn't have to break into the MREs yet.

There were still no other people.

Maybe this was what he deserved, something whispered.

It sounded like Margaret.

How long had he been here? Weeks? Months? The weather was getting colder, which suggested it was September or October, but was that even something he could trust? Everything else seemed to have gone wonky; there was no reason to believe the weather was any different. It wasn't like the leaves on the trees were changing color yet. Or the shadows beneath them.

Shadows didn't change color like that. What on Earth was he thinking?

It was time to go looking. Maybe he could find answers, and maybe he couldn't, but at least maybe he could figure out where the hell he was and resupply some.

But that meant going into the woods.

He studied the trees warily from the house.

The leaves rustled mockingly at him.

Wow, okay. Fine.

He found himself scowling at the foliage as he pulled on his tactical gear. The woods couldn't tell him what to do, but there was no telling what was out there if the thing on the beach was any indication, and he'd rather be safe than sorry.

He shuddered at the thought of that skeletal arm snapping out to grab the poor bird. He'd have to pay very close attention to his surroundings.

He put on a black trench coat to stave off the cold; the temperature had dropped what felt like twenty degrees overnight. After considering what he had available to him, he took two Glocks and a rifle.

He tried the radio again before he left. Still static.

His compass was also unreliable, swinging every which way and refusing to settle on north. Whatever, he'd figure it out as he went.

He stepped outside, taking care to close the door behind him. Then he squared off with the tree line.

The leaves made sounds like whispers in the wind. Warning him off? Or daring him to try?

Through the woods to Grandmother's house we go...

And so, an indeterminate amount of time after the world ended, Jak set out to explore what was left.

It was like the land itself was more alive.

The foliage was just a little bit greener, the animals a hair bigger, the air a smidge cleaner. Everything was wilder, untamed by people. Maybe this place had never even seen people before.

Maybe that was why it still felt so unfriendly.

He kept an eye out for any pockets of Rot as he navigated the dark forest. There hadn't been any infected land areas in central Wyoming when they'd retreated to Berke's cabin, but who knew what was around now? Things had clearly changed, and Jak wasn't interested in falling into a decaying pool of Rot by accident, especially after having avoided it for so long.

He made himself look for any other signs of people passing through the area despite how unlikely that was, but it seemed to be virgin woods. If anyone had come through here recently, they'd been skilled enough to pass without a trace, or at least skilled enough to seem to be an animal.

If others had come here, had they also felt the tingle of static in the air, seen how unwelcoming the dark shadows were, and understood the warning to leave?

Or was his imagination making things up after being alone for too long?

What was real, and what wasn't?

He was relieved to see that there were plenty of signs of animals, even if he wasn't entirely sure which animals were making all the signs. There were definitely deer, raccoon, and rabbit tracks, but some he couldn't identify. Hoof prints that weren't cloven and were too large to be deer. A bit of fur caught in a bramble that was unnaturally blue. The imprint of claws over six inches deep. He hoped none belonged to bears. At least none of the markings looked like a large eel had pulled itself through the woods.

But then, where *were* the animals?

Why were the woods so quiet? He couldn't even hear the birds anymore.

Some fairy tales warned that the animals that lived around certain mythological creatures gained magic of their own, learned to disappear into the leaves and shadows of the woods.

He shook himself. Ridiculous. Magic wasn't real. Animals were just animals.

But knowing that didn't stop the feeling that he wasn't wanted here.

He was looking over some maybe-deer tracks when he heard the faint sounds of someone crying.

It was the first sign he wasn't completely alone in this zip code.

He redirected almost without thought, quickly but carefully, fairy tales of creatures who lured the unwary to their deaths refusing to leave him alone. And humans weren't above ambushes either. There were probably good reasons for the existence of fairy tales that weren't supernatural, now that he thought about it.

Still, he couldn't shake the feeling that there was something unsettling about the whole situation, even more so than before. Hopefully it was just his nerves getting to him, but he wasn't willing to bet on it.

He quieted his approach as the sound got louder. He crept forward, paying more attention to the area around him than to the clearing he was approaching. If this was a trap, the crying was probably the bait.

But there was nothing. Just the sounds of heartbreak and loss.

He could empathize.

Satisfied for the moment that there wasn't anything coming closer, he peeked around a tree.

There was a naked woman crying in the center of a clearing.

Part of Jak's brain struggled to process that while the part that refused to be taken by surprise continued to observe the situation. Woman, age uncertain due to her hands covering her face but likely young considering the rest of her skin, kneeling in a shallow puddle that spread around her several feet in diameter. Reconsider the age;

could be old, hair was white and… very, very long, partially obscuring her body as it fell into the oddly clear water around her.

When was the last time it had rained? Jak wasn't sure.

The woman was just sobbing by herself in a clearing.

If there was ever a setup for an encounter with some fey creature, *it was this one.* That weird tingly feeling was stronger here, and Jak felt more and more on edge. He should just ignore this, pretend he hadn't seen anything, write it off as the product of an overactive imagination that hadn't seen another person in who knew how long, because if he were telling this story to Rachel it would not end well.

Except there was a naked woman crying alone in the middle of the woods.

Goddamn it.

Jak fought with himself as he observed her, but she gave no indication she had noticed him, continuing to sob. He watched as he tried to make heads or tails of the situation, giving another sweep to the area around them, but as far as he could tell they were alone. The crying continued, going on for long enough that his own eyes began to ache in sympathy.

He should walk away.

But…

Naked woman. In woods. Alone. Naked.

Part of him wanted to grieve with her, for everything that had been lost.

He pushed that away. She was still potentially a threat.

Oh, for the love of... he wasn't going to be able to just leave her here, was he? Fairy tales were just that – make believe. This was a real person in distress. If he left her here he'd never forgive himself.

And he did have guns, while she was – again – naked. He could shoot her if she tried to eat him or whatever. Bullets were pretty reliable like that. He readied the rifle before stepping out from around the tree. "Hey."

She didn't react at all, continuing to sob into her hands.

"Miss? Ma'am?"

Nothing.

Okay, then. How many other women were in this area? "Hey, crying lady in the middle of the woods."

Her head snapped around to look at him, revealing eyes that were way more purple than could be natural. They stared at him, almost accusatory, as tears continued to fall. Her hands dropped to the ground beside her, and–

Oh hell, he was *not* going to be able to have a conversation this way. Juggling the rifle to keep it pointed in her direction, he slid his coat off and tossed it at her. He thought her form seemed to flicker for a moment as he watched, but it happened so quickly he wasn't sure he hadn't imagined it. She seemed solid enough the more he looked at her. "Take this."

"You can see me?" Those violet eyes bored into him.

"Way more of you than I should. Put the coat on. Please."

She took it and held it in front of her, looking at it like she'd never seen a coat before. After a moment, she draped it around her shoulders, playing with the sleeves in front of her.

He firmly squashed the feeling of dread that was trying to surface. At least she was mostly covered now.

"Interesting," she murmured.

"What on Earth are you doing in the middle of the woods... like this?" he asked, firmly keeping his eyes on hers. She was younger, maybe in her early thirties, so... bleached hair? She looked kind of like one of the princesses in Rachel's cartoons. "It's dangerous out here." Probably.

At least she wasn't threatening him, but she also wasn't acting like a normal woman would who'd been found naked in the woods. Drugs, maybe? Mental illness? He was not equipped to deal with that.

She sniffed, wiping at her eyes with one of his sleeves. He felt some relief at the fact that she seemed to be calming down. "You can see me," she repeated. She squinted and tilted her head to the side. White hair contrasted with the black of his coat – that hair had been in the mud; how was it still so clean?

"Yup, we covered that already." She wasn't surprised to see him, but was surprised he could see her. That wasn't a great sign, but Jak pushed it aside for now. "What are you doing out here?"

"Mourning."

At least nothing had sprung out and tried to murder him yet, though her complete lack of regard for the gun was unnerving. "Okay, why are you doing that here?" And naked, but he couldn't bring himself to ask it out loud.

"I am a little bit... more than I usually am."

What was *that* supposed to mean? "O...kay?"

They stared at each other.

Then her expression brightened. "You can *see* me!"

Maybe she wasn't wearing any clothing because she thought people couldn't see her. "Still yes. Do you have any family or friends around?" It felt like a stupid question as soon as he asked.

Her face fell. "But what if it is just due to the excessive ambient magic resulting from the reaping?"

"Magic isn't real," he pointed out, ignoring the shiver down his spine and Rachel's giggle in the back of his mind.

"If you truly believed that we wouldn't be talking," she mused, pulling the coat around her a little more snugly as she studied him. "No, I think you *are* actually mine. What are the chances of that?" She looked down at the coat. "And you gave me a gift!" Her hands clenched around the material as she grinned.

Okay, this was rapidly spiraling out of control. "I didn't– look, do you have clothes somewhere nearby?"

She blinked at him. "No."

Maybe she was crazy?

He looked around, suddenly uncertain. What was he doing?

Well, he'd gotten himself into this situation. He'd have to get himself out. At least she wasn't crying anymore.

She didn't seem dangerous, but she also didn't seem quite right. He couldn't just leave her here in the middle of nowhere like this; she would die from exposure if an animal or something didn't get her. He could–

No. He was absolutely not going to live with this weirdo. He was lonely, sure, but was he *that* lonely? No, no he was not. She was just a random woman who needed help. If anything, she was in a worse situation than Jak was. He'd bring her back to the cabin, get her some clothes, and then trot her back out and hopefully find someone else to foist her off on.

Even if he should actually just leave her here.

She was still the only other person he'd seen since everyone else had... disappeared. Proof he wasn't alone. Someone else had survived the end of the world. Surely there would be others? He felt comforted by the thought.

He wasn't alone.

He sighed. "Alrighty then, let's... get you something to wear that isn't my coat. What's your name?"

Her eyes closed. "My name is... Hades."

Ah, he'd been wrong. This wasn't a fairy tale; this was a Greek myth. That was *much* worse. Luckily, strange women doing weird shit in forests had probably come before the myths, and not the other way around.

"Great. My name is Jak. Let's get going."

He was already regretting this.

Jak couldn't help but feel relieved when Berke's cabin came back into sight, still overlooking its impossible cliff and impossible ocean. It was the only thing left that was familiar, a piece of something that was otherwise gone. Maybe the memories of his friends still haunted it. The thought was oddly comforting.

The woman was looking around curiously, still gripping his coat tightly around her as she followed him inside. "What a pleasant little cottage. Nice scenery."

Jak headed for one of the bedrooms in the back; Lian's clothing would probably fit her. "The scenery is new."

"New? Ah, yes. The reaping." Her voice turned sad.

It was the second time she'd mentioned that. Jak didn't want to think about it. He stared at the drawers and realized he didn't want to pick out a woman's clothes. "Hey, come in here."

She poked her head around the door frame. "Hmm?"

He gestured. "Here. Take what you'd like and get dressed." He headed back to the kitchen without waiting for a reply and decided he needed something to drink. Unfortunately, his options were pretty limited nowadays. He glanced out the window and frowned. They wouldn't be going anywhere else today either; sunset would be in an hour or so. He sighed and lit the gas burner with a match so he could boil some water.

She padded back to the kitchen on bare feet after about five minutes. He glanced over to see she had chosen a baggy pair of jeans and a flannel shirt she was awkwardly buttoning. The black-and-white plaid blended with the strands of her hair, creating a weird optical illusion.

"I've never had to wear real clothes before."

"You've... only worn... imaginary clothes?" He wasn't sure what to make of that.

"Hmm, I suppose you could say that. The little water elementals – they tend to be fashionistas of a sort. I ask for a certain style or feel, and they deliver." She peered at one overlong plaid sleeve. She was even tinier than Lian had been. "They are incredibly distressed by this, but I think it is quite the novel experience!"

He shook his head slowly. If this had been pre-Rot Wyoming, he'd have taken her to a hospital at this point. Surely someone would have been looking for her. But the Rot had destroyed a lot of their infrastructure and systems merely by proving to be the greater threat, and Jak didn't know what they would have done with her if she'd wandered up to the cabin in those last few months. It had been kind of a mess.

Hell, he didn't know what to do with her *now*.

He poured some of the hot water into a mug as she took a seat at the table. Squashing down a feeling of disappointment, he ripped open a packet of instant coffee and added it to the water, stirring to mix it in.

Her eyes widened, and she leaned in far closer than he was comfortable with, inhaling the steam wafting from the cup with obvious pleasure.

"That's, uh, coffee," he said slowly.

"I know what it is. It's just been a long time since I've smelled it." Her eyes were closed and a wistful smile played at her lips.

"Uh huh. Believe me, this... isn't *good* coffee. And it's decaf." He'd had to rely on the instant crap for a while now. This stuff didn't deserve that reaction.

Her smile didn't fade at all. "It still smells wonderful."

To each their own. "Would you like some? To drink, I mean. Or smell. Whatever floats your boat, I guess."

Violet eyes blinked open at him. "Thank you. I would like that very much."

He shrugged and grabbed another packet and cup. "How do you want it? You seem like a cream-and-sugar kind of girl, but I haven't had real milk in a while. Got some of the powdered stuff, though."

She watched him prepare the second cup and hummed softly, nostrils flaring. "We'll start with black, and go from there."

He gave her Lian's room for the night. Lian wouldn't mind; she'd have probably loved the weird lady going by a Greek god's name.

He'd never had the chance to teach the old myths to Rachel. Just fairy tales.

She'd have liked the woman too. Granted, she'd have liked any lady with long princess hair like Rapunzel.

He spent the night wondering what the hell he was doing.

What was real, and what wasn't?

Did it even matter?

What if she wasn't human and tried to kill him? What if she *was* human and tried to kill him?

Would *that* even matter? What was there to lose? There was nothing left.

One of Rachel's stories whispered through his mind, telling him he had let his own doom in by the front door.

But she was still a person, right? Even if she brought doom, at least Jak wouldn't meet it alone.

He didn't get much sleep.

The next morning found him cooking breakfast early. The woman padded out of Lian's room shortly after he started, silent as a shadow, and sat down at the table watching him.

Her eyes lit up at the slab of venison he put in front of her, but then she frowned. "I do not wish to take your food. Do you have any of the skin or bones? You could just burn that; I'll be perfectly fine on the fumes. It's more than what I've had recently."

What the hell? "Absolutely not. Eat the meat."

What if that was true? His mind wandered back to stories of fey. Did they eat? He couldn't remember.

She was eating now, a little clumsily perhaps with the fork and knife, but she clearly knew what they were and how to use them. She was taking her time, savoring each bite of the meat with quiet little sighs.

Weird.

He pushed the thoughts of fairy tales from his mind and tried to focus on his own breakfast.

He found himself frowning as they ate. There was something familiar about her, but he couldn't put his finger on why. Surely he would remember white hair and purple eyes. No, it was something about the face. "You look like..." he mused out loud, causing her to blink up at him. But the answer was slipping away the longer he looked at her. "Someone famous, probably," he decided. Someone he'd seen on TV. Someone he'd seen on TV a lot, and then... forgotten about?

The hair on the back of his neck prickled, though he couldn't understand why.

The woman bit her lip and looked down, then went back to eating her food with far less enthusiasm than before.

They didn't speak for the rest of breakfast.

After breakfast she went and sat by the cliff, arms wrapped around her legs and chin resting on her knees as she stared at the ocean. Her long hair spilled and pooled onto the ground around her. She was wearing his coat again – thankfully over Lian's clothes.

He sat in one of the lawn chairs. "I haven't found a way down yet, and I don't recommend you do so." What was he doing? They should be leaving to get more searching in today.

She turned to look at him. "Oh?"

"Something was down there a few days ago: kind of like a big black eel with arms. It did not look friendly."

She smiled. "There is nothing on this planet that can harm me, but thank you for your concern." She turned back to the ocean. "It's quiet here. I like it."

Nothing that could–? "What?"

She hummed, glancing at him out of the corner of her eye. "Nothing will hurt you while I am here, either. There is a lot of ambient magic around right now. It would be very easy for me to deter an attacker."

His eyebrows shot up. "That's what the guns are for." Even if they were in the cabin at the moment.

She shrugged. "That'll probably do too, I suppose." A beat. "You don't believe me. About the magic, I mean."

"Should I? Magic doesn't exist." An echo of what he'd told her the day before. But then...

"There's so much magic in the world right now..." Her head tilted up to the sky as her eyes fell closed. "Can't you feel it?"

Aside from the unease he'd been living with the past few weeks or so?

Violet eyes shifted in his direction. "Yes, that."

He felt ice go down his spine. "What... how–"

"You are very close to me and you are thinking very loudly. Most mortals do nowadays; the ability to hear thoughts was bred out long ago. I wonder if it will come back now that magic is saturating everything." She tilted her head to the side as she twisted to face him. "The world had been dying for a long time. It's actually not that surprising that such concentrated magic might feel odd to you, now that I think about it."

They sat in silence while he considered that. "Magic isn't real," he decided to challenge her. He could hear her theories if nothing else. It wasn't like he had anything else to go on. Hell, when was the last time he'd had a real conversation with someone? And something *was* weird with the world, he'd known that before he found her in the woods.

"Where there is life, there is magic," she denied gently.

"You said 'the world had been dying.'" Something about that made him think of–

"Yes, the Rot." She agreed with his unspoken thought. He felt another chill. "But it is gone now. Abomination has been forced back once more. It will be a long time before it returns, and I doubt it will take the same form."

His eyebrows rose again. "The Rot is gone?" he asked disbelievingly. They'd been fighting it for years, and... just... "Gone?"

She nodded, face solemn.

"How?"

Her eyes closed. "Sacrifice."

Something in the world *screamed*–

Jak found himself reeling. "What...?"

"The magic remembers what was given in its defense, and it grieves for the loss." She lifted a hand in front of her, cupped upward as though to hold something. In that moment, she was almost translucent again, ethereal. Like they should be having this conversation under starlight instead of the morning sun. And something in him knew.

Whatever she was, she wasn't human.

This *was* real. And fantasy, both.

Then he made the connection. "Like you were, in the woods?"

She nodded.

"How long were you there for? Alone?"

How long had he been alone?

She made a soft sound of understanding, then her eyebrows scrunched together as she bit her lip. "I believe it was nine years, as you count time," she finally said.

He felt his stomach drop as his eyes widened. "No way. That's not possible." He looked at the cabin. "There's no way I had enough food to last *nine years*. It's been... weeks, maybe months, but..."

And yet... how long had he drifted, knowing something was wrong, but not what?

She cringed. "What I did to destroy the Rot... it was like a flood of my power, all of it in one moment, to call upon one of my domains utterly and utterly *destroy*. To a world that had lost its memory of magic... to be so saturated in it so suddenly..." She waved her hands about as though that would help her find the words. "I was the second of my siblings. I exist to balance the one who came first, and time is part of our makeup, even if I choose not to use it. Time is complicated, and it is very possible that things went a little... off, especially with the overabundance of magic. I do not usually have such strength, so these effects are new to me."

He didn't understand that explanation at all. "Wait, back up a step." He paused. "Maybe several steps. Let's go back to the beginning, actually. *You* destroyed the Rot?"

She nodded. "With the aid of a willing sacrifice, a part returned unto me. I could never have done it alone." She shuddered. "I never want to do it again."

He squinted at her. "Okay, we didn't go far enough back. Maybe... let's start with *what* are you?"

She went still, a white statue draped in a black coat. "What do you want me to be?"

"No, no, that's not how this works." He shook his head. "There is a right answer; what is it?"

She held his gaze for a moment longer, then turned away, sighing. "We don't really call ourselves anything. We just are. We have always been."

He grimaced. "You didn't choose the name 'Hades' at random, did you?"

"No," she agreed wryly.

Okay then. "But are you, like, literally a god? All powerful, all knowing, all that jazz?"

"None of us are all powerful or all knowing," she said with a shake of her head. "Though an argument could be made that we are when it comes specifically to our domains. None of us have ever been in the musical *Chicago*, as far as I'm aware."

"Got it." He was just going to let that one go. "And your domains are...?"

"I am usually associated with death."

"Awesome." He guessed it tracked with the name. "And you destroyed the Rot." He let his gaze sweep out over the ocean. It was still an impossible ocean, he decided. None of that explained why there was an ocean in the middle of Wyoming.

"Yes. All traces of it, and anything infected."

They sat together in silence for a while as the sun climbed high in the sky and then began its downward track.

Everything was gone, then. This was a world made anew, whether it wanted to be or not.

She wasn't human. That left him back at square one – were there others who had survived the end of the world? He didn't think a god counted, though he found himself grateful for the company.

Was he still alone?

He could ask, but... he was afraid of the answer.

Around dinner he went inside to make more coffee and grab a pair of MREs. He brought them out to where she was still sitting on the edge of the cliff, and they ate in silence, lost in their own thoughts.

As the sun began to set, something black cut through the surface of the waves to wash up on the shore. Thin, bony arms pulled the creature's torso towards the rocks, head still hidden by a mass of seaweed. It settled with its tail still in the water, exactly as it had before.

"That thing," Jak said, pointing like it wasn't the only thing on the beach. "Do you know what that thing is?"

She hummed thoughtfully. "One of my sister's creations. My siblings never hesitate to seize an advantage, and I'm sure the amount of magic present at the moment is proving too tempting not to use." She studied the form far below. "She is hunting. Death hangs around her like a cloud. I think she and the rest of her kind are meant to be something of a gift for me." She grimaced.

"How nice," he said with a wince. "Murder eels."

She laughed. "My sister tries, but sometimes her enthusiasm runs away with her."

He tried to figure out how he wanted to phrase his next question. "Those arms look... kinda human."

"They do," she agreed.

He let that hang while he gathered his courage. "Are there any other humans left? Humans that are still... well..." He looked down at the creature waiting on the rocks. "...Human?"

She blinked. "Oh! Oh yes, certainly. Scattered about, probably struggling or adapting, but my siblings specifically did put in effort to save who they could. The world has not fallen to Silence, and not all were changed."

Jak felt a huge weight ease off his shoulders, the relief making him lightheaded. He wasn't alone, not really. There were others out there somewhere. Somehow, humanity had survived. And still...

So much grief, for those lost. His eyes strayed back towards the cabin, all that was left of his friends.

And pity, when he thought of the creature down below on the shore. Did it even remember being human? There was nothing human about its actions, only its form. What else had been lost?

"I will help you remember those who have gone, if you wish. You are not alone," Hades offered gently, but Jak got the impression she wasn't just talking about the other humans. "You will never be alone again, as long as you wish it."

"Let's not go quite that far yet," he muttered as the sun finally sank below the horizon, leaving them in the inky blackness of a moonless night. For all that he didn't want to be alone, part of him whispered in Margaret's voice that he deserved it.

Hades turned to study him and he realized she was glowing in the dark, illuminating their little area. "Rachel's death was not your fault."

It was, but he wasn't about to argue with a god over it. That was something he was going to live with for the rest of his life.

But... were there other children out there who had survived the... what had she called it, the reaping? Were they as alone as he had been? Struggling to survive in a world that bore little resemblance to the one they had left behind? That didn't sit well with him. He could never atone, but maybe he could help prevent someone else from going through what he had. He was no knight in shining armor, but he did have a certain skillset. "Tomorrow we should try to find... someone. Or something. I think it's time to try to figure this out. Especially the provision issue; how the hell has my food lasted nine years?"

She hummed. "Yes, we can do this. Together?"

He nodded slowly, chewing on that. A goddess was probably the best companion he could ask for, all things considered. "Yeah, sure," he agreed. "Together."

Scarlet

"And you will search out that which demands an end, and return with trophy and story?"

"With trophy and story I will return, Hemjer." Sukra kept her voice low to suit the sanctity of the ceremony though she was practically vibrating with excitement.

"With trophy and story, and the world made safer?" With her head down and on one knee, all Sukra could see was the hem of Emeru's embroidered scarlet robes pooling on the sandstone floor, but she could hear the smile in the hemjer's voice.

"And the world made safer, with the hunt completed," she repeated dutifully. Almost done.

"And so the hunt may only end thus." Emeru's fingers touched Sukra's forehead, marking it with oil. "Hunt well in the Faleri's name, sister, and return a Warrior."

"This hunt is mine, and it is begun." Sukra stood, joints protesting after having held their position for so long. She met Emeru's eyes, letting the blazing flames in her own show her determination.

The traditional hood and veil hid much of the hemjer's expression, but the blue and green flames in her eyes signaled her joy regardless. Ceremony over, her tone shifted to a less formal one. "It is. And you have a ship to catch, no? I hear the *Sun Star* leaves in less than an hour. I hope you've packed."

Sukra laughed awkwardly at the reference to her last-minute attempt to plan her hunter's ceremony and departure. "One does not control when the call comes! I did the best I could."

"Most do take more than two days before dashing off into the unknown," Emeru said, voice dry as sand. "I'm surprised there even was a ship willing to take you."

"That's why I *really* needed the ceremony to be today. Who knows when the next ship will come?" Sukra ignored the soft laughter from the other robed hemjer who had been present for the ceremony.

Emeru took her arm as they began to walk out of the temple. "I think they are fairly common, actually. Trade is a thriving enterprise here. The short notice is what they do not tend to like."

"But they do like money, and I was willing to pay." Sukra shrugged. "I've been preparing for this. For a long time." She pushed away the sting of shame. It didn't matter anymore.

"No one doubts your dedication to the hunt," Emeru soothed. She had been privy to Sukra's doubts and tears for some time. "The call comes when it comes. You will do well, and when you return to us, you will have left a community a safer place. I know this. There is no need to rush, though."

They could agree to differ on that point. Sukra had waited long enough. She wanted to get out there and do things now! "I can rest on the boat. I have already rushed to get there; the past cannot be changed. And I stand by it anyway."

Emeru simply hummed as they exited the temple into the near-blinding morning sun where Sukra's mother-sisters were waiting.

"Sukra! Did you really do it?" Kari was the youngest, having just celebrated her thirtieth birthday the week before. Still too young to truly understand, she'd thrown a fit when it was explained to her that Sukra would be leaving, and Sukra's hopes that they might avoid another such display were rapidly being dashed by the tears beginning to well up in the little girl's green-and-gold eyes.

Faja, who had Sukra's bow and quiver slung over one shoulder, pulled Kari close and ruffled her hair. "Of course she did; she's wanted nothing else for years." The fifty-eight-year-old had completed her hunt the year before, having heard her call slightly earlier than most. Sukra appreciated that her sister never rubbed her new Warrior status in Sukra's face.

"And we are going to have to hurry, if you want to be on the *Sun Star* before it sails," Ivka warned. The oldest at ninety-seven, she had darker red hair than her mother-sisters, more ruby than scarlet. It fell in exotic waves down her back, and her wiry build and beautiful scattering of dark marks around her purplish-red eyes ensured she never lacked for suitors – something she took advantage of often. "I have your pack and spear. I'm sure Avhad Paeru is already waiting to see you off."

"But..." Kari's face started to crumple.

"Ah ah!" Sukra swept in and picked Kari up to rest against her hip. Her youngest sister was slightly too big for this to be comfortable anymore, but Sukra would rather deal with some mild awkwardness than a meltdown. "Come now, you can walk with me to the pier, hmm? We don't want to keep Avhad Paeru waiting."

Kari threw her arms tightly around Sukra's neck and buried her face against her shoulder.

Sukra glanced back at Emeru, who bowed. "May the Fires light your path, Hunter. We await your return."

Sukra inclined her head, the best she could do with Kari trying to strangle her. "May the Fires light your path, Hemjer. I will return." She turned and walked away, hearing her sisters give their own farewells behind her.

She was grateful Emeru had not insulted her with a "be safe," no matter how sure she was the other woman had wanted to say it.

Despite everyone's warnings, the Flame Temple was not that far from Weiba Port. The walk passed quickly, though Sukra could hear Ivka and Faja whispering behind her. Hopefully they were coming up with a plan for how to keep Kari calm when Sukra had to put her down. She cringed slightly at the thought as the *Sun Star* came into view, Avhad Paeru indeed waiting for them, leaning against a stack of crates. Four other Warriors of their House lounged nearby.

The older woman merely raised an eyebrow at their approach, fingers tapping against her crossed arms.

Sukra glanced at the *Sun Star*, but the crew was still completing preparations. Good. They were not late. "Avhad," she greeted, bowing as well as she could.

Paeru's purple-and-gold eyes took in the oil marking Sukra's forehead. "Hunter. Well met." She stepped forward to take Kari from Sukra.

Kari made a sad whimpering sound. "Avhad, Sukra is really going to leave us!"

"Yes, she is. And we of her House will await her victorious return with trophy and story," Paeru said gently, touching the tip of Kari's nose. "That includes you, little one." The flames in her eyes flickered as they shifted to Sukra. "You are finally ready to go."

"I am, Avhad! I will bring honor to the House of Dawn with my hunt." Hands finally free, she reclaimed her things from her mother-sisters. She straightened the blue-green wrap around her waist as best she could.

Paeru smiled. "I have no doubt of that. I expect quite the story when you return." She tightened her arms around Kari. "Say goodbye, little one. Properly."

Kari sniffled, her lip wavering, but managed, "May the Fires light your path, sister." She didn't wait for Sukra's response, burying her face in Paeru's shoulder.

"May the Fires light your path, sister," Sukra repeated gently, ruffling her sister's scarlet hair. Kari hadn't been nearly so obstinate with Faja's hunt the year before, but then she wasn't as close with Faja, and their sister had remained within Dalmara like most hunts. Sukra's departure across the ocean was proving to be more upsetting.

"I hope you kill many things," Faja said gravely, ignoring their Avhad's eye roll. "You've been preparing for this for decades; whatever you've been called to hunt doesn't know what's coming."

"I, too, await your trophy and story with an eager heart," Ivka said, shooting an exasperated look at Faja. It didn't matter; Faja's status as an active Warrior allowed her to say whatever she wanted to a Hunter. "Hunt well, sister. May the Fires light your path."

Sukra appreciated Ivka's formality and Faja's confidence. "I will hunt well. May the Fires light your path." She bowed.

Then, suddenly, Ivka's face crumpled. "Oh, we'll miss you!" She pulled both Sukra and Faja into a hug. "Who's going to read to Kari before bed? She doesn't think anyone else does it as well as you do."

Taken aback, Sukra glanced at Paeru, but the Avhad was studying the sky like it was of particular interest. "I'll miss you, too," she whispered, soaking in her sisters' warmth for the last time. She would miss them terribly. The rest of the House, too.

But the part of her that heard the call screamed at her to get on the boat.

She shushed it firmly; she could have these few moments.

Finally she pulled away, quickly wiping at her eyes. Faja took a deep breath, looking away, while Ivka clasped her hands in front of her chest.

"You will return to us with trophy and story," she said firmly, tears still in her eyes. "The Faleri have a plan for you. That is why they waited so long to call you. You will do great things, sister."

Sukra bit her lip and nodded, trying not to cry again.

The sound of hoofbeats and shouting caused them all to turn.

A pitch-black camel was hurtling down the street, decked in the official livery of the House of Sand. An orange-haired man in black armor was urging it forward despite the early morning crowd of dock workers. He shouted something, pointing at Sukra's group, and the crowd parted in front of him.

Sukra rolled her eyes, cocking a hip and folding her arms. Aldoresh was always so dramatic. He'd probably timed his arrival to be as late as possible. Though, hadn't he been in Menph-Aisan? She glanced at Faja, the most likely culprit.

Her sister shrugged guiltily. "He'd want to see you off, too. Besides, I wasn't sure he'd get the time off to come... or even get here in time at all."

That did make sense. He'd grown up with them in the House of Dawn before leaving to become a maji in service of the House of Sand, where he'd been doing very well for himself.

The camel skidded to a stop in front of them, sides heaving, as Aldoresh vaulted from the saddle and landed with a dramatic flourish.

Sukra pressed her lips together, but internally she was glad he had come.

"Maji Aldoresh, I greet you," Paeru said, tone devoid of any inflection. "To what do we owe this pleasure?"

"Avhad Paeru, I greet you." He bowed so perfectly Sukra was sure he had been practicing. "I merely came to see a former House-sister off on her hunt."

Paeru raised both eyebrows, tilted her head, and gestured in Sukra's direction with one hand, still holding Kali.

Sukra saw him fight back a wince.

"Must you abuse the camel so?" Ivka sighed, coming forward to soothe the beast.

"I am not abusing the camel." Aldoresh frowned at her. "The camel is fine. It just likes to be dramatic."

"Then truly you must be meant for each other," Ivka said, voice cool.

"You know, those in Menph-Aisan are impressed by me." He folded his arms in front of him with a frown.

"Then they do not yet know you well enough."

He rolled his eyes.

Faja grinned. "Have you missed the verbal abuse?"

His mouth quirked into a smile. "A little." Gold flames met Sukra's green. "Well met, Hunter!"

"I greet you, Maji," she said, emphasizing the more formal greeting. This was a formal occasion, and he was no longer of their House, whether she was glad to see him or not.

"I greet you," he repeated dutifully, but while rolling his eyes. "In all truth, though – congratulations. It is long overdue."

She inclined her head. "It is, and I thank you."

A call from on deck for everyone to come aboard.

It was time.

Paeru stepped forward. "May the Fires light your path, sister, and Montu-Ra stalk your prey by your side. I await your trophy and story."

Sukra swallowed at the acknowledgement of "sister" from her Avhad. As a Hunter it was an appropriate address, but she hadn't realized how much it would mean to her to hear it. "May the Fires light your path, Avhad. I will return with trophy and story." One last bow to those gathered, and she turned to walk up the gangplank, hearing the final goodbyes of her sisters behind her.

She was almost to the top when Aldoresh shouted, "Sukra!"

She whipped around at the impropriety of it and found herself catching a woven bag inches from her face. Something inside clinked.

"I made those for you, just in case!" He was ignoring the glares from those gathered below.

She took the last few steps up the gangplank to stand on the ship proper before curiosity got the better of her. She peeked inside.

Spell crystals! Six of them, in the yellow of Aldoresh's magic. She looked down at him, surprised he had gone to such effort.

He shrugged. "Think of me when you cast them, hmm?"

Oh, this was a *courtship* gift. She studied the bag thoughtfully for a moment while her sisters' stares turned scandalized. A bold move, to give it to her now, as she left on her hunt. She turned to go and find out where she would be staying for the next week without acknowledging him.

She would see how well they performed before making any decisions.

Sukra did not understand what it was that called Aradians to the hunt, only that it was divine in some capacity. Some thought it was the Faleri who were responsible, others thought it to be Montu-Ra, and still others believed it to be something about the magic of the world itself.

Whatever it was, Sukra was beginning to hate it.

Everything here was *wet*.

Even when the natives claimed it was "dry," Sukra found it to be disgustingly damp. The ground squished, surfaces were moist in the mornings, the air *smelled* wet. At least it meant water was plentiful.

It was far colder here than in Dalmara as well. The desert could get very cold at night, but this chill was persistent... and also wet. She was grateful for the warm cloak Ivka had insisted she bring.

There was so much green though! Everywhere she looked there was green. The trees, far larger and leafier than those back home, forming dense forests. The grass. Bushes. Painted shutters on houses. The color seemed to take over everything.

She took shelter inside as much as she could, picking up odd jobs here and there as she tried to determine what it was that she was meant to hunt. She knew she was at a disadvantage. While not unheard of, hunts rarely occurred too far from where the Hunter hailed from. As such, Dalmara and the other countries in Falin had infrastructure to support Hunters, such as free nights at inns and the occasional free meal. The countries of Espon had none of that, leaving her quite on her own. She hadn't even seen another Aradian sister or brother since leaving the coast.

She was thankful Avhad Paeru had suggested she study languages when it became clear she would not be called at the expected age, but even so this language felt awkward on her tongue, and it sounded clunky. She missed the graceful sounds of home and the voices of her sisters.

She hoped they were doing well, and that little Kari wasn't missing her too badly.

She studied Aldoresh's spell crystals and determined that they contained concussive lightning spells. Heavy firepower, if they delivered on what they promised. Not that she doubted Aldoresh's abilities; he'd always been a very good maji. Not good at many other things, but he'd really tried with magic and his dedication had paid off.

But what was she to use them on?

There were a few things here and there: a bandit, a Lorn, a rabid bear. But nothing called to her. She hadn't found what it was she was meant to hunt yet. So she continued to wander west, listening to rumors and gossip.

Only one thing was certain.

She was going to need different shoes.

It somehow felt even wetter the farther west she went. Wetter and colder as another month passed.

Where did all the moisture go? Where did it come from? Why did it exist? Dalmara managed perfectly fine with a fraction of this much water. Sukra had even seen some sort of muck creature rise partially out of a lake, horse-like head draped in dripping debris. It looked like the sort of thing that a hunt would be called for, but it had just eyed her placidly and then sunk back underwater.

She'd moved on.

Now she was huddled inside a tavern with a hot cup of tea (though what she wouldn't give for Ivka's cinnamon tea right now) and a blanket near the communal fireplace as what seemed like an entire ocean's worth of water fell from the sky. *Where* did it all come from? How did it keep falling? She knew what rain was; *this wasn't it.*

She was glaring out the window petulantly, feeling a bit like Kari, when two men stumbled into the tavern swearing – she overheard them tell the bartender they had been caught in the storm with no shelter in sight. They shook out their cloaks and laid them by the fire to dry, taking seats near her as the barmaid brought over two bowls of stew. Sukra went back to staring at the abomination of nature falling from the sky.

It wasn't long before one noticed her. "Hey, miss."

Her skin crawled at the informality, but that was the way things were done here. She turned to look at them, wondering if this was going to be another conversation about consent. "Yes?"

"You're an Aradian, right? Gotta be with those eyes." The Avari squinted at her as she nodded. "I know your kind is tough and all, but a young lady like you has got to be careful out here."

A "young lady" like her? She was seventy-five, probably twice his age. It could be hard to tell. Aradians lived much longer than Avari.

But his friend was nodding in agreement. "Yeah, there's been a number of girls gone missing the past few weeks 'round these parts."

And that part of her that demanded she go west began to burn.

"Girls gone missing?" she repeated, hoping for more explanation.

"Yeah, rumor has it that it's to do with the black wizard tower that sprung up to the north a couple of months ago, but who knows, really. Mages like being hard to know."

She thought of Aldoresh's spell crystals on her belt. Was it literally a black tower, or did they assume the maji was evil? Perhaps the magic was black in color. "A mage tower to the north? Where, exactly?"

The first man shrugged. "North somewhere. I haven't gone looking for it, you can be sure of that."

"Weird things have been happening. Not just the missing girls, though yeah, that's bad. Stories of creatures in the forest acting odd, crops dying, storms like this one appearing out of nowhere. We're headed south to try to avoid it. Lyndiniam is protected by the Rose Queen and her forces; should be safer than whatever's happening up here."

She hummed. The Rose Queen was a name unfamiliar to her, but then she hadn't been paying much attention to the politics or borders of the countries she'd been traveling through.

"Oh, and there was that eclipse the other night!" the second Avari exclaimed.

"Right, that was also really weird."

Sukra frowned. She had noticed no such eclipse. Did that mean it was some sort of localized effect? She found her eyes drifting up to the sky, but the storm made observing any celestial bodies an impossibility.

The call burned.

So be it, then. That was her next destination. It couldn't be too far if the effects were localized to this region.

"Have there been any other strange things?" she asked. It didn't sound like they had any more intelligence on the matter, but it never hurt to ask.

The first man's eyebrows rose. "Other than everything we've just said? Lady, what more do you want to happen?"

"Bad enough the way it is now," the second muttered. "If it's going to get worse, it can do it without me around."

"I'll drink to that," the first man agreed, tapping his mug against his friend's before downing half its contents.

Not everyone was meant to face evil. She didn't hold it against them. She'd head north tomorrow, or whenever this miserable rain stopped, and see what she could find. For the first time since coming to these wet lands, she had the scent of her prey.

Perhaps she'd be able to return home soon.

It took three days for the storm to pass.

Sukra watched those who sheltered with her and determined that this was not a normal storm by any means. She considered braving the weather just to ascertain if it was a proper storm, or if something had trapped it in this area and the surrounding weather was clear.

Her call burned, which told her the storm was related, but it did beg the question – was it deliberate, or a side effect of some other magic? Aldoresh sometimes complained about maji who messed with the weather since it had a much more far-reaching effect than usually intended. Sukra thought that those who did not take the normal weather patterns into consideration were likely too self-centered to care about the effect the weather would have on others, but she wasn't sure – yet – what the purpose of this storm had been.

She left while the sky was still hazy before the dawn, the very air itself still wet.

She followed the now unceasing burn of the call north. Even the forest around her had suffered due to the storm – tree limbs were broken and dangled in her way, trees themselves had been uprooted, brush and debris were strewn across the roads, and paths were covered in mud. Bridges had been washed out. The natives were trying to clean up and make repairs, forming groups that each focused on different tasks.

Sukra left them behind, entering darker woods, less traveled but no less harmed by the storm. She picked her way through the trails, keeping an eye out for anything that might hint at her quarry as she followed the call. She wanted to surprise her prey, not the other way around.

But the forest was quiet aside from the animals that lived there.

She made a little camp when it became too dark to see, huddled at the base of a large tree. She considered trying to dry some wood for a fire, but quickly discarded the idea. Even for her it would be too much work. She could handle a few wet, cold nights if it came to it. She wrapped her cloak tightly around herself and gnawed on some jerky before closing her eyes to rest.

The next morning found her again stalking north alone through the woods.

Shortly after noon she paused, ears picking up the sounds of... some sort of high-pitched laughter, perhaps? It did not sound friendly. It was rapidly followed by a sound she knew very well: steel on steel.

The call burned hopefully.

Readying her spear, she moved forward silently towards the fight, wanting to assess the situation before she threw herself into it. As the sounds grew louder she became more sure this was what she was meant to hunt – something about those cackling laughs and screams was wrong, set her on edge as her mind screamed that whatever was making that sound should not be here.

She knew she was correct when she came across the first piece of carnage, a disembodied arm still weakly twitching among the remains of several destroyed trees, all painted with streaks of dark red, purple, and blue. The skin was black, the blood a dark purple ooze, the fingers thick, elongated, and sharp.

The fire within her, that piece of the Faleri that lived within every Aradian, *screamed* in fury at the sight.

Demons.

Suddenly the arm went completely limp, indicating that its original owner was finally dead. Feeling disgust, she called up her flames to burn the arm to ash, looking around in dismay at what then must have been demon blood splattered everywhere around her. And the more she looked, the more she saw pieces of black, red, purple, and blue skin.

The sounds of battle had not ended.

That would have to take priority. Quickly she followed the trail of destruction towards the sounds. It took less than a minute to find the source.

One Avari, facing off against three winged demons alone, a longsword against their wicked weapons and magic. One arm had a long cut that was bleeding freely and he was covered in gore, but his eyes were fierce and he moved like lightning.

The demons ranged from four to six-and-a-half feet tall, wings looking like they were stolen from bats, owls, or moths. They also looked like they were somehow *losing*, covered in gashes and clearly trying to remain out of the Avari's range. One with dark-red skin was missing a wing, the shortest one an arm and a foot. The uninjured one was vaguely feminine in appearance, long black hair tangled in the breeze and framing two horns, which curled around her face. The mangled bodies of their brethren littered the forest floor around them, and though they cackled still, their breathing was labored.

The swordsman had his sword up as two of the demons circled him, the third holding on to a nearby tree to stay out of range. Both sides were searching for an opening.

Well, Sukra could help there.

Fire was supposed to be far more efficient against demons than steel.

She felt the embers in her soul rise to her will, and she nocked an arrow, taking aim. She loosed, letting the flames consume the arrowhead as it flew straight into the least injured of the demons.

It screamed, immolating instantly before it could bring its own magic to bear against hers. The other two demons screamed in answer before the one missing an arm dove at her. She called up a sheet of flame in defense, cursing how wet the ground still was from the storm as the demon used its own magic to attempt to smother hers, barreling through to get to her. She spun to the side, grabbing another arrow and setting it alight before stabbing it into the demon's back like a dagger as it passed her.

The demon screamed in pain and fury as it fought back the flames, turning to look at her with a deranged grin. Its eyes were completely black, with an unsettling red light glowing from within, and there was a scattering of red scales across its face. It knocked aside her next arrow like batting a fly aside and tackled her to the ground, mouth unhinging as it bit down at her.

She breathed fire into its face.

It screamed again and fell off her, bashing its head into the mud to put the flames out.

Sukra grabbed her spear as she rolled to her feet, lighting the tip as she used all her strength to impale the demon through the heart.

It made one last shudder, then went still as the flames took it.

She switched back to her bow as she sought out the remaining demon, only to see the swordsman hacking it into pieces as though he wielded an axe instead of a sword.

The clearing was quiet around them.

"I believe it is dead," Sukra offered when it became clear he had no interest in stopping.

"They've come back from worse," the Avari disagreed, continuing his butchery.

"I can burn it, to be sure. It would be more efficient."

"Less satisfying, though."

That was reasonable, she supposed. Sukra studied him as he continued his gruesome work. He was on the shorter side for an Avari, with dark-red hair that reminded her of Ivka's pulled back in a long, knotted ponytail. Under the gore he appeared to be wearing a sleeveless leather tunic, light shirt, and gray pants with a few pieces of leather armor over a lean build. His blade carried no ornamentation. And though his opponents littered the ground around him, his silver eyes still shimmered with the rage he was taking out on the corpse in front of him.

Sukra frowned, studying the area. How many demons had there been? Fifteen? Twenty? More? Had he taken all of them on by himself? Though she looked, there only seemed to be demon corpses on the ground. She did not see any of the native races of Gaia.

One Avari against twenty demons was...

She glanced at him again. He had shown great skill with the blade from what little she had seen, but he would have to be a master to have managed this carnage by himself. He looked young, though. Older than Faja, perhaps, but younger than Sukra herself. Except Avari were all much younger, so... she had no idea how old he was. Did Avari learn that quickly? If so, she'd never heard of it.

She turned her attention back to where her opponent had finished burning up. The two horns were all that remained. Carefully, she picked one up to examine it. It almost had the texture of hair instead of horn, pitch black with threads of deep red spiraling through it. Her senses did not warn her of anything dangerous about it.

These would do for trophies, then.

At the thought she paused, listening inward.

The call was silent.

Sukra blinked back tears. She had done it! She could return home, with trophy and story – and what a story! *Demons*! That was a far more challenging foe than what most Hunters faced. She would need the trophies if she was going to be believed! Had the first one she'd brought down with her bow also dropped its horns? She would go and look. Having more trophies was always better.

The swordsman's silver eyes tracked her as she passed by, his motions finally coming to a stop. "What are you doing?"

"Looking for the horns of the first one I killed," she explained, and yes – there! Black like its hair had been, curved differently than the first set with fine purple hairs scattered throughout. Perfect.

"What do you want those for?" he asked with a frown, wiping his blade clean of the gore.

"To bring home, proof of my hunt." She had an empty bag that would be perfect to hold them. Where had she put it?

"Uh huh." His ears were still in that horizontal position that indicated negative emotional states in Avari. "You were hunting...?" He shook his head as he trailed off. "Well, take your pick, I guess. There's likely to be more where those came from."

Sukra frowned. "More?"

"I don't think Dae-whatever-his-name is going to stop with just this group." His mouth twisted and his ears twitched even lower. "Kind of seemed to me that he saw this as just the beginning."

Her stomach sank as she recalled the conversation from a few nights before. "The maji– wizard," she corrected herself at his puzzled expression, "in the tower north of here? The one who may or may not be kidnapping girls?"

"Oh, he's definitely kidnapping girls. Or he was; I don't know if he needs to do that anymore." The swordsman's expression darkened further. "My sister was the last one taken."

Sukra frowned. More demons? The call had gone silent, the sign of a hunt completed. Technically, she was to return home with trophy and story. But she couldn't just *leave* if there was a rogue maji kidnapping girls and summoning demons. That... she would not have left the world safer. Not by any metric she might use, anyway. But if she killed the maji... She looked at the Avari, who was sheathing his sword, then turned to the north as she placed her trophies in their new home. "Then we will save your sister," she declared.

"She's already dead," he spat. He turned and started walking... east?

Sukra shouldered her bow and checked to make sure the demon remains had burnt off her spear before following. "Then we slay her murderer."

"Yeah, that's the plan," he muttered, silver eyes sliding in her direction. "Except you don't need to be part of it."

"You wish to take on a demon-summoning wizard by yourself?" she asked, turning and taking a moment to whisper a prayer to the Faleri for assistance. She felt the embers inside her dance, eager to cleanse this place. She touched a nearby tree, spattered with demon ichor, and focused.

The tree caught instantly, the flames jumping from tainted tree to tainted tree, from corpse to corpse. Sukra kept hold of the tree, directing the flames only to destroy the corruption, imposing her will on that which desired to consume – and reminded the flames that they were hers to command, not the other way around.

She and the swordsman watched it burn.

"Handy ability," he said after several minutes. "Can all Aradians do that?"

Just a moment more, and then... yes, it was done. The flames went out, leaving a new grove of charred wood in its wake, embers still glowing scarlet across the ruined bark. She felt herself sway for a moment, lightheaded with the effort of controlling that much flame for even those few minutes. "To one degree or another. Did you really kill all those demons on your own?"

He shrugged. "It was kill or be killed, and I refuse to go down before Daem-whoever does."

She could appreciate that sort of focus, or maybe spite, but still. "Your mastery over the sword must be counted among the legends, then, to kill so many while remaining so unharmed."

His expression blanked to one of confusion as he glanced down at the cut on his left arm. "I think that might be overstating things."

She started to shake her head but stopped, regretting it as the lightheadedness returned. She was going to have to rest soon. "To kill so many on your own... how long have you devoted yourself to studying your blade?"

He looked down at said blade as though he had never seen it before. "I don't think I've ever 'devoted' myself to it. I've always been a fair enough hand with it to chase off bandits or defend the animals from the wildlife. That's all I've ever needed it for before."

She stared at him. "Then... if not the sword, what is your profession of choice?"

"What is my...? I'm a farmer." He shook his head at her slowly. "Most people around here are in some capacity."

A farmer? She turned to look at the burnt remains of his battle. There was absolutely no way a *farmer* had done that. A group of Warriors would struggle with that many demons. "Is your blade enchanted?" she asked, groping for an explanation.

He scoffed. "This?" He inched the plain blade out of its sheath an inch. "Absolutely not; I'd never pay for one of those overpriced mage-blessed sticks. No, I've just always been good with a weapon."

Ah. That made sense. "You are a prodigy, then." She tilted her head and squinted at him slightly. With that red hair, perhaps he even had Aradian blood somewhere in his line. She nodded decisively. "Good. We may need that against demons."

"There is no 'we,'" he corrected with a frown. "Go back home to your desert. You don't need to stick your nose where it doesn't belong."

She hummed, considering. Prodigy or no, if he was going to set himself alone against a maji that summoned demons, he was going to die. His sister and any others the maji had killed deserved to be avenged, and the maji needed to be stopped. Demon summoning was such forbidden magic that the last demon summoner recorded by her people had been millennia ago, during the Era of War. This could not be allowed to continue. And while she was glad she wouldn't have to do it alone, how to convince him to join her?

Ah, she could use the hunt. It only required her to stretch the truth a little.

"Have you ever heard of an Aradian's hunt?" she asked, leaning against one of the intact trees. The heat from her fire had dried out this area; for the first time in months she felt dry, even if she had demon ichor on her.

"No, and I don't really care."

That was fine, she could make him care. His sullenness reminded her a bit of Kari when the little girl was in a bad mood. "It is a divine mission of sorts, given to certain Aradians by the Faleri," she explained. "Those who are meant to become Warriors are given a quarry to hunt. Successfully killing this prey is meant to make the world safer in some way." So what if the normal quarry were things like Lorn the size of a story-tapestry or alligators who had mutated due to too much magic in an area? "Should we succeed, we return home with trophy and story, and we may take up our new title. Those who become Warriors may even one day form their own House." Oh, maybe that was too much; she could see from the confused tilt of his ears she was losing him. "My hunt has brought me here. The call drives me to bring an end to these demons and the one summoning them."

There. Not quite true since her call was silenced, but she'd never forgive herself if she left things the way they were now.

"If your gods chose to send you on a suicide mission that's not my problem."

Not very religious, then. "Furthermore, if one of my sisters had been killed by a rogue maji..." She trailed off, shuddering at the thought of little Kari dead. "My other sisters and brothers and I would track that maji down to the ends of the earth if need be and bring them to a painful end. But you are alone. Have you no other Warriors in your family to help you bring this man to justice?"

His jaw tightened as he looked away. "It's just been us for a long time. We didn't need anyone else."

Until something beyond them both had stolen her away. Sukra closed her eyes and bowed her head. "What was her name?"

There was a pause. "Aria."

Sukra nodded decisively. "Then since you have no House to hunt with you, and since my hunt for trophy and story aligns with your hunt for vengeance, it only makes sense for us to hunt together."

He stared at her, silver eyes puzzled. Finally he shrugged. "Do whatever you want. But I'm not going to slow down for you." He turned away from their battlefield and began heading east again.

Sukra pushed herself off the tree, a little regretful she couldn't rest yet, but there would be time for that eventually. Avari needed to sleep just like Aradians did. "Acceptable. I understand completely."

She took a few quick steps to catch up. "I am Sukra, Hunter of the House of Dawn. What is your name?"

"Ebryn." The word was clipped.

Just "Ebryn"? Most of the Avari she had met had given two names. Perhaps he *truly* had no House of his own. No matter, such a journey as this was bound to give him one. "Well met, Ebryn."

He grunted at her.

Not terribly talkative. Perhaps they could work on that. It was clear to her he needed a distraction of some sort, lest his anger consume him the way her flames had consumed the demons. "If I may, why are we heading east? It was my understanding that the wizard lived towards the north?"

Silver eyes glanced at her before returning to the path in front of them that only he could see. "I've already fought what's-his-face. I need something more if I'm going to kill him for good."

"For good?"

"I must have killed him at least four times, but he just shrugged the wounds off like they didn't even matter. And that was before the demons." He scowled. "So we are going to Norik."

She wondered if this maji practiced necromancy in addition to demon summoning. "What is in Norik?"

"A temple of the Three."

"Ah." That made sense. "You are going to ask for divine aid?"

"No." He snorted.

"I'm going to demand it."

Yellow

"Little sister, I can provide you the opportunity, but it must be your choice."

Dying, dying, dying, she was dying, it was dark and cold so cold a sharp pain at her neck–

:*Jeri Vulpeta, this is my gift to my children. To you the choice is given; make it freely.*:

She chose–

"Looks like it's taking!"

"That's it, little sister. Come back to us." The cajoling tone turned harsh. "I need a blood bag over here, now!"

"What kind–"

"She fledged thirty seconds ago; it does not matter. Blood. *Now!*"

Jeri whimpered. Everything hurt. And she was cold. And... naked? Lying on stone? What... what had happened? The last thing she remembered... what was the last thing she remembered? Everything was a confused blur in her mind...

"You could feed her that guy."

"Absolutely not. We have no idea where that's been. And first blood from a body sets a bad precedent."

She'd been going home from a weekend in Vaslu on the train? She'd been with Mellanie and Fortuna, hadn't she? How had she ended up here? Where was here? Oh Goddess, she was so hungry... How long had it been since she ate?

"I'd take a step back, Johanen," the female voice said cooly. "Fledglings are dangerous at this stage."

There were people here. Surely they understood what was happening? Jeri fought to open her eyes, but they were so heavy.

"It's okay, little sister. Rest for a moment."

Who was this woman? Finding strength she didn't know she had, Jeri forced her eyelids open, blinking slowly to clear the film from her eyes. Trying to raise a hand to wipe at them felt like an impossible task right now. Why couldn't she move?

"Uh, maybe, like, a coat or something?"

"Are you offering? And where the hell is that blood?"

Some sort of stiff fabric was laid over her and Jeri tried again to see, this time with more success. A woman with long, wavy, pale-yellow hair in Watch Blacks was leaning over her, dark-blue eyes filled with concern. Jeri was lying on some sort of gray stone, head turned to the side. There were deep marks on her visible wrist, from where it'd been... tied tightly with rope? And... there were red swirls of dried something along the length of her arm... something about it smelled...

The hunger surged to the forefront, and she found herself trying to move her arm closer to her face, her tongue stretching out for just a taste–

"No," the blonde woman said firmly, pressing her arm back onto the stone. "We don't know what's in that, either. Johanen-"

"My people will be back as quickly as possible, but this isn't the center of town; it's going to take them some time, even with the wargs' help."

The male voice came from her other side. Jeri tried to turn her head to look, but the woman stopped her from doing that, too. Why did she have no control over herself?

"Just ignore him for now. Focus on me, all right? What's your name, little sister? Can you tell me that?"

She tried to answer, but her mouth felt like it had been stuffed with cotton. She was so thirsty...

"I know, but not yet. What is your name? Focus on that."

She whimpered, trying to make herself say "Jeri." Why couldn't she say it? What was wrong with her?

"Ah, Jeri. What a pretty name. Do you remember what happened? How you ended up here?"

Had she actually said her name? What was going on? She felt her lower lip begin to tremble. She wanted to go home.

The woman made a soft sound and gently stroked Jeri's hair. "Oh, I know. I'm sorry, Jeri. It's going to be a little while before we can do that. I'm sorry. My name is Mircalla. I'm a member of the Black Watch. Do you remember Her voice? Do you remember making the Choice?"

What was she talking about? Jeri blinked rapidly, still trying to clear her vision. The soft yellow glow of candles was not giving her enough light to see by.

"Jeri, this is important. Try to stay with me, okay? You were attacked. Do you remember that?"

Fuzzy flashes, a tall man with fangs, Mellanie had screamed–

"Yes, that's right. He's gone now; he can't hurt you anymore. But you had lost a lot of blood by the time we got here–"

"Which is probably not helping things either, now that I think about it."

Blue eyes flashed dangerously, but before the woman could continue Jeri whispered, "I died."

The woman's expression softened. "Yes, you did."

"And I... I..." It was hard to get the words out around the sandpaper taste of her mouth and around the horror building in her mind.

"Confronting it now will be better, I promise," the woman murmured.

Vampire. She had become a Vampire.

"Mmm." The woman – Mircalla? – hummed in agreement. "You are a fledgling now. My fledgling."

Jeri tried to push it aside, look around. What had happened after she'd been attacked? A flash of gold from behind Mircalla caught her eye and she focused on it.

It was a long golden braid. A long, familiar golden braid, lying severed on the floor behind the woman. Jeri managed to shake her head weakly and was horrified when a few golden strands brushed against her face, much shorter than they had been before.

It was too much. She felt her eyes well with tears.

"Oh, no, no, don't cry yet, please–" The woman looked behind herself and cursed, seeing the hair. She shifted herself so it was out of Jeri's sight. "We need that blood!" she hissed, eyes snapping to the person behind Jeri.

"I can't materialize it, I'm sorry. It should be here soon."

Jeri loved her hair. Her mother loved her hair.

Oh Goddess, her mother. She wanted her mother. Twenty years old, but she wanted her mother to hug her and tell her everything was going to be all right. She wanted to wake up and discover this was some horrible dream that she could forget, fading into the morning light.

"Oh, little sister—"

Mircalla was cut off by pounding footsteps as Jeri began to sob. Someone skidded to the ground beside the Vampire—

The next thing Jeri knew, she was screaming in Mircalla's arms, trying so hard to get just a sip of what was beneath that fragile skin. She was so thirsty. Just a taste, she'd be okay if she could have just a mouthful... but Mircalla was keeping her away from that sweet, sweet scent that promised salvation.

"Holy... you said to keep my distance, but..." The man swore, sounding farther away than before.

"Yes, this is what happens." Despite Jeri's thrashing, Mircalla's voice was calm and her grip firm. "Why do you think we try to keep fledglings isolated from non-Vampires? They don't have any control yet. Officer, if you do not in fact have a suicide wish, just place the bag on the ground and remove yourself."

A shaky voice rose from the direction of the one thing Jeri wanted more than anything right now. "Yes, ma'am."

Another few moments passed while Jeri fought with strength she had not thought she possessed. She found herself crying more as that sweet scent moved farther away, and she wailed in distress.

"He won't make that mistake twice," the other man muttered as Mircalla attempted to shush Jeri. "For that matter, neither will I. I didn't think she could move."

"There is nothing more motivating to the newly fledged than a meal." A tendril of shadow reached out from behind Jeri to grab the far less appetizing bag on the ground. "I know, my dear, but you will like this, I promise." The tendril ripped the corner of the bag open inches from Jeri's face.

Mircalla let go as Jeri lunged for it. Now that the bag was open she could smell it, and she *wanted* it. Greedily she sucked the red liquid into her mouth–

She almost immediately threw it up, the cold, viscous liquid making her stomach turn. She felt almost impossibly betrayed, but despite that she could not stop drinking it even as her stomach rebelled.

"It is better warm," the Vampire admitted, taking out a small orange crystal. She crushed it in her fist over the bag, and as motes of yellow-orange light drifted down, the contents began to steam.

The liquid went down much more smoothly, coating the inside of her mouth and throat with sanguine relief. Ignoring the part of her mind that was screaming at her for drinking blood, she downed the rest of it.

"Um, here's the coat again."

Jeri felt Mircalla drape the fabric across her shoulders as her eyes grew heavy again. "Thank you, Johanen."

Even through the exhaustion, Jeri found herself aggressively trying to consume every last drop.

"Doesn't look like her body is going to reject the transforma-
tion?"

"No, the immediate danger is over. It's all right, Jeri, you can rest
now."

Had she been in danger? She couldn't remember, the hazy feeling
of warmth traveling from her stomach lulling her to sleep.

"Excellent, that means we can actually start processing this crime
scene once you get her out of here. Where are you going to take her,
anyway? It's been so long since there's been a turning in this town
that I haven't bothered to look up the protocols for it for years."

Jeri felt Mircalla cradle her against her chest. "Home, of course."

Home sounded nice...

Jeri fought back tears as she looked at her reflection in the mirror.

She had several large bruises, one by her temple, one on her back,
and a few on her arms. She looked gaunt, as though she hadn't eaten
in weeks, hip and collar bones unnaturally pronounced. Someone
had done their best to remove the paint – blood? – that had been
used to mark her body with arcane runes, but the skin had been
stained and faint red marks remained against the stark pallor of her
skin. Angry red welts marked her wrists and ankles from where the
rope had been tied too tight. Scabbed-over cuts stretched from the

inside of her elbows almost to her wrists where she had all but been bled dry.

Her hair was mostly chin-length, uneven chunks a result of her hair having been cut while in its typical braid. It was *ruined*. Was it a silly thing to cry over? Perhaps, considering that she had literally died, but for Jeri it was just one thing too many. She loved her hair. The deep golden strands were something she took pride in, something she loved about her appearance. It didn't seem fair to both die and have her hair be ruined.

She shuddered at the thought of a shadowy, faceless man cutting her hair off. She'd tried to remember, but couldn't recall what he'd looked like. In some ways it was almost worse, as her mind supplied all sorts of frightening possibilities. Every time she looked at the ragged edges of her hair she just imagined a dark shadow with teeth holding her down as the knife came closer...

The tears welling up in her eyes had a decidedly red tint to them. Lady, she'd never look pretty when crying again, would she? She'd be a bloody mess from here on out.

And what was she supposed to do with herself? She'd liked working as a maid in the Palace of Dusk under her mother, who was the head housekeeper. Vampires didn't do such mundane tasks, though. Instead they mostly became healers or joined the Black Watch, neither of which sounded appealing to Jeri.

She'd met many Vampires while working in the palace. She'd never even dreamed she might become one. The Lady's gift was rare, and sometimes the turning just didn't take. Sometimes fledglings just... faded and died anyway.

She shuddered. Would that be her fate?

The room she had woken up in was a comfortable size, similar to her room back home, with an arched ceiling. Against one wall was a delicate desk made of dark wood with a matching chair next to a full-length mirror. A door to an adjoining bathroom was next to that. Two small dormers jutted out from the wall opposite the door, windows covered in heavy dark drapes. A little bench with cushions sat in front of one, a plush ivory armchair in front of the other. The hardwood floor was covered with a black, cream, and brown rug covered with tessellating diamond patterns. Across from the desk was something of a dais recessed halfway into the wall, forming a comfortable nook. Set into the dais was a plain coffin made of pale-yellow wood, with soft sheets and blankets and a plethora of pillows.

Jeri had woken up in the coffin.

She wasn't stupid; she knew Vampires slept in coffins. It was just surreal for *her* to be sleeping in one. At least it had been comfortable, and the top had been left cracked open so the room's soft lighting could filter in, provided by several electric lights shaped like candles.

There was a knock at the door, and a muffled, "Jeri? May I come in?"

Mircalla.

She wiped at her eyes angrily with a tissue and grabbed the soft, pale-green robe that had been left for her. She couldn't hide the travesty of her hair, but at least she could hide her body. "You may."

The door opened, revealing the beautiful Vampire who was now Jeri's Mistress. A delicate-looking woman with soft, pale-yellow hair in long waves down her back, Mircalla was wearing a deep-blue gown with white leather and gold accents. She had a box wrapped in golden paper under one arm, which she put on a nearby table before closing the door behind her and turning to her fledgling. Her dark-blue eyes were full of concern as she took in Jeri's appearance.

"Good evening, little sister. You look like you are feeling a bit better today?" Her soft voice rose at the end, making the statement a question.

Jeri had, very briefly, met Mircalla before at the Palace of Dusk, though she hadn't recognized the petite woman in her Watch Blacks. One of the oldest Vampires in the Lord's court, Mircalla was deeply respected by her peers. Though technically a member of the Black Watch, Mircalla was rarely in Tarvishte, more often watching over her estate in the Carpas Mountains south of the capital city. When she did come to the palace, it was more often due to issues of governance or social events, from Jeri's understanding.

"I feel terrible," Jeri said honestly, pulling the robe tighter around herself. She glanced at the mirror again, the sight of her hair making her blink back tears again.

"I am sorry, Jeri," Mircalla said, true sympathy in her voice. "If it helps, your hair will grow back. And we can trim it to make it look more intentional."

Jeri blinked. "How did you...?"

The Vampire smiled. "You are my fledgling now. Sires are connected to their fledglings, so I have a basic sense of your feelings, which will ebb with distance. This close I have a pretty clear idea. How about physically, though? Are your wounds healing? I still see bruising." The woman gracefully twisted the chair from in front of the desk and folded herself into it, indicating with a wave of her hand that Jeri should also sit.

Jeri shrugged as she sat in the plush armchair, pulling it to sit farther into the room. "I'm covered in all sorts of marks, but I'm not as sore as I thought I would be."

Mircalla nodded slowly. "Hmm. Usually feeding helps heal wounds, but you had lost a lot of blood, and it is likely your first feeding went to replenishing that instead of healing the more superficial damage. I am sure subsequent meals will help."

"What... what exactly happened?" Jeri had been trying to remember, but most of it was a blur. "I thought I was on a train, coming back from Vaslu to Tarvishte with two of my friends. Are... are they all right?"

Mircalla's blue eyes were sympathetic. "From what the local police have managed to put together, the three of you got off the train in Navodar during a stopover, where a Vampire kidnapped you."

A *Vampire* had kidnapped her? Perhaps that was why the shadow in her mind had such pronounced teeth. But even with that information, the image did not become any more clear. "Why?" she asked, aghast.

"He was a follower of Kaldor."

Jeri shuddered. The dark god of the Distant Trinity was a nightmare to imagine. "A Vampire worshiped Kaldor?"

"It can happen. Vampires are individuals too, and sometimes we do not make the best choices."

Jeri remembered the cold stone slab and the odd marks on her skin. A feeling of revulsion washed over her. "He was..." It was difficult to complete the thought.

"A sacrifice ritual," Mircalla finished for her. "He needed blood from three unwilling sources. I am sorry, Jeri. You were the only one still fighting when we found you."

Jeri felt tears prickle her eyes again. "Mellanie and Fortuna...?"

Mircalla shook her head.

A sob welled up in her chest, and before she knew it Jeri was crying again. Desperately she wiped at her eyes with her sleeve, only to be horrified at the red marks now staining the fabric, making her cry even harder.

"Ah, little sister, it is okay to weep for this loss." Mircalla was beside her, sitting on the arm of the chair and wrapping Jeri in a hug. "Your friends were dear to you. Do not worry about the robe; Vampires have all manner of spells to remove blood from fabrics. Just cry for now."

When Jeri had cried herself out, pulling away as she sniffled, the sight of blood everywhere made her heart sink. It was on her, some had gotten on the chair... it was even on Mircalla.

The Vampire clucked her tongue. "Ah ah, I told you not to concern yourself with this. I know you are a maid, so cleanliness is important to you, but I promise I have access to things that will make it as though this had never happened."

Jeri sniffled. "The Vampires at the palace never make such messes."

Mircalla smiled. "I assure you they do on occasion, but we are accustomed to cleaning up after ourselves so as not to traumatize the staff. In fact, here."

There was a soft woofing sound at her door, and the handle turned, letting in a large gray warg. It padded over to them and dropped a pale-pink spell crystal into Mircalla's hand before turning and leaving the two women alone again.

"This spell crystal has a cleaning spell in it, hmm?" The Vampire activated it and the blood faded away, leaving the fabrics untouched.

Jeri felt like far too much had happened all at once, but she focused on the one thing she knew. "That kind of spell is expensive."

"It is, yes, but very worth it when you cry bloody water," Mircalla said reasonably. "I don't want you to feel like you should be repressing your feelings because of such a thing."

Jeri supposed that made sense. Her eyes traveled back to her door. "You have wargs here?"

"Ah." Here Mircalla hesitated a moment. "Not usually, I will admit. But I am normally attended to by the citizens of Karnstejn, and with you so newly fledged I cannot risk having them here. The local warg pack agreed to aid me while you learn to control yourself."

Mountain wargs! Notoriously more aggressive and isolationist than their city counterparts, but if they had agreed to help Mircalla then surely they must be safe?

Then the first part of Mircalla's statement caught up with Jeri's brain, and she flushed. "I wouldn't harm anyone!"

Mircalla hummed, wrapping an arm around Jeri again. "You absolutely would in your current state. You would not be able to stop yourself. It is all right; you will learn control with time. As your Sire it is my duty to teach you."

Jeri thought about it, eyebrows scrunching together, but could not even conceive of attacking another person. "I don't understand."

Serious blue eyes considered her for a moment. "Follow me."

Mircalla brought Jeri to the castle's kitchen and had her sit at the large wooden table near the fireplace while the older Vampire went out through a heavy stone door to what looked like a small courtyard. A fire crackled cheerfully, warming the room. Two wargs were stretched out in front of the flames, and Jeri was starkly reminded of the palace as a feeling of homesickness washed over her.

But the kitchen at home would never be so empty. This kitchen was waiting for people – pots and pans and other bakeware neatly hung in their places on the walls; a large butcher's block of knives, jars of condiments, and a bowl of fresh fruit sat on the counters; barrels and crates rested in the corners. But Jeri and the two wargs were the only ones here.

It was sad.

After a few minutes Mircalla came back inside, something small cradled in her hands. She placed it on the table in front of Jeri.

It was a baby chick, soft yellow down making it a puff of feathers. It cheeped.

"Oh!" Jeri exclaimed, reaching forward to stroke its head. "What is this for?"

"Because if you can't find it in you to spare something so helpless, a non-Vampire will never stand a chance."

Jeri's brow furrowed. "What do you mean?" she asked, cupping the little bird in her palms. There was something about it...

Before Jeri knew it she was coughing up feathers, the memory of blood on her tongue screaming at her to get more.

She stared at her hands, stunned. "What...?" She coughed, the feeling of small bones going down her throat extremely unpleasant.

Mircalla hummed soothingly, taking Jeri's hands in her own and wiping them clean with a damp handkerchief. "It's all right, this is why we practice with chicks and not people, hmm? And I know that probably felt uncomfortable but it is perfectly safe for you to consume them whole, I promise."

Jeri felt a growing feeling of horror. Why in the Lady's name had she eaten the chick? She had felt no desire to do so at all, and then... it was gone. It was as if her body had not stopped to consult her brain at all. How was she supposed to stop herself from doing that when she had no memory of either the motivation or performing the action? She met Mircalla's eyes desperately.

"It is hard. I know. I remember," came the reassuring words as Mircalla gently rubbed Jeri's wrists with her thumbs. "But it is not impossible."

Jeri was coming to the terrifying realization that this was the reason new fledglings were kept away, sometimes for years, after their turnings. She had always thought it had more to do with coming to terms with what they were, but no – it was so they wouldn't *eat* anyone.

She didn't want to be hidden away for years.

"I want to go home," she whispered after a moment. "I want to see my mother."

"Which is completely understandable," Mircalla agreed immediately. "But until you learn control it is safer for everyone if you remain here."

"Alone?" Jeri asked, feeling tears begin to well up again. Learn control? Everything felt like it was spiraling out of control. "With just you and... and the wargs?"

"Oh no, no, of course not," Mircalla hastened to reassure her. "I would never dream of isolating you so thoroughly; that's not healthy at all. Had you been Sired by a Vampire with a larger Court, we would not be so alone in my house, but... well. No, we will have visitors, but they will be other Vampires. In fact, one of my friends will be coming by in a day or two with your clothes from Tarvishte."

A Court was essentially a family of Vampires, related by blood turning. Some Courts were extensive, others quite small. "Oh." Jeri was beginning to feel overwhelmed. "My clothes?"

"Indeed. I thought you would be more comfortable in your own things, so I sent for them." The Vampire stood, prompting Jeri to stand with her, and began to guide her out of the kitchen. "Your mother has also been made aware of the situation, and I expect there will be a letter for you along with your belongings. And of course you may write to her and anyone else you wish as often as you like. I have plenty of stationery, and should you go through it all I will be happy to acquire more."

It wouldn't be the same, but at least Jeri would be able to communicate with her mother. She wasn't cut off completely. "Thank you."

"And you are also free to explore the castle to your heart's content," Mircalla continued. "There is even a small chapel to Hades in the west wing, if it would ease you to pray to the Lady. Tomorrow I will give you more of a tour; you are still exhausted right now, and rightfully so. Your next proper feeding will also be tomorrow, and that is sure to help."

"Not another chick," Jeri said, blanching.

Mircalla smiled. "No, not right away. Just a regular bag of blood. We can hold off on that for a while; no one expects you to learn control in less than a week. It can take some time, but do not worry – I will be here for you while you learn. You are my fledgling. It is my honor to prove myself a worthy Sire to you. And on that note" – she pushed open the door to Jeri's room and settled her down in the chair – "I have this for you." She picked up the wrapped box she had brought earlier and handed it to Jeri.

"A present?" Jeri asked, brushing a finger along the smooth gold paper. A small bow of sheer cream ribbon sat on top.

The Vampire nodded with a smile, stepping back to give Jeri her space.

Carefully, Jeri peeled back the paper to reveal a pretty wooden box. Opening it, she was surprised to see a stuffed golden-yellow warg, the same shade as her hair. She took it out gently, examining it. "A stuffed animal?" she wondered aloud as she stroked the soft fur.

Something about the stuffing felt a little strange, firmer than most stuffed animals she'd owned when she was little.

"I know it may seem strange since you are an adult," Mircalla explained, "but this is actually a traditional first gift from Sire to fledgling. It is partially stuffed with dirt from Tarvishte, so sleeping with it will aid your ability to rest." She gestured towards the dais. "This has also been filled with dirt from your home city. You will find that being surrounded – even partially – by dirt from home will make it *much* easier to rest. And of course, the other part of that is your coffin."

Both women looked at the pale-yellow casket set into the dais.

"My apologies for the low quality of this one; it is only meant to be temporary. I am having one made for you specifically, but it will take a few weeks to be ready."

"Oh. Thank you." Jeri hadn't thought about where the coffin had come from. It was odd enough she had one at all. "This one is fine, though. It was very comfortable to sleep in." She found herself wrapping her arms around the stuffed warg.

"No fledgling of mine will rest in a plain pine box," Mircalla said with a sniff, causing Jeri's eyebrows to raise just a fraction. "But it couldn't be helped in the short term." The Vampire shook her head, lips pressing into a thin line before her expression smoothed out. "But all of that aside, it will be dawn soon. You should get some rest. Also, I would leave the curtains as they are for now – the touch of sunlight will burn you quite badly, and Karnstejn is not a large enough settlement to warrant a solar aegis."

Jeri frowned. That was right, most Vampires couldn't go out in the sunlight until they were old enough to withstand it without the complex spells that protected the major cities.

Another thing she'd lost. Of all things, the *sun*.

She found herself clutching the stuffed warg.

"And please, Jeri, do not hesitate to reach out to me if you need anything." The Vampire clasped her hands together in front of her chest. "Anything at all. While I know some things are not possible in the immediate future, that does not mean they will always be, and I want to make your stay here with me as comfortable as possible. I know this is a turbulent time for you, and I want to help in any way I can."

Jeri bowed her head. "Thank you very much. You've done so much for me already."

Mircalla smiled. "Rest well, little sister." She swept from the room in a swirl of deep-blue skirts.

Jeri looked around at her room again. She *was* tired; Mircalla had been correct about that. She looked towards the bathroom. She should try to wash and see about getting more of those red marks off, but the very thought made her even more exhausted. She could do it tomorrow.

There was a small dresser next to the dais that was mostly empty, but it did have a couple of nightgowns in it. Jeri slipped out of the robe, draping it on the desk chair, and changed into a long white gown. She turned off the lights and slid into her coffin.

She stared up at the cover for several minutes. To close it, or not to? Closed meant safety, but the dark...

A shadowy figure held her down, knife glinting impossibly in the dark as her hair fell in chunks…

She found herself getting up again to turn the lights back on, the soft yellow light soothing for reasons she didn't understand. She crawled back into her coffin, cuddling the stuffed warg. She decided she could leave it partially closed, as it had been when she'd awoken.

It was still a long time before sleep found her.

And so Jeri found herself not-a-prisoner in Castle Karnstejn.

She felt bad even thinking that – Mircalla had done nothing but be welcoming and as supportive as possible – but she still could not do the one thing her heart yearned for.

Go home.

Every time she thought *maybe, maybe this time*, Mircalla would offer her a chick.

And every time Jeri devoured it without a second thought.

She tired quickly of the taste of feathers.

It was depressing, even though Mircalla constantly reassured her that this was not unexpected. Most fledglings did not attain control for the first three years. Some managed in as few as one, but some also took longer, going as long as seven or eight years before passing the test.

Jeri could not imagine being separated from her mother for that long.

She found herself in the chapel often, praying to Hades for help. The death goddess was also the goddess of order, protection, and healing, and Jeri hoped the Goddess's support could help her achieve control faster. Sometimes she prayed instead for the Lady to banish the shadowy figure she still could not remember clearly. But though she prayed and prayed and prayed, she did not hear the Lady's voice again.

She also took up cooking for Mircalla and herself, as the kitchen sitting empty was far too sad for her to ignore. Most of the normal food she made ended up turning her stomach, but Mircalla said that too would pass, that her body just needed time to acclimate.

She rested, let her body heal from the experience that had killed her. Let her Sire's friend look her over to make sure everything was as it should be.

The wargs followed her from place to place, but she found with great disappointment they were not as interested in pets and cuddles as those she was used to. Instead, it felt like they were judging her for her failures, settling across the room and staring at her.

And on top of everything, she *hated* her new short haircut. Every time she looked in the mirror she felt a wave of impotent rage that her hair had been cut off without her consent, and then her mind tried to recall the man who had taken it from her. She still could not remember much of the attack and subsequent blood-draining ritual, but her unconscious mind was trying to fill in the gaps no matter how much she wished it wouldn't. She often found herself jolting awake in a cold sweat, clutching the stuffed warg and grateful for the light filtering into her coffin.

Sometimes it felt like everything she'd loved before turning and everything she'd tried since was ruined for her. Mircalla kept telling her to give it time, that things would even out, but...

Jeri didn't want to wait.

How was she to learn control when it felt like everything she tried was outside of her ability to do so? She could not control her body's reaction to blood or food; she couldn't control where she went or who she could see; she couldn't even control the length of her damn hair.

Just about the only thing she felt like she *could* control was the laundry. A few days after waking up in Castle Karnstejn she had taken charge of it after realizing Mircalla intended to send it down to the village. Jeri had been doing laundry for as long as she could remember; there was no reason to have someone else do it for her just because she was now a fledgling. It was a small piece of her old life that she could hold on to, just one small piece of normalcy.

She clung to it.

Mircalla tried to help ease her into her new life. The "traditional gifts" continued. The new coffin came in, this one of a different yellow wood with subtle speckling and gold accents. A fresh bouquet of sunflowers was placed in her room every week. A topaz and peridot necklace signifying her adoption into Mircalla's Court was presented to her after a month in the castle.

She wrote to her mother constantly, sharing the new things she was learning and trying to put a positive spin on the situation. Her mother wrote her back, glad that she was as well as she could be, and sharing gossip from the palace.

Jeri missed her fiercely.

But the dead chicks reminded her that she could not go to see others who were not Vampires.

Not yet.

Jeri couldn't help but sigh as she sauteed the onion and rice together.

"What is the matter, little sister?" Mircalla asked from where she was sitting at the kitchen table, papers spread across the wooden surface in front of her as she searched through them.

"This is one of my favorite dishes, and I just know I'm only going to be able to eat one roll before I won't be able to have any more," she explained, taking the pan off the heat and setting it aside to cool.

Mircalla hummed thoughtfully. "Have you tried adding blood to the dishes? Our Lord Vlad often adds blood to his hot chocolate. It is a unique taste."

Jeri almost gagged at the thought. "No, that's gross."

"It is odd, but then, Vlad often is. But this dish already calls for tomato juice, does it not? That seems a less egregious pairing."

Jeri frowned, forcing back the instinctual "no" and trying to look at it from her new point of view – that of a Vampire. Was that pairing less awful? "I am going to be cooking the tomato juice. Can I cook blood in the same way?"

Her Sire looked up from her papers, turning to look at the spread of ingredients on the counter. "I'm honestly not sure. I do not often cook, never mind with blood. I enjoy the simpler methods." She gestured towards her wine glass, filled with her favorite O positive. "I suppose you could always add it in at the end? Or perhaps dip the rolls in it like a sauce?"

"Perhaps," she answered noncommittally. She'd see how it felt when she got there. She began mixing together the pork and spices.

"Have you had your blood today?" Mircalla asked, turning back to her papers. "If you are satiated it might help. And you have favorites! That is an excellent sign."

Jeri glanced at the cold box where her bag of B negative was waiting for her. "Because I'm drinking it slowly enough to actually taste it?" she asked dryly. And how odd was that, that the different blood types all had different tastes? B negative was by far her favorite. AB negative tasted terrible.

Mircalla was nodding excitedly. "Exactly so! It is one of the earliest expressions of control that a fledgling can show."

"So when healers say they can taste what is wrong with you, they mean that literally," Jeri realized, adding the rice and onions to the pork mixture. "I always thought it was more of a 'this is the best way to explain it' explanation."

The older Vampire put down her pen and stretched. "It is very literal. It's something to keep in mind if you ever feed directly from a live source, because sometimes you end up with something unexpected. Sometimes even the person doesn't know about whatever has caused the change. You could be their first warning that something is wrong."

"But Vampires don't feed from live sources very often anymore. We don't need to, right?"

"That is true." Mircalla drifted over to the counter where Jeri was wrapping her filling in cabbage leaves. "But depending on what you choose to do once you have completely fledged and left my side, you may find yourself in situations where you need to feed directly. And sometimes – rarely, but it does happen – blood is offered freely."

Jeri's mouth thinned, and the roll she was making got wrapped tighter than it needed to be. "Sometimes it feels like I will never fully fledge."

"Jeri, you have been here just over a month. Do not become discouraged." Mircalla reached over and tilted Jeri's head to look at her, fingers under her chin. "We have plenty of time. I would even go so far as to say that you are ahead of schedule if you are tasting the blood."

Jeri felt a little part of herself warm at the praise, but still. "I miss my mother."

"Which is completely understandable. Would you like me to fetch another chick?"

She heaved a sigh. "No, I don't think I can handle any more failure today." She pulled away to cover her rolls with shredded bacon.

"What have you failed at today?"

"Well, I think these will probably be a disappointment." She poured in the tomato juice and sprinkled more cabbage on top. "And I did not sleep well, either." Just the thought conjured an image of a man, blurry on the edges and pure shadow in the middle, teeth and knife both standing out starkly against the darkness...

Mircalla frowned. "The nightmares still persist?"

Jeri was never completely sure what to think about Mircalla's ability to all but read her mind. "Yes."

"I suppose that is not terribly surprising," her Sire said slowly. "The situation we found you in certainly qualifies as traumatic. Perhaps you would be willing to speak to a mind healer about them?"

A mind healer? Jeri hadn't considered it before, but if it made it easier to sleep... "If you think that would help?"

"Almost certainly." The Vampire nodded decisively. "I will make the arrangements. It is no trouble."

"Thank you," she said, sliding the dish into the oven. She fought back annoyance as her short hair swung into her face. "I know he is dead, but sometimes it feels like my mind refuses to acknowledge that."

"Our minds can be tricky things," Mircalla agreed, going back to sit at the table. "It can be difficult to figure out how to... reset them, if you will. Do you need more exposure to it, or less? What is the true core of the problem? But mind healers are good at that. I do not wish for that sorry excuse for a Vampire to be haunting your steps. You are my fledgling. You will be meant for greater things."

As Jeri set the timer for her rolls, she found herself wondering if that was true.

Two more months passed.

More chicks died.

The mind healer had been an excellent idea. Flaviu was kind and endlessly reassuring, and one of the first things she had done was prescribe Jeri a sleeping aid. Jeri hadn't even known there were any that would work on Vampires, but Flaviu reassured her that it was perfectly safe and that getting a good night's sleep was important while they worked on untangling the root cause.

Not that it was a secret or difficult to uncover, but Flaviu reminded her that traumatic experiences left mental marks as well as physical ones, and that sometimes it took work to help those heal. And while acknowledging the root of the problem was important, there was usually more work to do for true healing.

So the Vampire came once a week and spent a few hours with Jeri, strolling around the castle gardens or through the halls, and Jeri felt a bit better afterwards.

But it was only a matter of time before the shadows began to close in again. And while the sleeping aid helped, it could only do so much.

And so she found herself wandering through the halls one day when she should have been sleeping. One of the wargs – this one quite a bit smaller than the rest – was following her at a distance. Whenever she turned to look at him he would sit and wag his tail twice. If she tried to approach he would stay out of reach, but if she continued on he stayed within sight. She started to turn around on purpose just to see him sit and wag his tail, and though he was not interested in her coming closer, he also seemed to be enjoying the game.

As she explored, she wondered what the castle was normally like. Was this quiet darkness normal, or had Mircalla just made sure her fledgling could not be harmed by the sun in her castle? The Vampire had said she was normally attended to by the villagers – did that mean the castle was usually busy the way the palace was in Tarvishte? Or was it a smaller group of people who came by occasionally to help Mircalla take care of the estate? What would it be like after Jeri attained control and the villagers could return?

Jeri noted that she was finding it much easier to see in the dark than before her turning.

As she and the warg continued their silly game, she heard voices drift down the hallway from the direction of Mircalla's office. Bored and a little lonely, she decided to head that way. Perhaps it would be a good distraction.

She knocked on the smooth, dark grain of the door and waited for Mircalla's "Enter!" before going in.

Mircalla's office was large, and in Jeri's opinion it was more like two rooms without a wall dividing them than one unified space. One side was the office – a dark wooden desk with a single neat stack of papers; a desk chair with pale-blue upholstery; two comfortable armchairs across from the desk in the same shade. A gold-and-blue geometric rug covered the hardwood floor, and a side table with a number of bottles sat on it against one wall. The other side was more like a sitting room, with a thick, plush rug in cream, two pale-blue velvet couches with a scattering of pillows, and two more armchairs. A low, round coffee table made of dark wood sat in the middle. Plants were scattered about both halves in decorative vases, and the area was lit by the soft yellow glow of candles in addition to the dim electric lights. There was a large set of floor-to-ceiling windows behind the desk that were covered by heavy blue curtains. Mircalla liked to open the curtains on clear nights to let the moonlight in, but always left them drawn during the day.

The office's owner was currently sitting on one of the couches, the shape of her bronze gown suggesting that her feet were tucked up beside her. Across from her in one of the armchairs was Morden, a Vampire Jeri had a passing familiarity with from the palace. His long black hair streaked with white was pulled back into a neat ponytail, and his mustache and beard were trimmed short. Kind brown eyes regarded her over a steaming mug of coffee. His overcoat was draped on the back of the chair – whatever he was here for, he did not expect it to take long.

"Jeri!" Mircalla exclaimed, patting the couch next to her. "Come sit! Have a maple candy. Morden brought them from Gallia. Would you like some tea?"

She glanced back into the hallway, but the warg had already padded off somewhere else. "No thank you," she said, crossing the room to sit beside her Sire, considering the candy. She had been doing better with food; surely one little piece would be fine.

"And how is our newest fledgling doing?" Morden asked. He had been the one who had brought Jeri's clothes and checked her over in the beginning. He was also one of Vlad's oldest friends and a member of the king's Court.

"I am still working on control," she admitted with an annoyed twist of her lips as she took one of the candies from the plate on the coffee table. "But otherwise I feel that I have been settling in as well as possible, given the circumstances. How is my mother?"

"She is doing well, from what I can see, though I know she misses you. I would be happy to pass along a message for you, if you'd like. I leave to return to Tarvishte shortly, and I expect I'll be back there by tonight."

Oh, that was much faster than the normal mail! "Yes please, if you could take a letter before you go I would appreciate it greatly!"

He smiled and inclined his head. "Of course. Though if I may, it might perhaps be serendipitous that you've joined us. I've been investigating your case."

She glanced at Mircalla, but the other woman only nodded in encouragement. "In Gallia?" she asked, confused. "I thought I was found in Navodar?"

"That is correct," Morden agreed, pausing to take another sip of his coffee. "But we've been trying to figure out what Alec was trying to do, exactly. We know it was a ritual in the name of Kaldor. But what was its purpose?"

"There seems to have been some evidence that he wasn't working completely alone," Mircalla explained at Jeri's puzzled look. "So understanding the 'why' may help us to catch other conspirators."

Morden shook his head. "But the trail appears to have gone cold in Gallia. Kaldor's adherents are not numerous and do not advertise themselves to begin with, so they are difficult to track down by design, but I had hoped... for something, at least." He scowled into his mug. "But since you are here, perhaps you've managed to remember something from that night?"

She looked down at the partially unwrapped candy in her hand, stomach turning to lead. "No, I'm sorry. That night has never really gotten clearer. It's just... shapes, and feelings. I don't even remember why we got off the train."

Mircalla drew her into a hug. "Likely Vampiric suggestion. Which could also explain why you don't remember; sometimes it does odd things to people's memories if the Vampire tries to force it or over-does it."

"Don't concern yourself with it," Morden said gently. "The thing that was of most concern was the bloodletting, but it's possible that wasn't even Kaldor-specific, and instead something Alec threw in because he was a Vampire." He paused. "Which is why it was concerning."

"Why would he do that? Did he drink any of it?" Jeri asked with a frown.

Morden stared into his cup for a moment. "It's hard to tell if he did or not at this point, though my instinct is to say 'yes.' Remember that Alec was a Vampire, and if the opportunity presented itself..."

"Alec wasn't terribly old," Mircalla explained to Jeri. "Just under a century. And you have first-hand knowledge of how hard it can be to resist blood when it is in front of us."

"Though Vampires – the good ones, anyway – don't want to bring harm to those around us, to some degree the violence is in-nate," Morden mused. "The first thing a fledgling will do is try to kill. We have to acknowledge that is a part of us, too. Our mother is the Goddess of death, and our makeup reflects that. Like Her, we have both the power to heal and the power to kill."

Mircalla snorted. "All living beings have that capacity."

"But it's so much more pronounced in Vampires, you must admit." Morden was actually pouting.

"I don't think either of us are terribly interested in philosophy right now," Mircalla said dryly, smiling at Jeri.

Jeri managed a weak smile back.

"Oh, all right, fine then. Have you two any plans for the Longest Night?"

Jeri felt her heart sink at the reminder. It would be the first time spending the holiday apart from her mother.

"I've sent a few invitations," Mircalla said, accepting the change in subject with grace. "I hope to make a little gathering of it here. Anna and her fledgling Kaeden, Waylon, Esther, Jayne, and a few others... You are also invited, though I assume you'll be joining the king's vigil?"

"Ah, if you sent an invitation it is probably awaiting me along with a pile of other mail. One of the hazards of being gone for an extended period." Morden sighed. "Though yes, I will probably be attending the king's vigil."

"You know mine will be more fun." Mircalla winked with a playful smile.

Morden shook his head. "Please don't tell me you've been listening to Jak."

"There's no greater authority to consult," she said with a laugh.

Jeri ignored the banter, trying to push past the disappointment. Mircalla had promised to make the holiday fun, but it wasn't what Jeri truly wanted. Not that she could have what she truly wanted.

"Well, I should be on my way," Morden said, standing and placing his mug on the table. "I'll have to report to Vlad and Primrose as soon as I get back, and I'd rather get that out of the way sooner rather than later." He looked at Jeri as he swung his coat on. "Would you like to get your letter for your mother?"

"Oh, yes. Thank you!"

She ran to her room to get her letter and delivered it back to the study, out of breath. Morden accepted it with a flourish, promising to deliver it promptly, and bade the two women farewell. Mircalla offered to see him to the border of her domain, and told Jeri to try to get some sleep before dusk.

Rather than going to bed, though, Jeri ended up drifting through the empty hallways again, thinking over the elder Vampire's words.

Eventually she found herself in the kitchen, a warg dozing in front of the embers in the hearth. The dishes from dinner were still by the sink; perhaps cleaning them would give her something to do while her mind refused to settle. She added a few logs to the fire, and before long the kitchen was almost as cheery as the palace kitchens.

But Jeri was still alone.

She scrubbed at the pots and pans in annoyance.

She wanted to be able to spend the Longest Night with her mother.

She did not want that Vampire to ruin her life any more than he already had. He had achieved control, yet he had still done horrible things to her and her friends.

She refused to be a lesser Vampire than him.

Her eyes caught on the door to the courtyard.

Morden's words echoed in her mind: *"To some degree the violence is innate... We have to acknowledge that is a part of us, too."*

Control, but while acknowledging the potential for violence.

She pulled a bit of the curtain aside from one of the windows with the fireplace poker, but it only confirmed what her instincts were telling her – night had fallen. She looked at the warg, but though it raised its head it made no move to stop her.

She pushed open the door and looked around. The courtyard was fairly large, with a gate on the other side. There was a well, a stack of crates, bags of grain in one corner, and the coop.

The coop was large, and Jeri wondered how many chickens it housed. Thirty? Forty? That was a lot of chickens. No wonder Mircalla was never lacking a chick to sacrifice.

Jeri took a deep breath and went in.

When Mircalla found her, Jeri was kneeling in the center of the coop, hands cupped in her lap. Blood, bones, and feathers were everywhere, spattered on the floor, the walls, the nesting boxes. Jeri herself was covered in bloody pieces of chicken, her arms red from her hands almost to her elbows. She'd thrown up a pile of feathers and bones in the corner, the pure amount too much even for her new stomach.

The coop was silent.

Mircalla knocked on the open door to the coop. "Jeri?"

Jeri looked up from her hands to her Sire. "I did it." Everything felt sharper, clearer, more... real.

"I can see the red in your eyes. You've drunk much tonight," Mircalla said, voice calm. "Probably a little too much. Fledglings don't know when to stop."

"No," Jeri whispered, bringing her hands up and opening them. "I did it."

One yellow chick, sleeping peacefully in her palms.

Mircalla blinked, then smiled, kneeling next to her fledgling. "Yes, yes you did. Proof of control."

Jeri looked at the ball of yellow feathers. Though she keenly felt the desire to drain the creature, she was able to control the feeling – and so the little chick slept.

"Congratulations, little sister," Mircalla murmured. She reached forward to stroke the chick's head with one delicate finger. "Now the real training can begin."

Green

I

One of Ander's earliest observations was that his eyes were as green as his mother's hair.

The other was that he wasn't like everyone else.

It was more than his appearance – the ears, pointed, but not fully Avari, despite his white hair, or his eyes, which were almost a Human green but not quite. It was more than his lack of a father. (People had whispered about the man's disappearance for as long as Ander could remember. He didn't care. The man was gone; there was no use dwelling on it.)

It was something about how people interacted, how they seemed to know how to communicate with each other in a way that allowed for connection and led to desired responses.

Ander couldn't figure it out.

The six-year-old watched his mother speak with the woman standing behind the bakery counter, a hand fisted in her long dark-gray skirt, standing just a bit behind her.

"Good morning, Leyna!" the woman greeted her, her smile smaller than the one she had greeted her previous customer with. "What are you looking for today?"

His mother smiled back. Her eyes crinkled. "Good morning, Etta. Just two loaves of rye; I don't think I'll have the chance to come back until next week."

The woman's smile brightened. "Of course, of course." There was a pause, and her smile faded slightly. "Would you like to wait a few minutes? We have a few coming out of the oven shortly."

His mother smiled again but shook her head. "Those two there will be just fine."

Ander, who preferred the warm bread straight from the oven, tugged on his mother's skirts.

She just ran a hand over his hair, patting it gently. She did not change their order.

"I'll wrap these for you, then." The woman's movements were quick and precise, her smile returned to its earlier size.

Ander watched closely, impressed with how the brown paper sheets were deftly wrapped around the loaves. It was almost mesmerizing. He liked watching the woman wrap their bread.

The woman glanced at him but looked away quickly. "Odd eyes, for a child to have."

His mother hummed. "Green ones?" Neither her tone nor her ears changed.

"No, no, of course not." The woman spoke quickly, smile twitching a little wider. "It's just... very... intense."

His mother wrapped an arm around him and pulled him closer to her. "He's just curious. He likes watching people."

The woman's eyes flickered towards him again, but the moment they met his she looked down at the wrapped loaves. "Of course." She held out her hand.

His mother handed over a number of bills before placing the loaves in the bag she carried on her arm. "Thank you, Etta, as always. Have a nice week."

"Of course, Leyna! You as well!" She waved at them as his mother guided him out of the shop into the damp, cold air of their little town.

Ander frowned at the bag. "Mama, why not the warm bread?"

Now his mother's ears did twitch downward, ever so slightly, but she still smiled at him. "Because she did not want us to stay, little one." Her voice was low, and she ran a hand over his hair again.

What? "But she said…" He scrunched his eyebrows together, displeased and confused.

"She was just being polite."

Ander understood "polite." That was all the meaningless words his mother told him he had to start and end conversations with instead of simply saying what he wanted to and being done with it. His mother and the woman had said the words. What did the offer of warm bread have to do with it? She had offered. His mother should have accepted. Then they could have had superior bread.

His mother shook her head with a soft chuckle at his expression. "When you are older, you'll understand." She nudged him towards the next stop on their list.

No, Ander did not understand people.

School was equally perplexing.

Not the content, that was... fine, even if Ander felt they moved far too slowly and repeated the information too often. It was the people at the school that confused him.

His mother had told him school was a place for learning. Why, then, did his teacher keep answering his questions with "we aren't learning that yet" or "you won't learn that for a while"? If he asked the question, it meant he wanted to know the answer. Why was that difficult to understand? Why should he have to wait – in some cases *years* – for the answer?

He asked his mother instead. She might not be able to explain how people worked to him, but she always tried to answer his other questions.

(He didn't blame her. No one he asked seemed to be able to explain how people worked. Perhaps it was something he would have to figure out on his own, even if everyone else seemed to understand it without knowing why.)

And then there were the other children.

"Do you want to play?"

No he did not. Most were sitting in a circle, with one child patting the others on the head until they chose one to chase them around, trying to avoid them long enough to get to the vacated place. It was completely devoid of any sort of value. Most of their other games were the same: jumping rope, throwing balls to each other, singing rhymes that ended with them collapsing on the ground. Ander wanted no part in it.

"No," he said after it became clear the boy wasn't going to leave without an answer. He looked back down at the collection of shaped blocks he was arranging into a new pattern. At least this was entertaining in its own way. He'd already managed to create over thirty different designs over the past week.

The boy tugged at the hem of his long jacket, shifting his weight from one foot to the other for a moment, before shrugging. "Okay!"

Ander did not watch him leave, already resetting the blocks to find a new pattern.

His mother bit her lip, then smiled at him as he walked over to her. "And how was school today?" she asked, brushing a few strands of green hair that had escaped their braid behind a pointed ear. She looked around at the other parents, but they were all focused on their children, or in conversations with each other.

"The same," he answered with a shrug, as he always did. He didn't know why she always asked.

She ruffled his hair, ears twitching upward, before placing a hand on his back and guiding him towards home. "Oh? What did you learn?"

Ander frowned. "Nothing. We reviewed the words we're supposed to be able to read again, and did some practice adding. Then

Ms. Schreiber made us practice writing. But I did make four new patterns at recess today."

"That sounds like a busy day." They waited for a carriage to pass before crossing the cobbled street. "Was anyone interested in helping you make more patterns?"

"They can't make patterns I haven't already made," he said, dismayed that she would suggest it.

"Oh? Are you sure?"

"Yes." They weren't very smart from what he could tell, and any creativity they had went to all the wrong things. "They make boring patterns when they move the blocks."

His mother hummed, a soft sound he was long accustomed to. He knew what that one meant; she didn't agree with him. "Sometimes, working with someone can create something new and unexpected. Everyone sees things differently. You can't know everything that goes on in their heads, little one."

He spared a thought to the boy that had approached him today, and the children playing the circle game. Ander didn't know anything about what went on in their heads, except that it could not be as interesting as what went on in his own. "I like my patterns better," he said instead.

She chuckled as they came up to the door of their little two-room house. It turned into a cough, but she recovered quickly. "Who knows? You should give it a try. Maybe one of them will surprise you."

Ander doubted that very much.

Ander was arranging the blocks into his forty-second pattern, displeased that he was running out of options. He would have to find a new activity during recess soon.

A pair of black leather shoes entered his field of vision, but they stopped a few feet away. Ander spared a glance; it was the blond boy who had asked if he wanted to play the circle game a few days ago, the boy who didn't look at him the same way the other children did out of the corners of their eyes. Ander didn't know his name. They weren't in the same class.

"You're very pretty."

Ander blinked, then looked up at the other boy. Was that supposed to be a compliment? Mother said that when people complimented you, you should say "thank you," but she wasn't here and Ander didn't want to. He didn't think of himself as "pretty" and wasn't sure why anyone would. He settled for staring at the boy instead.

The other boy clasped his hands behind his back, grinning. "Your eyes are really pretty. Green, like the glass vase my mama likes to put fresh flowers in sometimes."

"They're green like my mother's hair," he corrected with a frown.

The other boy shrugged, dropping to sit next to Ander on the ground. "Same thing. What're you doing with the blocks?"

Ander looked around, but everyone else was either playing tag, jumping rope, or drawing in the sand. "Making patterns," he said after a moment.

"Oh." The boy leaned over Ander's design, squinting at it with the tip of his tongue sticking out of the corner of his mouth. "That's pretty too."

"Why are you here?" The words slipped out without much thought. Didn't the boy have something better to do than annoy Ander?

"You seem lonely."

Ander wasn't sure he understood what that meant. He understood the definition of lonely, of course, but it certainly didn't apply to him. He liked being on his own. "I'm not lonely."

"You're over here by yourself every day!" The boy added a block to the design Ander had laid out and twisted another, which made it a pattern Ander had created four days ago. "That's okay; I'll play with you!"

"I'm not playing," Ander denied, a sinking feeling beginning to make itself known somewhere in his chest. "I'm finding new patterns, and I've already found that one." He reached over to fix it, glaring at the blond.

The boy nodded, blue eyes meeting Ander's steadily. "You'll have to show me all the ones you've made, then, so we don't repeat." He grinned again, sudden and bright. "My name's Fredrik; what's yours?"

Ander was certain this was going to be a problem.

Despite Ander's best efforts, Fredrik became a constant presence over the next few years, even as the other children seemed to pick up on Ander's desire to be left alone. He heard them whisper things about him sometimes. Some of it was true, most of it was made up – a continuation of the pretend stories they'd been telling each other since the beginning. Ander gave it the exact same lack of attention he'd given to the puppet theater they'd played with in the first years of school.

But Fredrik would not be swayed to leave Ander alone, to his mother's delight.

Like now, when the blond refused to leave their house, and his mother insisted on feeding him.

Ander sighed, very put out that his plans for a quiet evening were completely shattered as his mother put a plate filled with potato pancakes in the center of the table. Potato pancakes were his favorite, and now he had to share.

"Thanks, Frau Haas!" Fredrik clapped his hands together, eyes sparkling.

Ander's mother smiled, before coughing into her elbow. It took her a moment to recover. "You're welcome, Fredrik. Enjoy!" She ruffled Ander's hair. "You, too, little one."

"I'm going to," he asserted, eyeing the plate. Which one was the best one? They were all going to be good, since his mother had made them, but still...

Fredrik did not share Ander's hesitation, grabbing the one precariously balanced on the top and shoving it into his mouth, to

Ander's despair. "Mmmm!" was the only sound that came from the boy as he chewed.

Ander finally selected a pancake, neatly breaking off a piece and popping it into his mouth. Delicious.

Fredrik swallowed dramatically, twisting to face Ander's mother. "Amazing! If I didn't know any better, I'd say you used magic to make these, Frau Haas."

She coughed again, but Ander could see the smile through it. "Thank you, Fredrik, but no magic involved. Just cooking. Science, really."

Ander hummed, considering. "Could magic be used for cooking, do you think?"

Fredrik blinked at him. "Maybe. All the stories have magic being used for really big and awesome things, though! Like lightning being thrown at dragons, or people raising mountains out of valleys."

"If it can be used for big things, it can be used for little things," Ander pointed out.

Fredrik shrugged. "Could be. It's not like we'll ever know."

"Oh? You don't believe there's still magic?" his mother asked as she began cleaning the pan she had fried the pancakes in.

Fredrik's eyes went wide. "You do? Is that an Avari thing?"

"It's a logic thing," Ander muttered. "There's absolutely no reason for magic to have just stopped existing over a hundred years ago." Then again, logic wasn't really Fredrik's strong suit. Hadn't he just been talking about the Three the other day? If the gods existed, then why not magic?

His mother's pale-green eyes found his bright-green ones. "That does seem like a strange thing to have happened."

"But if magic still existed, we'd be seeing it, right?" Fredrik said, face scrunched up. "Why would everyone just stop using it? That doesn't make sense, either."

Ander had already thought this through years ago. He might not understand what magic was, really, but that it was some sort of force people had been able to access in the past was indisputable. "The public knowledge of how to perform it must have been forgotten," he explained. "I would bet there are still groups out there that do practice it, but they do so secretly."

"My mother explained magic to me as a part of the life-force of the planet itself," his mother hummed, turning her attention back to the pan in her hands.

Ander considered that. "Then it can't be gone," he reasoned. "If it were, we'd be gone, too."

"Really? Then do you think we can learn magic, too?!" As usual, Fredrik was missing the point.

His mother coughed again, but her smile was still the one he always associated with her.

Fredrik found a lot of people pretty, Ander had come to realize. It was just a part of who he was. And he never seemed to hesitate to ensure people knew he thought they were pretty.

Ander fought not to roll his eyes as Fredrik sidled up to a pair of girls, complimenting everything from their dresses to their hair to their smiles. They giggled, hiding their smiles behind their hands, cheeks reddening. Fredrik leaned in closer.

Ander just shook his head from where he sat on a nearby bench and turned his attention back towards his book. Books, he had discovered, were remarkably helpful in ways people were not, and plentiful from the library as long as he treated them well. If only there were a way to make a book that answered direct questions...

Loud laughter from the trio. Ander glanced back up and caught the eyes of one of the girls. Her smile disappeared immediately, and she said something to Fredrik and her friend. All three looked at him.

Ander blinked slowly, then deliberately returned his attention towards his book.

After a few minutes, Fredrik's shadow fell across the page. Ander glanced around, but the girls were gone. Unfortunate; Fredrik wouldn't likely let him read in peace now.

Fredrik took a seat next to him, leaning back with his hands behind his head, blue eyes staring at an equally blue sky. "You know, you don't have to scare them off like that."

"What do you mean?" Ander turned the page, determined to at least finish this chapter. There were a lot of bones in the hands, it turned out, and the way they all interconnected and functioned together...

Fredrik chuckled, but it was softer than usual. "You glared at Mina."

"No I didn't," Ander denied. "I looked at her."

"Have you ever tried looking at someone in a nicer way?" Fredrik's voice warbled a bit at the end of his question. "I just mean, I'm your only friend! But maybe you could have more if you just... came across a little less... ah..." The blond boy glanced away.

"A little less...?" Ander prompted.

Fredrik winced. "Creepy, maybe?" He shot back up, waving his hands in front of him. "Not that *I* think you're creepy! I think you're great! But... other people..." He glanced back towards the place the girls had been.

"Other people don't matter," Ander reminded him, turning another page.

"What are you going to do?"

Ander didn't answer, continuing to stare at the book in his hands. He'd already read it four times, and the words were beginning to swim in front of him.

Fredrik continued when it became clear Ander wasn't going to answer. "The university won't take anyone younger than eighteen, even if you are the smartest fifteen-year-old in the history of Elbe. And... the rumors..."

Ander didn't care what the rumors said. They weren't true. If he'd been killing small animals in the woods, no one would know. He'd never be so sloppy as to leave proof.

Fredrik cleared his throat. "And, ah, and even if they did accept you, I don't think your mother has that much time left." His voice lowered in that way it sometimes did when he thought Ander might take offense to whatever it was he was saying.

He needn't have worried. It was true. Ander already knew it. He turned the page deliberately.

It didn't mean he couldn't try.

If the university wouldn't take him, he'd teach himself.

He'd been doing it for years anyway.

In the end, she withered away no matter what he or anyone else did.

"It's okay to cry, you know," Fredrik whispered, tears streaming down his own face as they sat next to the body on the bed. "She can't see anymore. You don't have to be strong for her."

Ander rolled a couple of long green strands of hair between his fingers. It was dull, no longer the same color as his eyes. It was what it was. They had known it was coming, even though he had tried to stop it. They'd been able to say goodbye.

So why did he feel so angry?

Why was there a part of his chest that hurt? Was there something wrong with him, too?

He couldn't afford that right now. There was so much he was going to have to do. Arrangements had to be made. She'd worked hard to save up enough money that he'd be able to cover the rent until he could either get a job or move to the university, so at least he didn't have to worry about that.

She'd known it was coming a lot longer than he had.

Why hadn't she told him? If he'd known sooner, maybe he could have found a way to help in time.

Lips touched his cheek.

He snapped his head around to Fredrik, who was still crying. "It's okay," he whispered again. "I'll stay. You'll always have me."

II

Ander was fairly certain Fredrik chose to go to university simply to flirt with everything that moved.

(But it never goes beyond that, never – Fredrik is loyal to Ander, his promise binding. But a Fredrik who does not chase after "pretty" people is not Ander's Fredrik, and it doesn't bother him anyway. Fredrik, Ander has come to realize, has flirted for as long as Ander has known him.)

Ander's days were filled with memorizing anatomical drawings and names of medicines and tools. He preferred the vigor of the program to the much more lax schooling he had received previously. Even if he still felt miles ahead of everyone else, at least there was always something to move on to.

He had absolutely no idea what Fredrik did during the day.

At night, they returned to their shared apartment. One of them, usually Fredrik, would cook dinner, Ander would listen to him recount stories of the "interesting" people he had met throughout the day, and then they'd clean up. Ander would try to study for a bit; Fredrik would read or try to distract him. After a while they'd retire to their bed. Eventually they'd sleep.

In the mornings, Ander made sure both of them were up in time to go to class.

He discovered coffee during their first semester.

Twice a week they were able to meet for lunch.

Ander always got there first, sitting with his back pressed against the old ash tree they had more or less claimed as "their" spot, medical text of the day propped open against his knee. Fredrik would arrive shortly after with sandwiches or sausages or pretzels. Sometimes he brought people to join them, sometimes they ate alone.

One day he brought a girl with long brown hair and dark eyes, wearing a green dress.

"Ander, this is Ida! She's in my poetry class; I've told her all about you and she wanted to meet you!"

Ander glanced at her, and she smiled at him, blinking her eyes slowly. "He has told me a lot about you," she agreed, settling on the ground nearby. Though her name was Elben, her accent was Gallian. "Mostly about how pretty you are."

Yes, that tracked. Fredrik would always be Fredrik. "Sorry to disappoint," he said absently, taking the small wrapped package from Fredrik. Potato pancakes. Fredrik usually brought these when he wanted something. Ander raised an eyebrow in question.

Fredrik shrugged. "She likes them too!"

"And I wouldn't say I'm disappointed," Ida added, tilting her head to the side. "There is a certain... something about you that is aesthetically captivating."

Oh, she was like Fredrik, then. Ander hummed noncommittally and turned his attention back to his book.

She chuckled, quiet and low. "Oh, he is very much like you said!"

"Yeah," Fredrik agreed with a grin, plopping himself down on the ground right next to Ander and wrapping an arm around him. "You are getting a very typical Ander reaction right now. It's okay; I love you anyway."

Ander offered a hum in response, shifting his weight slightly to lean against Fredrik in the way he knew he liked.

Ida chuckled again. "Too cute."

Ander suppressed a sigh for Fredrik's sake.

Like Fredrik had long ago, Ida slowly began to creep her way into Ander's life.

He was fairly certain Fredrik and Ida shared a number of classes together, chasing the same ephemeral degree in who-knew-what. She began to show up for more lunches than not, occasionally even finding Ander on days Fredrik couldn't join them. She claimed someone needed to make sure he ate, even though he assured her he was eating just fine. Sometimes she joined them after classes, able to convince Fredrik to study when Ander could not. Sometimes she convinced Ander to – if not enjoy himself – put the books down and go out to a party or bar.

When the semester came to an end, she started coming to their apartment for dinner, too.

Ander wasn't sure what, if anything, he should do about this. Ida was not like Fredrik except in that they both appreciated the things they found "pretty." Fredrik seemed to brighten a room with his enthusiasm and large grins. Ander couldn't possibly explain how that was the case – the room did not literally become brighter; he'd checked – but nonetheless, Fredrik's effect on a room was much like the sun's.

And if Fredrik was light, Ida was shadow. Her movements were always more subdued, more purposeful than Fredrik's. Languid, perhaps. He couldn't explain this, either, but there was something about her that seemed to sap the light from a room. Fredrik gave, but Ida seemed to take.

In this sense, Fredrik and Ida balanced each other out. Was that good? Ander wasn't sure, but they both seemed to enjoy each other's company, and Ander had never been very good at figuring out people anyway.

There were a few classes he was looking forward to taking in upcoming semesters. He had some hope they might be able to finally explain "people" to him. The few books he had found on the topic were woefully lacking in detail.

"What do you want to do, after graduation?"

Ander didn't bother to look up from his textbook. "Be a doctor."

Ida snorted. "Obviously. I meant–" She paused, then shook her head. "Why medicine?"

Ander thought back to dull green hair spilling over the side of the bed. He didn't know how to express it.

"His mom died a few years back," Fredrik explained. "She'd been sick for a while, and no one could fix it." He grinned at Ander. "But Ander's really smart. I bet he'll discover a whole bunch of cures for a whole bunch of diseases no one else has figured out yet!"

That didn't seem to match how Ander felt exactly, but it seemed close enough. He tilted his head in acknowledgement.

"What about you, Ida?" Fredrik asked.

"I want to travel!" she exclaimed, her eyes lighting up. "I'd like to go back to Gallia, visit some of the places I remember going to as a little girl. Then maybe travel the Empire, go to the Nyphoren Islands, or Cartago-Mir. Maybe even go to some of the other countries like Dalmara or Ni Fon!"

"Those are on the opposite sides of the globe from each other," Ander observed.

"That's the fun of traveling! Getting to a destination can be just as exciting as the destination itself."

Ander, who had never been anywhere other than the northern part of Elbe and had no desire to go anywhere else, wasn't sure that was true.

"What about you, Fredrik?" Ida asked, poking the blond's arm.

"Hmmm." Fredrik dropped back so he was lying on the ground, staring up at the sky through the leaves of the ash tree. "I don't know yet. I think I'm still figuring it out." Blue eyes flickered in Ida's direction.

Ander hummed, unsurprised, and turned back to his book.

Ida surprised him when, as they were cleaning up one night after dinner, she kissed him on the mouth.

Ander froze, not prepared for whatever this was. Fredrik did too.

Ida smiled that same slight smile, lips painted red. "Fredrik and I have a proposition," she began, stepping back to give Ander some space. "But your attention can be hard to get a hold of."

He grasped for something to say. Was this normal? If not, who was the outlier – him, or her? "You have it now."

"See, all three of us have been getting a lot closer," Fredrik began, coming around the table to lay a hand on Ander's arm.

"And we thought we could make it a little more," Ida added, gracefully sinking down onto the couch. "In Gallia, such arrangements are more common than they are here, but they do work."

Oh, okay. Ander was the odd one out then. He wondered how long they had been planning this. What even were they really asking? He frowned at Fredrik for a moment, then said "Excuse us" to Ida as he pulled the blond into their bedroom. He shut the door firmly behind them.

Then he just stared at Fredrik.

Fredrik laughed, higher pitched than usual. "Look, I know you're probably concerned–"

Concerned? Should he be? Of what?

"–but it really *is* up to you." He sighed and ran a hand through his hair, mussing the short waves. "This isn't you or her. It's you, me, and her, or just you and me."

Oh. Ander considered that. "You like her."

"Well, yes?" Fredrik chuckled again, eyebrows raising. "I was kind of hoping you did too?"

Ander studied him while he reviewed the relevant information. He certainly didn't like Ida the way he liked Fredrik. Her form held no real appeal to him, and while he didn't mind her company it didn't melt away as seamlessly as Fredrik's did when they were together. But... she also made Fredrik happy, he was pretty sure. In a way Ander wasn't sure he *could*. And Fredrik and Ander hadn't always been so seamless. Perhaps in time, Ida would fit in the same way? At least she was more intelligent than Fredrik. "She'll be sleeping with us too?" he asked, just to be sure.

Fredrik choked, and from the other side of the door came Ida's voice. "That is the idea, love!"

Ander shrugged. If it made Fredrik happy, so be it.

III

"And Ander, can you pick up some bread on your way home? We're almost out."

Ander hummed in acknowledgement, mentally adding it to his ever-expanding list of errands for today (being a third-year med student was both more and less effort than he had expected – while the amount of work required of him was plenty doable, there were only so many hours in a day to complete it and everything else he needed to do). When Ida wanted bread, she usually meant foreign, expensive bread. It would be a little out of his way, but he could stop by the bakery on Saalgasse. They usually had something she liked. He was certain they still had three quarters of a loaf of rye for himself and Fredrik.

"And maybe some pickled herring?"

He blinked, put the book down, and looked over at her. She'd been lying with her head in Fredrik's lap since she'd finished her lunch, staring up at the sky through the leaves of the ash tree. Ander was pretty certain the way Fredrik's eyebrows were squished together meant he was also confused. "You hate pickled herring," he reminded her.

"Ah, well, you know," she murmured, draping an arm over her eyes as a sunbeam drifted into them, "I just really feel like pickled herring."

He met Fredrik's eyes, and the blond just shrugged a shoulder, mouthing a word that was probably "women." Though Ander usually didn't see any point of making such generalities based on gender, in this case, he felt unsure.

Because Ida loathed pickled herring. Had nearly thrown a fit the one and only time they had included it in dinner.

"Okay," he agreed after a long moment.

"Thanks, love!" came the enthusiastic response.

Ander picked his book back up, making a mental note to pick up some pickled onions as well, for when she remembered how much she hated herring.

"Ander, have you seen Ida?"

He paused just inside the door of their apartment. Fredrik looked like he'd been pacing back and forth. His hair was a mess, probably from running his hands through it so many times; his vest was unbuttoned, his shirt rolled up to the elbows and coming untucked.

"Not since lunch. Did something happen?"

"She wasn't in philosophy. And she hasn't been home either, from what I can tell."

Philosophy? Fredrik was in a philosophy class? Was he actually passing it? Ander shook his head. "She didn't leave a note?" He decided to ask the obvious question, as sometimes Fredrik didn't actually check these things. He moved into the room, putting his bags down on the table and starting to put things away.

"No, she didn't leave a note, and how can you be so *unconcerned?*" came the wail.

"Because Ida likes to go out with friends," Ander reminded him. "And it's not like both of you haven't occasionally skipped class."

"But we usually skip class together," Fredrik muttered, looking down and scuffing a foot at the floorboards, hands sliding into his pockets.

Great. Sometimes Ander wondered if he was going to be the only person making money for this family.

Was that what this was? A family? He supposed it fit the definition, even if none of them were technically married. They'd all been living together for two years, and he'd lived with Fredrik for longer than that. They ate together; they spent a large majority of their time together. They even had shared finances. And, well, he didn't really mind supporting the other two. Maybe that was how he best fit into this arrangement anyway.

Yes, he could work with that.

He idly scanned for a note Ida might have left as he put things away, but he didn't see one. Unfortunate, because that would have been the fastest way to reassure Fredrik. But Ander wasn't worried; Ida was more than capable of taking care of herself, and despite Fredrik's dramatics she did occasionally go out without them. She liked to do things like this to remind them that she was "an independent woman." Ander wasn't sure why she felt the need to assert this, especially when all it actually did was distress Fredrik, but it was what it was.

Maybe it was a space thing? Fredrik could get a bit... clingy.

The blond dropped his head on Ander's shoulder from behind as though summoned. "What should we do?"

"Eat?" Ander suggested, getting out a pot of water to boil the sausage.

Fredrik raised his head and took a step away. "You really aren't concerned?"

Ander glanced over his shoulder. "I'm not," he tried to reassure him. "I'm sure she's fine."

Fredrik was frowning. "That's a little harsh, even for you."

Ander blinked, turning to face Fredrik a little better. "What do you mean?"

"She could be in trouble out there!"

"Technically true, but knowing Ida, statistically unlikely."

"What if she gets hurt? Or lost?"

That one was just ridiculous. "She doesn't want you to treat her like she's made of glass."

Fredrik's lips thinned, and his expression became pinched as the tone of his voice dropped. "What would you know about what she wants?"

Ander just stared at him, eyes wide, uncertain how to respond to that. It was suddenly difficult to breathe.

They stood like that for several moments, then Fredrik turned and left, slamming the door behind him.

Ander swallowed, finding it surprisingly difficult, then turned back to the stove. Mechanically he picked up where he'd left off. They'd probably want to eat when they came back.

Later that night, lying alone in bed, he pretended not to hear the shouting in the other room.

Neither of them came to bed after.

Four days later found him kneeling next to her in the privy as she threw up.

"I think I might be pregnant," she admitted before heaving again.

Ander considered that possibility as he held a cool, damp cloth to the back of her neck. "Are you late?"

"By two weeks, yes." She closed her eyes and sat back on her heels, slumping against him.

Ah. "I believe there's a test with urine and wheat you could try, to be sure?" Pregnancy wasn't one of the things he'd been studying; he'd have to double check. "There are books – some doctors are beginning to specialize in it."

Her eyebrows lifted as she looked at him. "It's always books with you, isn't it?"

He shrugged. "They've proven to be helpful in the past."

"Yeah," she sighed. "That makes sense."

Fredrik was... Fredrik about the whole thing, even as Ander tried to caution that it was too early to know for absolute certainty.

"Is it a boy or a girl?!?" he exclaimed, clapping his hands together as he bounced in his seat.

"It is far too early to tell with any accuracy," Ander said, repressing a sigh as he tried to rein in Fredrik's expectations. "Ida might not even be pregnant, though the signs are pointing that way."

"I think... it'll be a girl," Ida said, completely undoing Ander's work.

Ander made a mental note to check the library for books on obstetrics.

"I think I'm going to need new dresses."

Ander glanced over to where Ida was struggling to button up her dress in front of the mirror. She was definitely starting to show now. At least she had given up on the corset.

Fredrik came around behind and wrapped his arms around her, both looking at their reflection. He kissed her temple. "Of course, whatever you'd like."

Ander watched from where he sat on the bed behind them.

Obstetrics was a growing field in the medical community, and as a result there were many recently published books on the subject, as well as some older ones. Ander found himself having to sift through theory and some... truly amazing leaps of logic in order to ensure what he was learning was both pertinent and accurate. There was something to be said for the older advice as well – the writers may not have understood why some things worked and others didn't, but there was some advice that had been proven time and time again regardless.

Maybe he could figure out the why?

Ander's head snapped up at the squeal Ida made. "What's wrong?" he asked, alarmed.

She was standing in the middle of their living room and kitchen, hand on her stomach, eyes wide.

Fredrik was right next to her, hovering, hands moving without any obvious direction to guide them. "Does something hurt? What's wrong?" he echoed.

She turned wide, dark eyes up to Fredrik. "I felt it kick!"

Ander felt a significant amount of tension leave him. That was normal. He turned back to dinner preparations, willing his heart rate to return to its normal pace.

Fredrik gasped. "Oh oh oh! I want to feel!"

"You might not be able to for another few weeks," Ander warned, mashing the potatoes. "It's easier for her to feel it since it's in her."

"She," Ida corrected firmly.

Ander did not know why Ida kept insisting on the gender when it was impossible to know for certain, but fine. If it made her happy. "Since *she's* in her."

"That still sounds…" Fredrik trailed off, tilting his head at Ander and squinting.

"Sounds?" Ander asked, feeling a pit appear in his stomach. These interactions were becoming more common. Fredrik had always seemed to understand Ander in the past. What had changed?

"It's fine," Ida declared, drawing Fredrik out of the kitchen half of the room and onto the couch. "Here, sit with me while he makes dinner, and maybe you'll feel her too!"

Late that night, when they lay curled around each other and Ander was certain the other two were asleep, he put his hand very, very carefully on Ida's stomach.

He didn't feel anything.

"Can I get you anything?"

"Hmm… maybe just some tea for now?"

Ander rubbed at his eyes as Fredrik jumped off the couch to fetch Ida some tea. He would be thankful for the upcoming winter break; trying to keep up with his med studies and the extra research and Ida was starting to take its toll.

At least Fredrik seemed pleased to be waiting on her hand and foot.

Ander was doing what he could to suggest ways to make Ida comfortable and ensure the baby was developing well. The extra time he'd been spending with the pregnancy books was paying off, at least, and he'd managed to corner one of the professors who specialized in obstetrics last week to clarify a few points and run a couple of theories by her. Aside from the creeping exhaustion, he was feeling more confident in his ability to take care of Ida.

He'd have more labs in the upcoming semester, though, and those tended to be far more intense than just class.

He made a mental note to pick up more coffee.

"Have you checked to see what arrangements can be done for classes?" he asked.

Both Ida and Fredrik blinked at him as she took the tea cup, and Ander realized they had been speaking about something else. Ida took a very deliberate sip of tea, but she cut Fredrik off just as he began to speak. "I'm just not going to enroll for next semester."

Ander nodded. That made sense.

"Is that really what you're concerned with right now?" Fredrik asked with a frown. "*School*?"

It was an important part of their lives. Should he not be concerned with it? "It's one of many things I'm concerned with right now," he said slowly.

Fredrik's eyes narrowed, and Ander's stomach dropped. What had he done this time?

"Ander, I know you've always been a little confused on how priorities work–"

He blinked. Was he? He didn't think so.

"–and I think maybe we should all be taking a break from school right now."

"I can't." Ander felt blindsided. How could Fredrik ask that of him? He *knew* why Ander had chosen this profession. "This program doesn't just let me skip semesters–"

"Gods damn it, Ander, there's more important things–"

"Stop it, both of you!" Ida snapped, dark eyes flashing. She took a deep breath, then a deliberate sip of her tea. "I'm the only one who needs to take a semester off, Fredrik. Though you might want to try a lighter course load, Ander; you've been exhausted lately. Maybe it's a little too much for you? Right now?"

He stared. "It's not the classes, I've been trying to–"

"Yes, research, because it's always about books with you." Fredrik interrupted. "That was all you did when–" He abruptly cut himself off.

Ander closed the book he was holding and stood up, grabbing his coat as he left. He could study at the library.

"Things are going to have to change, Ander."

Ander was not and never had been religious, but he spared a moment to pray to any deity that might possibly be listening for patience as he put his bag down on the kitchen table. Fredrik liked to spring these sorts of conversations on people as they entered the apartment.

The pit was back in his stomach again.

"What do you mean?" he asked.

Fredrik stood and placed his hands on the table, leaning in. "I mean with the baby."

Ander was sure he had a better idea of the amount of work a baby was than Fredrik. "Of course. There might be some trial and error in the beginning, but I've drafted a possible timetable of–"

"No, I don't mean schedules, Ander," Fredrik sighed, hanging his head for a moment. "Well, I guess I do kind of mean schedules, that's part of it, but I mean you can't be so..." He waved a hand in the air.

Ander waited as the feeling in his stomach intensified.

"So... ah, damn it, you're going to make me say it, aren't you?" The blond ran both hands through his hair with sharp, jerky motions.

"I have no idea what you're implying," Ander admitted.

"Selfish!"

Ander frowned. "How am I being selfish?"

Fredrik stared at him for a long moment, squinting ever so slightly with his mouth hanging open just a bit. "What do you mean, 'how'? All you've done since we found out was read somehow more than before and tell us what we should be doing."

How could he say that? "I make dinner at least five nights a week. I clean. I helped Ida through her morning sickness–"

Fredrik drew back. "Ida had morning sickness?"

"Yes, but you slept through it–"

"And neither of you *told me*?"

"What would the point of that have been? You've never been good at getting up in the mornings and I was already helping–"

"Have you been keeping anything else from me?"

Ander was getting very tired of not being able to finish a sentence. "We haven't been keeping *anything* from you."

"Well, of course you'd say that! Why would you admit to it?"

"Then why did you ask me in the first place?" Ander pointed out, turning his back on Fredrik and beginning to grab what he needed to make lentil soup. "Ask Ida."

"Maybe I will," came the response. The door to the apartment opened, then slammed shut.

"Please do," Ander muttered tiredly to an empty room.

The next day Fredrik made potato pancakes for dinner.

They didn't discuss it again.

Ander felt dead on his feet. All he wanted to do was collapse and sleep for the next week. But at least midterms were over, and he could join the other two for lunch.

No one was waiting beneath the ash tree.

Ander stood for a moment surrounded by the green of spring, trying to process this. No, neither of them was here. He checked his watch; he was later than usual, but he had made sure to let them know the time the exam was likely to let out.

He scanned the area again, just to make sure, then headed home to their new, larger apartment.

They weren't there, either.

But there was a note.

Ander went to the hospital.

"Well, she's definitely Fredrik's daughter," Ida murmured later that night, a small, still bundle of blankets and baby nestled in her arms. She touched a curl of blonde hair sticking out.

Ander had never doubted whether he or Fredrik had fathered the child. He didn't think she did either. While they did sleep together, the activities they usually engaged in couldn't result in babies.

"Still," she mused, "I think some of you ended up in there anyway."

"That's not how genetics works," he said after a moment. He'd been awake for over forty hours at this point, but he was still sure of that fact.

"For gods' sake, Ander..." Fredrik sighed, but there was a small smile on his face as he gently shoved Ander's shoulder.

"It's not, though." Ander craned his head to get a better look at the baby. "What..." He paused, quickly sorting through his memories to see if they had discussed this previously. They had not, to his knowledge. "What are you going to name her?"

Ida had yet to take her eyes off the baby. "Alice."

Fredrik made a small sound, but when Ander turned to him he was smiling. "An Elben name! I thought you wanted to go with Aalis?"

So maybe they had discussed it, just not with him.

Ida just hummed.

"Can I hold her?" Ander asked curiously.

Ida froze for a moment, then slowly looked up at him. "Okay," she finally said.

Ander carefully bent down and took the bundle from Ida, holding it exactly the way he had learned to while Fredrik fussed around him. He looked down at it, unsure what he had expected – he was now holding a baby. There was nothing specifically special about it.

What was he supposed to do now?

Very small eyes opened, just a tiny bit.

They were blue-green.

If Ander thought he was tired before, it was nothing compared to the exhaustion of the next few weeks.

And there were three of them taking care of one baby. How did couples do it? How had his mother done it on her own?

Had she been on her own? Ander actually wasn't sure. Maybe she had help.

Maybe *they* needed help.

Ander felt like one of the mindless living dead, which he tried to offset with an unhealthy amount of coffee. Former conversations in mind, he tried to bear the burden of the baby's care when he came back from class to give Ida and Fredrik a break. But everyone was near breaking point – the number of arguments he walked in on was increasing, everyone was tripping over everyone else, and he did need to sleep at least occasionally.

At least three months until the little one would begin to sleep through the night. That wouldn't help him with his classes at all – the semester would be over and summer break would be in full swing – but at least that would give them all time to breathe.

Ida always watched them very closely whenever they held the baby or came into any sort of contact. She was sleeping the least out of the three of them even with the tea blends Ander had procured, she was barely eating the carefully constructed meals Ander was preparing, and she refused to let anyone other than Fredrik and Ander near Alice at all.

Ander was fine with that – he hated having people in the apartment – but it was odd that Ida felt that way. She normally loved people.

And something about that sounded familiar. Had he read it somewhere?

"What are you doing?"

"Changing her," Ander said absently, even though he thought it was pretty clear what he was doing. He wasn't sure what else this could be.

"Without asking me?" Ida's voice rose behind him.

"You were asleep. You're exhausted; I thought it better to let you rest." He finished pinning the diaper in place and tilted his head as the little one gurgled at him. He had enough difficulties figuring out what adults were thinking; there was no way he was going to know what was going on in *that* head. He decided it was thanks for changing her diaper. "You should go lie down; I can watch her for a little while."

"Get away from her! You just want to dissect her the way you dissected all those little animals! That's why you keep trying to drug me!"

Ander felt a chill go down his spine; Ida's voice was far too shrill, and it wavered strangely. He hadn't even known that Ida had heard those rumors; he thought they'd died years before he met her. He turned. "Ida–"

"Get *away!*"

He grabbed her wrist just in time to partially deflect the knife she was trying to put through his skull. Pain blossomed across his face as the tip of the blade found skin, slashing down from his forehead almost to the corner of his mouth. "Ida!" he shouted, shaking her, trying to get her to snap out of whatever this was–

Oh, yes. Some women suffered hallucinations, panic, depression or mania, and a number of other symptoms after giving birth. It was rare, but there were reported cases.

"What on Gaia–"

"Fredrik, *help me,*" he snapped as Ida continued to struggle in his grip, screaming at him to get away from her baby. Blood was starting to drip into his eyes, but he increased pressure on her wrist until she dropped the knife.

Fredrik grabbed her from behind, freeing Ander to run to the kitchen, grab a glass of water, and throw it in her face.

Silence.

Ander had never been so tired in his life.

"She feels really bad about it, you know."

Ander hummed in acknowledgement but kept his eyes closed. He really wanted to get at least an hour of sleep in while the painkillers were still strong in his system.

"Are you okay?"

"She said I wanted to dissect Alice the way I 'dissected all those little animals,'" he said evenly.

Several minutes passed before Fredrik spoke again. "The doctor said she wasn't in her right mind. She doesn't really feel that way, Ander."

Ander knew that. That wasn't the problem. "How did she know?"

He heard Fredrik shuffle a bit before the blond dropped to the floor next to the couch Ander was lying on, leaning his head against Ander's arm. "I'm sorry. I never thought... there was no way to know..."

"Why?" Ander asked quietly.

"I don't really know."

IV

"Hi, Vater!"

Ander opened the white gate and stepped through as Alice ran up the path to greet him. "What are you doing outside, little one?" he asked, glancing around. Neither Fredrik nor Ida was in sight.

The five-year-old pouted, clasping her hands behind her and scuffing the ground with one foot. It was a very Fredrik-like action. "Mama and Papa are fighting again."

"Ah." Not much to do about that. He eyed the front door to the house, wondering if it was worth it to try to interrupt so he could start dinner, or if they should just eat later.

She tugged on one blonde pigtail, blue-green eyes looking at him intently. "Can we play hide-and-seek?"

Ander hid a wince. "Or we could play the memory game?" He could also try to start dinner, but he didn't want to get drawn into whatever argument was happening. He'd rather play hide-and-seek, but if he didn't have to...

Alice squealed, hands clapping together as she bounced up and down, beaming at him. The memory game it was.

He guided her over to the little garden bench by the ash tree in the yard (not the same ash tree as the one on campus, but it had reminded them of those lunches long ago, even if this one almost never served the same purpose). He opened his briefcase and took out the deck of illustrated cards he had made for this purpose. He separated out eight pairs, shuffled them, then laid them out on the bench in a grid. "All right, then. Which card first?"

"Ander, I picked up some sausage for dinner tonight."

Ander fought back a sigh. He was exhausted from working at the hospital and had hoped to take a nap, but... "Did you have anything specific in mind?"

Fredrik shrugged. "Not really." He grabbed his coat. "I'll be back in time to eat."

Ander stared. "Where are you going?"

"Just out for a bit. See you later." The door swung shut behind him.

Ida snorted from where she was leaning against the wall, but then disappeared into their bedroom without a word.

"Vater?"

He looked down at blue-green eyes. He sighed. "Do you want to help me get dinner ready?"

"Vater, where did you get your scar from?"

Ander hummed as Alice climbed onto the couch next to him, curling into his side. He closed his book. What should he say this time? "I was protecting a kitten from a dragon."

The eight-year-old giggled. "Mama says dragons don't exist anymore."

"They did when I got my scar," he affirmed. "Perhaps it was the last dragon."

She tilted her head to the side. "Was the kitten thankful?"

"Well, it was the kitten who scratched me, so it's hard to say."

She shrieked with laughter. "The *kitten* scratched you? Not the dragon?"

"It was a mildly vicious kitten," he informed her seriously.

She giggled again. "Vater, you let a *kitten* scratch you!"

"I had let my guard down. It was completely my fault."

She shook her head, grinning. Then her eyes landed on the book. "What are you reading?"

"*Diseases of the Nervous System.*" He tilted the book so she could see the cover.

Her eyes narrowed as her mouth moved soundlessly, trying out the shapes needed to form the sounds.

He waited patiently.

"Diseases of the Nervous System," she finally declared, pointing to each of the words as she said them.

Ander nodded. "Good job."

"What's a 'nervous system'?"

Ander lay on the couch in the living room, trying to ignore the shouting he could still hear through the walls. He needed to get some sleep tonight; he was scheduled to do surgery tomorrow.

At least there was always coffee.

He'd tried to stop the argument when he realized what was happening, but they hadn't been interested in any reasonable conversation, or even just leaving it for the next day. They could yell all they wanted while he wasn't there, though he would prefer that they stopped yelling entirely.

It wasn't about him, and there was nothing he could do about it.

There never was.

"Vater, Vater! Come see!"

Alice had a number of photographs spread out on the kitchen table. Ida was sitting next to her, smiling faintly.

Ander picked one up. It wasn't anything he recognized: a little café with wrought iron tables and chairs, blue umbrellas, green plants with colorful flowers. An ocean appeared just visible in the background.

"That wasn't very far from where I grew up," Ida explained. "I'm showing her some of the places I've been." She looked at the picture, but her gaze was somewhere else.

"These are so pretty!" Alice exclaimed, pointing to another image of rolling hills peppered by trees.

Ander hadn't known Ida had pictures like this. "You said you wanted to go back one day?" He remembered a conversation long ago beneath the ash tree.

"Yes," she murmured, voice soft. "That would be nice."

Ander wanted to ignore the shouting, but the house wasn't that big. The pit in his stomach felt like it was going to swallow him.

You never take things seriously! Losing your job is a big deal, Fredrik!

No, it's not! Ander makes enough to support us all anyway.

He barely *makes enough to support us; we need a second means of income–*

Well, if you're that concerned about it, why don't you get a job? What do you do all day while Alice is at school, anyway?

The house doesn't maintain itself, Fredrik!

Fine, let's switch! I'll maintain the house, and you–

We both know that'll never happen! You always have your head in the clouds, you never have any direction–

Oh, so now we're making assumptions? How about this one: if you didn't spend so much, maybe Ander's income would be enough!

How dare *you! After everything!*

Yes, *after everything!*

I've given up everything *I wanted to be here!*

It's not my fault you had a kid and trapped yourself here–

No, that literally is *your fault–*

Ander abruptly scooped up the papers Alice was drawing on.

"Vater?" she asked quietly, looking at him with those big, blue-green eyes.

"Let's go to the library for a bit, little one," he suggested. "You can draw there."

It had been a while since they all sat for dinner together.

Ander placed the plate of potato pancakes and the spinach and strawberry salad in the center of the table before taking his own seat, acknowledging the murmurs of appreciation with a tilt of his head. He placed two on Alice's plate before letting Ida and Fredrik serve themselves.

Alice and Fredrik dug into theirs; Ida pushed hers around the plate.

She'd never really latched onto many of the recipes Ander knew, but he'd hoped she would appreciate the salad. Strawberries were one of her favorite foods.

She didn't touch it.

"Hey, Ander?"

"Yes?" He had so little time to himself nowadays; he just wanted to finish this book.

Fredrik cleared his throat. "Well, uh, can we talk about something?"

He was not going to get that chance. He closed the book and set it down on the coffee table, already dreading whatever this could be about. "Yes?"

Fredrik's mouth twisted to the side as he bent down to pick the book up. "*Brown's Practice of Medicine*," he read slowly. "Don't you already know everything there is to know about this stuff? How are there still books you haven't read?"

"The field evolves constantly," Ander explained. "And I am very, very far from knowing *everything*."

Fredrik shook his head. "Was this what you were reading to Alice last night?"

"Yes."

The blond winced. "And, uh, you don't think that's a little... weird?"

Ander's brow furrowed. "What do you mean?"

"Ander... she's nine."

Ander was very aware of that. The scar on his face twinged. "Yes."

"A nine-year-old girl?"

"Yes." He wished Fredrik would get to the point.

Fredrik tossed the book back on the coffee table, making an incoherent sound as he scrubbed at his face with his hands. "She's not... she's not *you*, Ander. This kind of book... it's not really appropriate, you know?"

"I don't expect her to actually learn it, she just likes to follow along," Ander explained, feeling perplexed. "She's never asked me to read a different book than whatever I'm currently reading. There's nothing inappropriate in there; it's just a medical textbook out of Agale."

Fredrik huffed. "For gods' sake, Ander, could you just switch to, like, a story book or something? What if she gets nightmares from that stuff?"

"From a medical textbook?" Ander was completely lost.

Fredrik made an explosive sound before turning and storming out of the room.

Ander watched him go. He'd been reading various medical books to Alice for years. She had never indicated that she wanted him to stop or read something else.

It wasn't a total surprise to Ander in the end, though it did leave a hollow, aching feeling in his chest.

"Mama's going to be gone for a while, baby girl," Ida whispered to Alice as she brushed golden curls out of the ten-year-old's face.

"Where are you going? Can I come too?"

"I'm sorry, sweetie, but this is something Mama has to do for herself." Ander could see the tears in her eyes, but the decision had already been made. He suspected it had been made longer ago than any of them knew. "You're going to stay here, with Papa and Vater."

Alice turned her big eyes to where he stood leaning against the wall.

Fredrik wasn't here; he'd already said everything he was going to say to Ida last night.

Alice looked down at her feet, tried to suppress a cough, then turned watery eyes on her mother. "When are you going to come home?"

The feeling in Ander's chest intensified.

"I don't know yet. Probably not for a while. I'm sorry." Ida kissed Alice's forehead, then pulled her into a tight hug. Her eyes found Ander's.

They looked at each other for a long moment.

Ida looked away first.

Gently, she disentangled herself from her daughter, picked up her bags, and left.

V

Ander liked listening to Alice talk, but sometimes it was a little much.

"...And then Clovis was telling me today that his father had been talking to his mother about the new military division they're supposedly trying out in Agale even though he thinks they've actually existed for a while already and they're just going public now," Alice finished saying all in one breath. She wheezed for a moment, gasping for the air she had denied herself, which turned into a cough.

"You can use multiple sentences to get your point across," Ander reminded her. They were sitting under the ash tree in the yard, Ander with a book, and the fourteen-year-old with gossip. It was something she'd inherited from Fredrik. "At least make the attempt to breathe somewhere in there."

She scrunched up her face as she ran her hands through her ponytail. "But then you could *interrupt* me," she said as though that would be the worst thing in the world.

"I promise to allow you to talk at me without interruption, if it means you will breathe at regular intervals."

She giggled. "You're so funny, Vater."

"Am I?" He turned a page deliberately. "You may be the only person who thinks that." Even he didn't think he was funny.

"They just don't know you the way I do." She paused, tilting her head as she squinted at him. "By the way, Emma invited me and a number of other girls to a–"

"Yes, you can go," he interrupted. "You know I don't mind."

"You juuuuuust interrupted me!" She scowled and poked his arm. "Rude!"

"I won't interrupt your gossip, but you really don't need to ask me for permission to go out."

She sighed. "Can you convince Papa of that?"

He thought that through. "Considering the amount of time he spends out, you'd think I should be able to, but I don't think that sort of logic is going to work on him."

(Maybe Ida would have been able to convince him, but Ida has been gone for a long time now. Sometimes Ander wonders if there was something else he could have done to change how things turned out, but in the end, what's done is done. He can't bring her back.)

"Welcome home, Vater!" came the loud call from farther in the house, followed by a short series of coughs as smoke wafted from the kitchen.

Ander blinked, sniffing the air. It smelled like... food cooking.

Curious and mildly alarmed, Ander made his way to the kitchen. There was an ungodly number of pots and pans strewn about, some in use, others still clean. Most of the actual food looked to have been successfully contained to the part of the counter next to the stove and about a quarter of the kitchen table. Alice stood over a pan, carefully dropping a heaping spoonful of batter into the oil.

"You decided to make potato pancakes?" Ander hazarded after a moment.

"Yes! Well, I thought I'd make dinner, since you always make dinner, and Papa said he'd be out late again." She paused, then scowled at the sizzling pan. "He can't have any pancakes."

"He probably won't be home in time to have them anyway," Ander mused, watching her carefully. For her first time, her technique was pretty good. Or was it her first time? Fredrik went out most nights now, and often was gone by the time Ander got home from the hospital. Maybe she'd been practicing? He'd shown her how to make them before, but he'd always handled the frying on his own after Fredrik had almost thrown a fit about Alice being too close to the hot oil.

She seemed to be doing just fine now.

They watched the pancake sizzle for a few minutes, then she carefully used the spatula to flip it, the tip of her tongue sticking out of the corner of her mouth.

"Vater?"

"Hmm?" Yes, she was doing just fine. Fredrik had been worrying needlessly.

"Why do you always make dinner?"

He blinked. "It used to be a little more evenly distributed," he admitted. "But over time... I'm not sure. Things changed."

She considered that as she moved the pancake to a plate. "I'm pretty sure Papa's at a brothel," she said completely out of nowhere, nostrils flaring even as her brow furrowed. "I think he's been going for a while."

Ander pursed his lips, not sure what to say to that.

She glanced at him, then did a double take. "You already knew?"

Ander looked away, catching a glimpse of his reflection in the hallway mirror and the scar running down his face. "He's always liked pretty people."

Something was wrong with Alice.

How long?

Which coughs had been due to pollen, to occasional colds, to clearing the throat, and which to the rot now inhabiting her lungs?

He was a doctor, but he hadn't noticed. How? Had he simply been blind to it, the way he had been blind to his mother's illness, explaining away the reason for each cough? Or was Alice's sickness new? They shared the same symptoms, but was it even the same illness?

Because it was consuming Alice much, much faster.

"I don't want to go to the hospital, Vater. I'm just tired." She paused as another fit overtook her, settling back against the pillows on her bed as it subsided. "And coughing a lot."

"And running a fever," he pointed out grimly, pressing the back of his hand to her forehead. Too warm. "It's not just a cough, little one." He hesitated, suddenly uncertain if he should continue. He decided on, "I think you'd be better off in the hospital."

Fredrik was sitting on the other side of the bed, face pale. "Maybe just do it for Papa and Vater? Because we love you, and we want you to get better. Vater is an amazing doctor, you know? If he thinks you'll be better off in the hospital, then maybe just humor him?"

Green eyes met blue across the bed. Fredrik already knew.

"What are you going to do?"

Ander remembered the same words, being said by the same person about the same situation long ago. He refused to let it end the same way.

Fredrik's voice wavered as he continued, pacing in the hallway outside Alice's room in the hospital. "We can't lose Alice, Ander. She's all we have left of Ida. She's our little girl!"

"I don't intend to," he assured.

"But you said we still don't know what it is."

"We don't," he agreed, glancing at the closed door. "But medicine has advanced significantly in the past twenty years, and we can afford actual, good care for her. I have access to far more resources than I did. I can figure it out." He had to.

He knew it was in the lungs. That meant he just had to get it out of the lungs.

They weren't going to lose Alice, no matter what.

Ander was exhausted. When was the last time he had slept?

But he didn't have time for sleep.

She was slipping away from them.

Ander had nearly lost track of the number of things they'd tried. Some helped a little, others made no difference. Nothing was working well enough to prevent it from getting worse; they were only able to slow it.

Tiredly, Ander brushed a strand of blonde hair out of her face. She was sleeping now, face drawn and pale, breathing labored, looking small in the hospital bed. Washed out, like she was fading away before his eyes.

Fredrik was also asleep in the chair in the corner of the room. He hadn't left the hospital since Alice had been admitted.

Ander left the room quietly, not wanting to disturb them. He was running out of options, but he hadn't exhausted them all yet. He decided to go to the university. Perhaps someone there would have an idea. Something experimental that hadn't been tried before.

He was willing to try anything at this point.

"Yes, we did try that," Ander answered for what felt like the nine hundredth time. He was trying to remain patient, but he could feel the desire to *do* something eating away at his limbs, making him twitchy.

Seven of the medical faculty had joined together in Desiree's study with Ander to brainstorm ideas.

They had yet to come up with anything usable.

Desiree – the department chair – hummed and leaned back into the plush couch. "Anything more invasive will have a high possibility of death."

Ander nodded but felt his heart sink. "If it becomes clear that she is going to die either way, then I will try anyway. There will be nothing left to lose, at that point."

"That's drastic, but... it might be your best bet," Koten said, biting his lip.

"If only you could magic it away," Jeroen murmured, staring at Ander intently.

Ander tilted his head slightly, meeting his eyes. "If that were an option I would absolutely pursue it. I will pursue any avenue open to me."

Chloe snorted. "If magic still existed, it would make all of our lives easier, but we must rely on the sciences now."

Ander inclined his head, acknowledging her point. Whether magic still existed but the knowledge of how to use it was lost, or magic itself was gone, was an argument in semantics he did not have time for right now. "Then you think the surgery is the best option?" He himself didn't think the chances for success were going to be very high, but...

Chloe nodded. "It sounds like you've tried everything else."

Later, as they filtered out of Desiree's study, Ander murmuring the appropriate words to indicate thankfulness, he found himself walking out with Jeroen.

"I'm sorry about your daughter," the man offered.

Ander studied him a moment. Out of those who had come to help, he knew Jeroen the least. He had joined the faculty after Ander had graduated. "Thank you," he said, not actually sure if that was the right response for this situation.

They walked in silence through the halls of the medical department. Finally, Jeroen said, "You said you would pursue any option?"

"As long as it's viable, yes," Ander agreed, not sure where this was going.

"Literally anything?"

Ander didn't hesitate. "Anything."

"This isn't a surefire way to save her, but... I don't know. Maybe you can do something with this. Everyone says you're the smartest person to have passed through the university in the past fifty years."

Ander touched the book's cover, faded green leather and gold foiling and embossing. There was no title, just a series of concentric circles with symbols on the cover. "Where did you get this?"

Jeroen cleared his throat, tugging at his collar. "From... ah... a friend, in Noror."

Ander flipped it open, noting the gilded edges of the old parchment pages. Most of the pages were each dedicated to a symbol, with a list of meanings and explanations below; some had combinations of lines. "How do you use it?"

"I don't," Jeroen said with a shake of his head. "I've never been able to figure it out. Nothing works for me. And I don't dare ask around, really. Things like this tend to disappear, and the people attached to them, too. But I couldn't figure out how to get rid of it safely, either. I tried to burn it. It doesn't burn."

The Empire believed magic didn't exist, but here was proof. Validation, at least, that magic *had* existed. If it simply didn't work anymore, then why try to control the remaining artifacts? This book could not be an anomaly. If it existed, then there must have been others. Where were they?

"This is a dangerous thing to own." Jeroen cleared his throat again. Ander could see the sheen of sweat on his brow.

Ander didn't much care. "What do you want for it?"

The man pursed his lips. "A promise."

Ander spent the next week reading the green tome between caring for Alice, trying to ensure Fredrik occasionally ate something, and continuing to do his job. There was some explanation of theory and mechanics, but this book had not been meant for a beginner.

No matter. Ander had yet to be bested by a book.

It might not have worked for Jeroen, but he was going to *make* it work for him.

Three days later, Ander smiled grimly at the little floating ball of light, hovering about a foot over his desk.

It was intent and craft, something more artistic than what he had imagined magic was like before. The book didn't have a list of spells to cast. It had the building blocks of how to make spells. But that suited Ander just fine.

That meant he could create the perfect spell to save Alice.

Ander watched Alice cough painfully, tears coming to her eyes as the fit subsided. Fredrik was holding her close, rubbing her back, whispering softly to her.

He handed her a cup. "That should help with the pain in your throat."

She wiped at her eyes. "It hurts in my chest now too," she whimpered.

Ander felt his own chest tighten. "It will help with that, too."

She only had to hold on a little longer, and then Ander would fix everything.

Casting the spells seemed to take something from Ander, he realized quickly. The larger or more complicated the spell, the more tired he felt afterwards, though food and a quick break helped to alleviate it. He wondered if that could be trained the same way an athlete trained to increase their stamina.

And if it couldn't... it didn't matter. He'd give whatever he had to to save Alice.

The spell he finally settled on was complex. Multiple rings of glyphs, three overlapping bridging patterns. Some of the concepts he had wanted didn't seem to exist in the list in the book, so he was making do with careful modifications and being sure his intent was as clear as he could make it. As long as he held true to the desired outcome, there was no reason it shouldn't work.

He waited until late at night, when Fredrik and Alice were both asleep and activity in the hospital was low. He made sure the door was closed, then took out the square of paper he'd drawn the spell on. He placed it on Alice's chest. He looked at her face; even sleeping she wasn't free from the pain anymore. Her face was pinched and drawn, dark circles under her eyes.

He could ease that, now.

He placed a hand on the spell gently, and *willed.*

The circle immediately activated in a flash of green light, a larger version appearing above the paper. The rings of glyphs, beginning to rotate, linked bridging lines turning with them.

The drain was immediate and significant. Ander felt himself get lightheaded, but refused to submit, holding tight to envisioning the desired effect. He could not waver now.

The rings continued to spin slowly as Ander demanded of them to burn out the rot from Alice's lungs. Ander felt himself get weaker, but then the rings began to dissolve, their purpose fulfilled. He just had to hold on a bit longer, just long enough.

And then the light faded.

He blinked rapidly, spots dancing in his vision, either from the light of the spell or the cost of casting it. He closed his eyes, rubbing them to try to clear his vision, then looked back at Alice.

Her face had smoothed out, no longer looking pained. Her breathing looked easier, and her face had a little bit of color back.

Ander stuffed the scrap of paper into his pocket and stood, intending to get a stethoscope, but he felt himself sway in an alarming way. He stumbled over to the second chair in the room–

When he woke up, he was in an incredibly uncomfortable sitting position. Everything ached, and the light filtering in from the window had him snapping his eyes shut again immediately. At least he had made it to the chair before he passed out.

"Ander?"

Fredrik's voice. Ander felt a hand gently touch his shoulder.

"Hey, you awake?"

He blinked his eyes open again but tried to shield them from the light with his hand. "Alice?"

A watery giggle. "Ander, you won't believe this, but she's getting better. She's actually getting better!"

Alice was asleep in the bed, but his observations had proved true – she had much more color to her face now, and her breathing was easy. Ander felt a sensation of pure relief wash over him. It had worked.

"You can go back to sleep, if you want. You need it. I know you've been trying so hard to take care of our little girl." Fredrik was babbling. "And you look absolutely exhausted, but the nurse came in this morning and was amazed at how much better she looks, and then she went and got Dr. Marson who agreed–"

Ander was finding it difficult to keep up with Fredrik's excitement, though he wished he could share it. He was just... too tired right now. He'd sleep a bit more, then celebrate afterwards.

His hand found the crumpled piece of paper in his pocket.

Jeroen had said it was dangerous. Ander was forced to agree. It didn't make sense that all magic had suddenly stopped working for people when he had just proved it could still be done. That meant something else was going on, but what? He wasn't sure. He'd have to think about that later, too. It felt like a conspiracy of some sort.

It could be his secret for now. After all, Alice was safe, and that was all that mattered.

VI

"Yes, add twelve drops of the phenolphthalein," Ander instructed, keeping a close eye on Alice as she dripped one liquid into another. "Now three milliliters of the lime water."

Her eyes widened as the liquid turned pink. "Oh! That's pretty, actually."

Ander hummed noncommittally. "Now take this straw, and *do not drink the solution*, Alice, I mean it. Blow into the water gently."

There was a knock on the doorframe, and Ander looked up quizzically to find Fredrik standing in the opening between the kitchen and the hallway. "Please tell me that whatever you're working on is *not* dinner," the blond said, wrinkling his nose at the collection of beakers and other equipment strewn across the table.

"I wouldn't recommend it," Ander said, keeping an eye on Alice, though she had paused when Fredrik appeared. "Are you home for dinner tonight?"

"I thought maybe, but... is there going to be dinner tonight?" Fredrik asked after a moment.

Ander blinked. He hadn't expected that. He considered what they had on hand.

"I made some potato salad this morning; it's in the icebox!" Alice exclaimed. "And I picked up the ingredients for meatballs and caper sauce."

Ah, that was helpful. "Meatballs. We'll be eating a bit late."

"Right, uh, okay then," Fredrik said. "I'll just... come back later?" He shot one last look at the mess before disappearing.

Alice frowned after him. "Huh, I thought he'd want to go out and hear the gossip tonight."

Ander raised an eyebrow. "Gossip?"

"Yeah, about the news?"

He stared at her blankly.

"Vater, *the news!* It's been all over the place today; surely they were talking about it at work?" She hid her face in her hands.

"I don't usually engage in idle chatter at work," he pointed out mildly.

She made a sound that usually meant she was annoyed with him for some reason, setting closed fists on her hips as she stomped a foot down into a wide stance. "Vater, you'd have had to be actively ignoring people to miss this!"

He didn't grace that with an answer.

"The Crystal Light Blade was stolen from the museum in Norik last night!"

"So?"

She squinted at him. "You're half-Avari, Vater. Shouldn't you care about that?"

He shrugged one shoulder. "Not really. Are you going to blow into the solution to see what happens?"

She shook her head at him. "All right then, just take my word for it – that's a big deal. The last real magical artifact in the Empire was stolen. Everyone else is going to consider that news."

He filed that away for when someone else inevitably tried to bring it up. "Thank you for the warning. Blow into the solution."

She rolled her eyes at him but obediently picked up the straw and blew gently into it. "Oh!" she exclaimed after a moment as the pink liquid lost its color. "But why...?"

"The carbon dioxide in your breath reacted with the water to form carbonic acid, which neutralized the lime water," he explained.

"Oh, so the phenolphthalein no longer had a base to react to so it returned to being colorless!" She drew the obvious conclusion. "It's just like magic, though!"

"Science, not magic," he corrected, thinking of the green book hidden upstairs. He hadn't cast any other spells since he healed Alice a year ago, but sometimes, when he was sure the other two weren't home, he pulled it out and looked through the glyphs again, continuing to memorize them and their many meanings and applications.

Just in case, he told himself.

A knock on his office door. "Come."

"Would you mind if I shut the door?"

Ander looked up from the report he was reading to see Jeroen shifting from foot to foot in the doorway. "If you wish."

He hadn't seen the other doctor since a few days after Alice had been "miraculously" healed, when he'd come by just to "check in and see how his colleague's daughter was doing." He hadn't said anything at the time – Fredrik had been present, and Alice had been awake – but Ander suspected Jeroen knew he'd figured out the magic to some capacity.

"How have you been?" the other man asked, tugging on his tie. His sandy hair was a mess; for a doctor he looked fairly disheveled.

Ander wished people would skip all the formalities and get to the point, but his mother had been firm that even if he didn't understand why, the formalities were a necessity. "Busy; you?"

The other man smiled lopsidedly. "Well, well! Couldn't ask for any more. Well, you know, maybe just a little more."

Ander stared at him, silent.

Jeroen wrung his hands together, glancing back at the door.

"Can I help you?" Ander finally asked, wondering what this was about.

"Ah, well, since you asked" – Jeroen's voice dropped to a whisper – "you remember that book I gave you?"

"With crystal clarity."

"Shh! There's people about, no need to draw more attention than we need to." He glanced at the door again.

Right, because nothing was more subtle than two men whispering in an office with the door closed. Ander waited.

"Well, I've– we've– I've recently come into possession of something else of a similar persuasion. Like the book, though, I've failed to achieve any success in making it work."

Ah, now Ander saw where this was going. "You want to know if I can activate this artifact?"

"Shh! Keep your voice down!" He pulled out a handkerchief and wiped at his face. "But yes, that's the gist of it."

Ander did owe Jeroen; he knew that. "When and where?"

"You must be joking," Ander said, taken aback by the sight of the object Jeroen had pulled out of a cupboard in his office later that night. "How on Gaia did you end up with *that*?"

Three feet of pale-blue crystal, topped with a silver crossguard in the shape of a delicate pair of wings. A dull violet crystal rested between them, and the black hilt was topped with a smaller blue crystal.

The Crystal Light Blade.

"Are you *completely* insane?" Ander demanded, staring at Jeroen incredulously. He might not have cared about the fact it was stolen, but that didn't mean he wanted to be anywhere near it.

The man chuckled, wiping at his brow. "I acquired it quite by chance, you know? But that doesn't really matter. What matters is that it doesn't do anything."

"It's meant to kill demons!" Even Ander knew the story. "Of course it doesn't do anything; there *aren't any demons here.*"

"It's a magic sword; it should do magic," Jeroen argued.

"Like *what?*"

"I don't know. Light up, or something." The other man frowned at the Blade.

Ander wanted to strangle him. "What are you possibly even planning on doing with it?"

"Oh, you don't have to worry about that. I just want it to work," Jeroen said quickly. "You made the book work, so surely you can do the same with the Blade?"

"The book was literally a manual," Ander said through gritted teeth. "I don't see instructions written anywhere on the Blade." There weren't even any of the glyphs from the book. Maybe he could have done something if there were glyphs, but as far as he was concerned this was a very large paperweight that should have been left in its museum, where it at least served a purpose.

"Well, no," Jeroen conceded. "But I'm sure you can figure it out! After all, we wouldn't want to have people start wondering *how* your daughter miraculously recovered from her illness last year, would we?" He grinned.

Ander wasn't sure how to respond to that, but he finally settled on, "You are going to blackmail me into doing something I can't possibly do?" That was... ah, yes. Pathetic.

Jeroen's smile slipped a little. "Well, maybe just try your best?"

Ander had struggled to understand people for as long as he'd lived, but this was something else. Still... Jeroen had given him the means to save Alice's life. And even though Ander thought this was ridiculous beyond all reason, he had promised a favor in return.

Sighing, he resigned himself to stupidity for the foreseeable future.

Maybe Jeroen would realize it was futile sooner rather than later.

"Vater?"

Ander cringed as he shut the front door, turning to find Alice dressed in a nightgown on the stairs. "What are you still doing up, little one?"

"I wanted to see you." She was pouting. Not a great sign for him. "I don't like this university project you're consulting on. You're never home anymore."

"If it's any consolation, I don't care for it much either." He held an arm out and let her wrap herself around him like a limpet. "I'm sorry."

"Then why are you doing it?" Her voice was muffled by his shirt.

He sighed. "Because I have to."

Ander powered the spell, but even though it lit, the Blade remained dormant.

"How much more of this before you admit it's useless?" he asked Jeroen, who always watched him work.

The other man shrugged, face pinched. "I don't think it is."

Ander had even tried to teach Jeroen how to cast the spells, but no matter what, not even the simple light spell would activate for the man. Ander was forced to consider that whatever he had that the spells drained, Jeroen might not have.

And in fact... hadn't the Blade only ever worked for Ebryn?

"Perhaps it only works for the Hero," he suggested. "Ebryn forged it with the help of the Three; it is possible that they added some sort of failsafe to ensure only he could wield it to its full potential. Or maybe it does only work around demons. There are too many variables we can't account for."

"No... it has to work. It has to work!" Jeroen slammed a fist down on the table. "It has to work," he repeated, more softly.

Ander stared. He was missing something; he just didn't know what.

Ander was woken up by someone pounding on the front door.

"Who the hell is that?" Fredrik muttered, sitting up. "At this hour?"

"How should I know?" Ander rolled out of bed, grabbing a shirt and throwing it on. He glanced at the clock; it was three in the morning. "It might be an emergency at the hospital; I'll get it."

Alice popped her head out of her bedroom as he passed by. "Vater?"

"Go back to bed. It's fine."

"Okay." Her door clicked shut.

Ander opened the door and was shocked to see Jeroen, who looked like he'd dressed in haste in the dark, holding a suspiciously sword-shaped bundle in his arms.

"Ander! You have to let me in!" He tried to shoulder past him into the house. "They're here! They're looking for me!"

Ander blocked him. "What?" he asked, completely aghast. "Who?"

"The authorities!" the man whimpered. "Please, Ander, please!"

"So you brought it *here?*"

"I didn't know where else to go, please, you don't understand, *please–*"

"My family lives here!" he hissed, furious.

"There's a Truth Seeker, he's investigating the university, I couldn't stay!"

"A what?"

Jeroen kept twisting to look over his shoulder at the road behind him, but it was empty. "A Truth Seeker, one of those new troops, but I *know* they're the ones that are responsible for all the magic things going missing!"

"If they're new, how could they?" None of this was making any sense.

"Because they're not actually new, they're just new to the public." Ander realized Jeroen was crying, tears pouring down his cheeks. "Please, Ander, *please.*"

Ander hesitated.

Suddenly, Jeroen made an odd sound, and like a marionette whose strings were cut, he dropped to the ground. A small girl, around four feet tall, with golden-brown skin, dark-brown hair, curved black horns, and facial features reminiscent of a gazelle stood there, looking up at Ander with inscrutable large brown eyes.

Lowkeef.

"You may call me Sanne," she said without preamble, the low tones of her voice at odds with her childish appearance. She gestured with the hand not holding a bloodied knife. An Avari with reddish-gold hair and a loaded crossbow appeared from seemingly nowhere. "And this is Hendrik. You will let us in, for there is much to discuss."

A lot of Jeroen's behavior did make sense in retrospect. But while he had come across as something of an idiot, these two were dangerous.

Ander leaned against the counter, wanting to move over to where Alice and Fredrik were sitting against the opposite wall, but not daring to. Hendrik stood in the doorway; Sanne was sitting cross-legged on the kitchen table, the Blade unwrapped on the table in front of her. They had dropped Jeroen's corpse in the corner closest to the door.

Sanne and Hendrik were both Elben names. Ander would bet neither of them actually belonged to the two claiming them.

"The Blade is old elemental magic," Sanne was explaining. "It does not belong to the Empire as it is now, corrupt and waning. Its time will come."

"I still don't understand what that has to do with us." Fredrik's face was pale as he held Alice tight. "Why the hell are you *in our home*?"

Sanne tilted her head to the side. "Even though the Blade contains the crystal light of earth, a sacred relic of my people, I cannot resonate with it. Nor can Hendrik, whose Avari physiology should have worked." She gestured to Ander. "We need him to figure out why the Blade is silent."

"You need *Ander*?"

Ander refused to meet Fredrik's eyes. "I haven't been able to do anything with it for weeks. Whatever secrets it has, it keeps them well."

"What on Gaia are you talking about?"

Alice had remained silent so far, though her face was pale and she was pressed firmly up against Fredrik, and her eyes never left Ander.

"He figured out how to use the book," Sanne said, voice cool. "You do not know how rare that makes you."

"Trying to teach magic to people born in the Empire has like a point five percent success rate," Hendrik added. "Growing up in an environment that teaches that magic doesn't exist does something to people, makes it nearly impossible to learn later in life."

"But he did not just learn it; he taught himself," Sanne continued. "It makes him a prodigy."

Ander felt that was probably taking it a little far; the book had contained some instructions.

"Ander?" Fredrik's tone was questioning.

He cleared his throat. He owed them at least some explanation. "When Alice was sick, Jeroen gave me a book. I was able to use it to make a spell that cleared her lungs of the sickness."

"And that sort of healing magic can be incredibly complex." Sanne turned those large, deer-like eyes on him. "It is not something to be easily dismissed, that you shaped such magic on your own, and it was successful." She nodded at Alice. "So Jeroen told us, when we expressed our need for a mage."

"Ander, you *did magic* and *didn't tell me*?" Fredrik squeaked.

Ander looked down. To some degree, he found himself hating Jeroen for bringing this down on them, but mostly... mostly he hated himself. This was very much his fault in the end. A series of unbroken choices leading to this moment.

"So, you will activate the Blade. You have some Avari ancestry; it should be enough," Sanne declared.

Weren't all Lowkeef supposed to have some sort of animal companion? Where was hers? "What makes you so sure that is necessary?" he asked instead.

"Ebryn was Avari," she stated simply.

"And...?" he asked after a moment, unsure what that had to do with anything.

The large, deer-like ears twitched for the first time. "And that is how the magic works."

He'd seen absolutely nothing in the book that supported that theory. "You just said it didn't work for him." He inclined his head at the Avari standing by the door.

"He is not a prodigy. You are."

"Nothing I've done has affected it. Whatever it is the Blade requires, I don't think I can provide it." What would convince her?

Sanne hummed. "Well, there is another sort of magic that is strong. Perhaps strong enough to wake the Blade. I had preferred not to, but time is passing while the Liar hunts us, and if there is nothing else, maybe the Blade will remember the reason its original wielder forged it." She picked the Blade up and hopped off the table, landing in a crouch in front of Alice and Fredrik.

Hendrik frowned, straightening up and turning to face her. "Sanne, I don't think–"

She held up a hand and he cut himself off, though he did not return to his previous posture. "Girl-child, you have not yet reached the majority of your species, correct?"

Alice finally looked away from Ander. "What do you mean?" Her voice was steady, but quiet.

"You are not yet... an adult?" Sanne questioned.

Fredrik's arms tightened around her. "No, she is not."

Sanne nodded. "Good. For neither was Aria." She made a gesture, and a spell circle appeared on the wall behind Fredrik. Vines exploded from it, grabbing him and tearing him away–

Then Sanne stabbed Alice.

Ander felt as though time froze. He stared at the Crystal Light Blade, pinning Alice to the wall beside Fredrik, whose mouth was open in a scream.

And something in him broke.

The next thing he knew, Sanne was somewhere across the room and he was beside his little one, trying to stop the bleeding, glyphs blooming into existence and forming from green threads even though he knew a wound like that was fatal not even magic could fix this–

:No. We can save her.:

A wave of foreign understanding rolled over him, and a feeling of power that certainly was not his own. No glyphs could save her, but this power could. He gave himself to it utterly. *:Pull the Blade and repair the body; give her spirit a place to return to, and the choice is hers, always hers. It is not too late, beloved.:*

His magic bled from green to violet.

And the world was suddenly *saturated* with magic.

He did as the feminine voice bade and carefully pulled the Blade from Alice's body, tossing it to the side once free. The magic took its place, a feeling of clear determination and love and devotion and complete refusal of reality–

And then Alice was blinking at him. "Vater?"

Ander realized he was crying as he held her. He held her even more tightly, because–

The other being's understanding was his own, and he knew, knew there would be no return from this, understood the kind of magic this was, what the nature of this being was, and knew he couldn't stay here, he'd be hunted and they would forever be in danger–

A feeling of uncertainty. *:But we saved her?:*

Yes, he agreed fervently. And that was worth anything. Even if he had to leave.

:Hmm, a little more distance between the two of us will be better for you.: The feeling of Her presence lessened but did not leave, and he found it easier to think like himself again. Dark shadows were coalescing around him; he could feel their desire to protect, even as they shifted into shadowy skirts, worn by a pale woman with long white hair and violet eyes. She turned to where Sanne was pushing herself up from where she had landed when... Ander threw her? Was that what happened? He didn't have a clear memory of that moment.

Sanne looked up, saw the god, and screamed, backing away by pulling herself along the ground, eyes filled with terror.

She ran.

:Let her go,: Hades murmured dispassionately. *:She already hears the hounds, and she knows what they mean. She'll not outrun them for long.:*

Hendrik was in an unconscious pile by the wall, and Ander chose to ignore him too in favor of Alice.

The vines holding Fredrik withered and then he was also there, holding them both, and Ander tried to burn this moment into his memory.

:You will not be alone. It will not be the same, beloved, but you will not be alone.: A pause, and She spoke again, but Ander didn't feel that She was speaking to him. *:I know what you seek. It is not time yet. Withdraw. None of those involved here will remember; I will ensure your mandate remains upheld.:*

A presence Ander hadn't been aware of until its absence disappeared.

:Beloved, you must go. It is not safe for you here, though I have secured safety for them.:

:What do you mean?:

:They will not remember the magic. The memory must fade. For their sake:

Ander felt his breath hitch. The night had been *full* of magic. *:Then... what will they remember?:*

She hesitated. *:I'm not certain.:*

:They'll think I left them... they won't remember why?:

:Possibly.:

Ander swallowed harshly. Everything he'd done had been for their sakes. If this is what it took to keep them safe, then he would do it. One last moment, and then he began to untangle himself from them.

"Ander?" Fredrik's eyes were wide.

"I'm sorry," he whispered, pressing Alice into his arms.

"Vater? What's... what are you doing?" Panic was beginning to creep into her voice. She knew.

"Goodbye, little one." He kissed her on the forehead one last time, then stood.

"*Vater!*"

"Ander! What... you can't just–"

He met Fredrik's eyes. "I'm sorry. For everything."

"What? Ander–"

And then Her magic came down, and there was silence.

:*Could we...:* he began, looking around.

:*Of course.:*

She began to fade from view, but the kitchen returned to its former state. Jeroen's corpse and Hendrik disappeared.

:*The Blade... take it with you.:*

He eyed it distastefully. :*Where?:*

:*North.:*

North? Only the Wall was north.

:*Home is north, past the Wall,:* She stated firmly. :*I will not leave you here.:*

Past the Wall? Ander looked back at where Alice and Fredrik lay, minds learning a story he would never know, but which still ended with him leaving. He would remember the truth for them.

And maybe they would be able to move on.

He picked up the Blade, turned, and left, knowing he was leaving pieces of himself behind.

Blue

Mara breathed deeply as she hopped out of the boat and into the ankle-deep water. The scent of salt water, the sound of waves crashing on the shore, the caress of the breeze all welcomed her home. She'd spent most of the trip from the Emerald Shore daydreaming about finally coming back, but she had a little ways to go yet.

She'd been gone too long this time.

"You sure this is where you want to go, lady?"

She turned to the *Blue Iris*'s navigator, who was looking over the deserted beach with one raised eyebrow. He and a few of the other crew members had tried to convince her to let them bring her to the small port on the other side of Marcrae, but that wouldn't be as helpful as they thought it was. She flicked her long, dark-blue ponytail over her shoulder. "Yes, this is perfect, thank you very much!"

He turned back to her, and his tone became concerned. "You don't even have any... luggage, or bags or anything."

"Oh, don't worry about that," she said with a grin. She'd already dropped everything she'd been traveling with back at the apartment she kept on Crescent Island, bringing only a few things that she'd tucked into her clothes. "I'm all set. Safe journey back!" She gave him a jaunty wave, ears twitching.

He gave one last look at her feet – black socks completely soaked from the surf, no shoes – and sighed, rolling his eyes. "If you say so. Good luck to you, lady." He began rowing the boat back to the *Blue Iris.*

Mara waved for another moment, then turned and made her way to the beach to relax in the sun for a bit. She'd been given very strict instructions this time to wait for her escort, and she doubted they'd come while the ship was still in sight of the beach.

She found a nice spot and plopped down onto it, lying back with her hands behind her head. She closed her eyes against the glare of the sun, thinking about the message that had called her back to the Nyphoren Islands. Kaikani had begged Mara to return. It wasn't like her. And to wait for an escort… that indicated danger of some sort, but what? Mara had been a priest of Hades for almost eight hundred years; while she wasn't completely invulnerable she was pretty close to it, especially in the water.

Something had spooked the Veren. But what?

:Kaikani knows you are capable, but she also worries about you,: Hades observed.

:Worries a little too much, but that's part of what I love about her. Oh! I wonder if she's thought more about becoming a Dedicated.:

:It's been fifteen years since you left; I'm sure she's had the time to consider it.:

Mara pressed her lips together, annoyed with herself. *:I didn't mean to be gone so long. But there is always work to be done on the Shore.:*

:I appreciate your efforts there.: A brief feeling of a hug. *:I know what you sacrifice to aid them. But you should feel free to remain here for a time. Rest and recuperate. Maybe even return to Tarvishte for a visit. The Shore's problems are not new, and you made good headway there this time. It can be left for a while.:*

They had written each other letters while Mara was gone, but it wasn't the same thing. It would be nice to spend actual time with Kaikani again. *:I think I will.:*

Hades hummed, pleased, and then her attention faded.

Mara soaked in the sun and sand until a familiar brush of magic against her own caused her to spring up in excitement.

The sun was just beginning to set, and standing out on the water was a figure she'd missed more than anything. Orange and gold scales, fins tipped in teal running down both arms and legs, delicate gold jewelry with blue gems, and pale-green coral armor. Large electric-blue eyes sparkled with joy over a mostly flat face while her head tentacles twitched.

Kaikani.

Mara shrieked happily, running full tilt onto the water, jumping the waves as they came in to throw herself at the Veren. Kaikani caught her, arms holding her close as their lips met, distance and time melting away as though it hadn't been fifteen years since they'd last seen each other. When they broke apart, Kaikani's eyes sparkled with mischief as she pitched herself backward, pulling Mara with her. They crashed beneath the surface of the water, where four other Veren waited for them.

"Kaikani! You don't know how much I've missed you!" Mara exclaimed. As a Mer, her inherent magic made breathing possible underwater – convenient for when one's long-term girlfriend lived beneath the surface of the ocean.

"Who's to say I didn't miss you more?" Kaikani laughed, hugging Mara again. The tips of her tentacles squeezed Mara's shoulders.

They kissed again, basking for a moment in the joy of each other's presence.

One of the other Veren cleared his throat meaningfully. "Ladies, we should be returning to Ahulowaki. The waters are not safe right now."

Mara frowned, ears sinking as another one of the Veren handed Kaikani back her spear. This close to the surface and they were concerned? Was the problem Empire-related? If so, she wasn't going to be much help. "Your message indicated something is wrong, but you didn't say what."

Kaikani exchanged glances with the other warriors. "Yes. I'm sorry for being vague, but the king asked me to be, just in case the message was intercepted. He doesn't want it widely known how bad the problem is. You know the Empire will do anything in their power to make our lives difficult."

Mara tilted her head to the side, kicking her feet idly. "What is the problem?"

"Movorae." Kaikani shook her head at Mara's puzzled look. "No, it's not what you are thinking. This is not the occasional one rising from the depths. A swarm of thirteen or more has been spotted in the Nyphoren's eastern waters."

Mara blanched. She and the Veren were in the eastern waters right now. "*Thirteen?*"

Kaikani nodded grimly. "It gets worse. One is an Old One – at least fifty feet long."

"There hasn't been an Old One in the Mid-waters since..." Mara thought back, but she couldn't actually think of the last time.

:Not since Ebryn Stormlight came to these islands,: Hades murmured softly.

"Ebryn." Right, the Avari hero had slain an Old One for the Nyphoren, and they had given him the Crystal Light of Water in exchange. "This is..."

Kaikani nodded. "It's terrible. Potentially catastrophic. But..."

"But?" Mara prompted after a moment.

"It's odd. They've been spotted, but there have been no attacks."

"Huh." That was odd. Movorae were not known for restraint. But that gave Mara hope.

"That's why the king asked for your aid, High Priest," a Veren with pink scales tipped in green added. "We are trying to figure out what to do."

Mara nodded. Thirteen Movorae could kill a lot of Veren, even if they were trained warriors. Even with her help, dealing with them would be difficult. "Of course. I'll do everything I can to help."

Kaikani nodded again, but her eyes betrayed her worry. "He's waiting for us now."

Mara reached out and took Kaikani's hand, threading their fingers together. "Let's go."

The sound of soft voices floated through the throne room, mingling with that of falling water, but conversation ceased when the herald announced, "High Priest Mara and escort presents herself to King Kanahiku."

King Kanahiku sat on his sea glass throne, red, blue, and violet scales creating a striking look against the soft teals and blues of the grotto. Vibrant blue kilpe with its delicate white flowers spilled from the tops of marble pillars. Cracks in the stone walls allowed for gentle waterfalls to spill into the grotto, creating comfortable pools for the Veren nobility to lounge in at the edges. A large, shallow pool of water lined with white marble dominated the center of the room, lines of gold tracing astrological paths visible beneath the still surface. The king himself wore many of the delicate gold chains the Veren favored, spotted with pearls, rubies, and sapphires, and a half cape of elegant purple silk. The coral crown was bleached white with age.

Mara had pulled the water from her clothes and hair as soon as they had passed through the water gate at the entrance to the grotto, but the air was still damp, a fine mist rising from the waterfalls and pools – good for Veren scales. She gave a half bow to the king while Kaikani went down to one knee beside her, the other warriors who had accompanied them falling back. "Your Grace."

Kanahiku smiled warmly. "Mara, old friend. Welcome back to Ahulowaki."

She straightened, returning the smile as her ears twitched. "It is good to be back," she agreed, taking Kaikani's hand as the woman stood. She had first met the Veren king when he was a little tadpole trying to escape from the fry pools. It was hard to believe he was almost five hundred and seventy years old now, his own son preparing to take over in a few years' time. "I wish it were under better circumstances, though."

The look on his face became grim. "What has Kaikani told you?"

"Only that there is a swarm of Movorae in the eastern waters, and that there is an Old One among them. And that there have been no attacks yet. It's been centuries since more than one or two rose from the depths at the same time; I've never seen a swarm in the Mid-waters. Even the last Old One to rise came alone. Do you know what drew them from the depths?"

He snorted. "What drew them? It may be more accurate to ask what *drove* them. Not two weeks ago there was a series of explosions on Crescent Island." He gestured to a yellow-and-green Veren.

Penani, the king's spymaster, stepped forward. She cleared her throat, tentacles curling to show her unease. "We believe it to be connected to some sort of massive construction project the Empire is undertaking on the eastern side of Crescent Island's bay. There's been an influx of craftsmen and materials in addition to the detonations; it seems as though they were attempting to reshape part of the shoreline. Our current theory is that some of the explosions went deep and may have either driven the Movorae from their home or drawn them up to investigate."

"And while I wish we could just let the Empire suffer their own follies... we are between them and the Movorae," the king finished. "And who knows if more of the creatures will rise to the Mid-waters as the construction continues?"

Mara felt Kaikani's hand tighten around hers. "I can't help with the Empire," she reminded them gently. "They do not recognize a priest's authority. The Truth Seekers would try to kill me." It didn't help that communication between the Veren monarchy and the Empire had broken down five hundred years before. The Empire would probably be pleased to know they were making life difficult for the Veren. "But the Movorae... Kaikani said there have been no attacks?"

Kanahiku inclined his head, moving past her refusal to his unspoken question. "Not yet, though it is only a matter of time before a swarm needs to feed."

"We've been evacuating the nearby villages and bringing them to Ahulowaki," Kaikani added, turning to Mara. "But there's too many fish in the Mid-waters to hope they will return to the depths in search of food."

"But no attacks yet," Mara repeated thoughtfully. "From a species that normally kills on sight."

"We've been purposely staying out of sight, using the Lokanu's magic to track their movements as best we can," Penani explained. "But this is not sustainable."

Mara shook her head. "No, of course not. But I wonder if they *can* be tempted to return to the depths." That would be the ideal solution. No one was going to want to fight thirteen Movorae head-on, even with Mara's magic. That was suicide. And she didn't want to kill them anyway. "They've been in the Mid-waters for two weeks?"

The king nodded.

"How long before the Movorae start to put a strain on your food supply?"

Kanahiku shrugged. "They have not left the eastern waters, so the other quadrants can supply food if needed for a while. I am more concerned that the swarm may approach Ahulowaki itself."

"But the Lokanu are tracking them." Mara thought hard. "And I'm in the city. If worst comes to worst, I can cast an aegis to keep them out. All right, then. Tomorrow I'll go out and try to get my own eyes on the situation. I'm leaning towards waiting them out to be honest, but it might be possible to try to break up the swarm and kill them one by one if it becomes necessary." And *only* if it became necessary.

Murmurs spread throughout the grotto, and Kaikani's hand tightened in a death grip around her own.

Kanahiku tilted his head. "A High Priest's promise of defense does put an old man's mind at ease."

She gave a definitive nod as Hades hummed in agreement in the back of her mind. "It won't solve the issue, but it'll buy us time to find a solution."

The king nodded. Let us hope we can do so."

Kaikani dragged her off to the side as soon as they passed through the water gate out of the throne room. "Are you crazy? Offering to go out and look for the Movorae *by yourself*?"

"It's okay, I promise," Mara hastened to reassure her. "They won't see me, and I'm not going to engage. I just want a look."

"Can't you look through the viewing pools, like the Lokanu?" The Veren rested her head against Mara's shoulder.

Mara shook her head. "It's best to see things personally. And if there really is an Old One there... those aren't usually part of a swarm. Something weird is happening."

:Agreed.:

Luckily, there was nothing that could see Mara in the water if she didn't want it to. She would be fine. "But let's not worry about that right now. The swarm has yet to do any damage, and it might even leave on its own! Everyone's been evacuated, so... let's just relax tonight!"

Kaikani shot her a baleful look. "Only you could be so unconcerned with a swarm of Movorae nearby."

"But they're not, really." A feeling of agreement from Hades, which was... interesting. But she could use that. "Hades agrees. Ahulowaki is not in any immediate danger."

"Ugh." Kaikani pulled her to one of the nearby currents that would take them home. "Is it a priest thing, then?"

Mara considered that. "I mean, if Hades doesn't think there is any danger..." She shrugged. "Then I guess it kind of is. Though, speaking of that...?" She trailed off hopefully.

"Hm?" Electric-blue eyes blinked at her. "Oh! Your offer, about becoming Dedicated."

Mara nodded as they let the current begin to carry them through the city.

"I have been giving it a lot of thought. It is not... the kind of decision I want to make blindly," Kaikani said, waiting for Mara's nod to continue. "I went to one of the Lokanu and asked for a reading, even."

"Kai!" Mara exclaimed, fighting the impulse to hide her face in her hands as her ears sank. "You did *not* seek the opinion of a god on becoming dedicated to a *different* god."

"Don't be like that." She whacked Mara on the shoulder. "The stars are neutral on such things."

"The stars might be, but is Chatori?" Mara muttered, brushing a rogue strand of hair out of her face. "Though I guess it's more like you are dedicating yourself to me, and then through me to Hades." It was actually the sort of convoluted ridiculousness Chatori favored, so maybe it wasn't so bad.

Kaikani hummed. "Are you sure... Hades doesn't mind?"

Mara blinked. "Mind? Mind what?"

Her girlfriend looked away. "Her priests taking Dedicated. The way you describe it, my loyalty will first and foremost be to you, not to the goddess."

"If Hades minds she should really tell Daiyu. I think she's up to six Dedicated now," Mara said, voice dry.

:A whole school of them,: Hades laughed. *:But whatever makes you happy.:*

Mara took a moment to appreciate the mental image of Daiyu being followed around by a school of fish-Human hybrids before continuing. "But honestly, the whole point of the Dedicated – at least in Hades' mind – is to have someone support the *priest*. She is fine with the whole structure and kind of... second-hand worship, though, yeah. It is weird."

And really, only Daiyu made that much use of it as far as Mara was aware. Siva had a Dedicated as well in Dalmara, and Yafen had two in Cartago-Mir. Daiyu had once insinuated that Jak had a Dedicated kicking around somewhere, but then, Daiyu had also been very drunk at the time, and Mara wasn't sure whether or not to believe her. Even her hair had been acting drunk.

"Is Daiyu sleeping with all six?" Kaikani asked pointedly, pulling them out of the current and towards one of the market grottos, the one Mara knew housed their favorite food stall.

Mara opened her mouth to answer, but then paused. "I was going to say no, but actually I have no idea. Probably not. I haven't even met them all."

Kaikani's eye ridges raised as they passed through the water gate into the grotto.

Mara shrugged. "The Lady really doesn't care about that."

Many of the Veren called out greetings as she and Kaikani strolled past different stalls and displays. This was their neighborhood, and it was wonderful to see so many familiar faces and places after having been gone so long. Night was beginning to fall, and the soft glow of lumenpearls lit the grotto as the suncoral closed to sleep.

The grotto was busy, and Mara was reminded of the refugees. Life in Ahulowaki hadn't seemed to change very much, which Mara found comforting.

Her mouth began to water as Kaikani placed an order to-go. It had been literal years since she'd had Haloe's grilled fish and rice balls, and she intended to *savor* it.

They stepped off to the side to wait, and Kaikani put an arm around her. "To return to my earlier questions... what, then, if we break up?"

Everything in Mara rebelled at the thought, but the question was valid. "It's up to you. You could choose to remain as my Dedicated, or you could be released. Hades will not force anything on anyone."

Kaikani sighed. "Sometimes, I think maybe the Lady could stand to be a little *more* forceful. Perhaps then she would have a proper religion."

"Eh, it works for us," Mara said with a shrug. "Blame Jak. The rest of us do."

"Oh, I do." Kaikani laughed, and Mara enjoyed the way the light played off her orange and gold scales. "I would like to meet him one day. Some of the stories you've told me are wild."

Mara smiled slyly. "If you become my Dedicated, you have a better chance of that... if only because he only wanders through every few hundred years." Maybe he *was* keeping a secret Dedicated somewhere, and he spent most of his time with them. Though it would be weird for him to have never mentioned it, wouldn't it?

:Yes, that would be very weird,: Hades agreed wryly, but Mara noted she did not directly confirm or deny it.

Interesting. Mara wasn't sure which side that lent more credence to, but it was interesting nonetheless.

They were interrupted by Kaikani's name being called, and they collected their food before continuing home. Mara squirmed in delight as their grotto came into view, high on one of the living rock pillars, and darted for the water gate.

She was home!

Their little grotto was furnished differently than most due to Mara being an Avari. In addition to the sitting pools, there was a soft pink couch that had been actual hell to get in here, decorated with a pair of fuzzy pillows Mara had made. A crocheted green-and-blue blanket was draped over the back, another of Mara's creations. The mist-generating waterfalls were contained to one side of the room so Mara could actually be dry if she preferred. The kilpe and luminpearls decorated the walls next to two murals Mara and Kaikani had painted directly onto the rock, depicting dawn and dusk, iconography of Hades, the Nyphoren, and the Distant Trinity blended together.

She spun around in the greeting room with joy, pulling Kaikani into her arms as the Veren caught up with her. "Oh, I've missed this – and you – *so much*."

Kaikani held her tight. "I missed you, too."

They stood for several long minutes just holding each other, basking in each other's presence, until Mara's stomach rumbled. They laughed and headed to the kitchen.

"Hungry?" Kaikani teased, waving the kelp bag holding their food in front of Mara's face.

"Extremely. I haven't eaten since this morning!" Mara complained. "Oh, and that reminds me." As they sat at the low table, she pulled a small, waterproof box out of a pocket. "I brought you a present."

"A present?" Kaikani's eyes lit up and she opened the box. "Oh, it's beautiful!"

Mara smiled as Kaikani took the small charm out to examine it. Gold, inlaid with pearl, sapphire, and aquamarine in the shape of a four-pointed star overlaid with the glyph for water. "It made me think of you, and then I thought it should be on you."

Veren did not wear clothes the way land dwellers did, but they greatly enjoyed decking themselves out with jewelry and had a magpie's appreciation for shiny things. Kaikani stroked the charm for a moment, then attached it to one of the thin chains around her hips. "Thank you, beloved." She pulled her in for a kiss.

Later, after they'd eaten and retreated to the bedroom, Mara lay on her back on her sleeping mat next to Kaikani's sleeping pool. The Veren was curled up at the edge of the pool, fingers entwined with Mara's. An oddity of the Veren having both lungs and gills was that most Veren preferred to sleep breathing air, with the warm water of their pools acting as a blanket. It made sleeping together a bit awkward, but they made do.

"You're thinking too loud," Kaikani complained with a yawn.

"Am not," Mara protested, though she'd been staring at the ceiling, enchanted to mirror the night sky far above, for probably far too long. She didn't even know what was making her restless. Her mind refused to settle, jumping from the Movorae, to Old Ones, to Kaikani possibly becoming a Dedicated, to Daiyu's Dedicated, to being home for the first time in over a decade, to the Empire's dangerous building methods, to maybe getting a new fish for Ander the next time she went to Tarvishte. Idly her mind also pointed out that like the Veren, Movorae had both gills and lungs. Why did Movorae have lungs? They lived in the depths. Did they work the same as the Veren, with only the appropriate organ actually working depending on the environment while the other closed off?

It was a lot.

"Yes, you are." Kaikani's voice was fond. "What's wrong?"

Mara hummed, not sure how to answer, when a shooting star cut across the mirrored sky. "Oh!" she breathed, as Kaikani looked up and grinned.

"Star light," she began, singsong.

Mara smiled back. "Star bright."

"First star I see tonight."

"I wish I may."

"I wish I might."

"Have this wish I wish tonight."

They dissolved into laughter, the familiar lines of the old Veren lullaby rhyme soothing some of the restlessness, reminding her that she was home again.

"Then wish and go to sleep," Kaikani giggled. "You're the one who set up a busy day for herself tomorrow."

She closed her eyes and wished that they could stay like this forever.

Mara's eyes snapped open and she shot up, staring off into the distance. What on Gaia had–

:Death.:

"Oh no," she whispered. *:Where?:*

:Too far to make a difference, but closer than you'd like. If you go, wear your armor.:

"Mara?" Kaikani asked blearily, rubbing at her eyes. "What is it? Are you okay?"

"I need to go," she said, untangling herself from her blankets. Her soul armor was just a thought away, blue threads of magic wrapping themselves around her.

Kaikani stared for a second, then launched herself out of her pool, dashing for her own armor. "What happened?"

"I'm not sure yet," Mara whispered, still staring off into the distance. That direction, whatever it was.

But part of her knew it had to do with the Movorae.

"Go alert the king that something has happened. I'll come back with more information by dawn."

"You can't go by yourself!" Kaikani snapped, making the connection that it had to do with the Movorae. "Those things are dangerous, even for you!"

"I'm not going to fight them, I'm just going to investigate. They won't know I'm there." She was already building the array in her mind. "And remember – if it comes to it, I've killed them before. I'll be back!"

"Mara–!"

But Mara was already gone, running through their grotto and diving into the ocean outside, swimming through the city as fast as she could. She utilized the currents and small speed spells to give herself boosts, heading in the direction her Goddess's power was strongest.

Hades kindly did not reiterate that Mara was too late.

Still she swam, until she was on the outskirts of Ahulowaki. It was quiet, still several hours before dawn, and the waters were deserted. Mara paused for a moment, then drew her array in magic around her, activating it and letting the illusion conceal her.

She continued forward.

Another thirty minutes, and she found the remains.

A scattering of brightly colored scales in a rainbow of colors flickered in the cloud of maroon blood in the water. Mara guessed maybe five Veren had been viciously torn apart, and a scattering of weapons fallen onto the coral shelf below seemed to support that. Pieces of coral armor that did not seem fully formed were also strewn about the area, making Mara fight back tears.

These had been young Veren.

Why had they been so far out from the city?

She made sure to stay close to the coral and rock formations while her spell whispered to anything nearby that there was nothing here. The cloud of blood was dense, but it was barely large enough to conceal maybe one Movorae, never mind thirteen, and certainly not an Old One. Where were they?

A shadow passed over her.

Mara looked up, and there, far above her, almost to the surface of the water, silhouetted by the moon, was an Old One. Her long body hung peacefully in the water as she... just... looked up at the sky?

What on Gaia was it doing?

Mara had never seen a Movorae do nothing before. Where was the rest of the swarm?

She swam just a tiny bit closer, trying to get a better look. Whoever had estimated its size had underestimated – she looked closer to sixty-five feet in length. Probably a little over a thousand years old. Her scales glistened black in the moonlight; the seaweed that grew from her head continued on down her back and spread out around her, but her long skeletal arms and face were bare to the moonlight.

Mara retreated back down to the rocks, unwilling to disturb the Old One while she did nothing. She looked around again for the swarm, but there was nothing. The cloud of blood was dissipating into the waters, leaving a dismembered hand and a few fins slowly sinking. *:Can you tell where they are?:* she asked Hades.

The Goddess hummed thoughtfully. *:They are gone, content with the death they wrought. I can't tell any more than that.:*

It was more than Mara had hoped for, but then why was the Old One still here?

"Oh, shit."

She jumped at the whispered hiss, spinning around to see Kaikani hiding near a large outcropping of rock, apparently having seen the remains. She swam to the orange Veren, letting her illusion flicker. "Kaikani! What are you doing here?" It was hard to keep her voice quiet when all she wanted to do was yell at her girlfriend for being an idiot.

"Making sure you aren't doing anything stupid," she whispered back, shifting to hold her spear against the rock. "You can't go after a swarm by yourself!"

"I told you I wasn't going to!" Mara wanted to shake her. "My magic makes it safe for me; you are in danger here!"

Kaikani's eyes narrowed. "Two will always be better than one. Are you saying I'm not capable?"

"I'm not saying you aren't capable; I'm saying it would have been easier to remain unseen on my own."

Kaikani lifted her chin defiantly. "Do you want me to become your Dedicated or not?"

Mara felt instantly conflicted. "Yes, of course I do, but you *aren't* yet. You don't have access to my magic; you don't have any of Hades' protections."

"I am still a warrior of Ahulowaki," Kaikani said coolly, tentacles twitching.

"Of course you are, and I love you, which is why I wish you had stayed in the city! Wait." Mara paused. "Did you alert the king that something had happened?"

"Uh, yes, I did." Kaikani looked away with a wince.

Mara's heart sank. "And?"

"There's a band of warriors on their way to back you up. And no, I *did not* tell him to do that, and even told him you probably wouldn't like it. Didn't make a difference; four trainees were missing."

She wanted to scream. They'd asked for her help; was it really that difficult for them to let her deal with the problem? "I'm sorry, but they are gone." The words tasted like ash on her tongue, but they were true. "Any idea *why* they were missing?"

Kaikani ran a hand over her head, tentacles twitching in annoyance, but Mara could tell she was upset. "Some of the others heard them boasting about trying to take one down as a trophy."

"*One*? The reports said there were thirteen!" She felt sick. Four young Veren had died for absolutely no reason.

Kaikani just shrugged helplessly. "They made the decision." Her eyes traveled upward, then widened. "The Old One!"

"Yeah." Mara twisted to face the creature, but she was still just drifting near the surface.

Kaikani's expression shifted to one of confusion. "What is it doing? Is it dead? I've never seen one so still before."

"She's not dead, but I also can't explain the behavior." Mara shrugged. "The rest of the swarm was gone when I got here; I'm not sure where."

They watched the Movorae together.

"She's kind of beautiful like that, in an abstract way," Kaikani observed. "Still disturbing, but also beautiful."

Hades agreed.

The sound of a shell horn shattered the silence.

Kaikani swore as the Movorae came to life, tail churning the water around her. "Whoever is in charge of that squadron…" She swore again. "What idiot charges in against a Movorae and *announces* their presence first?"

Mara was already prepping spell arrays in her mind. "Someone who hasn't fought one," she muttered, looking around. "Over there!"

Ten warriors were just swimming over the coral shelf, spears and tridents ready.

The Movorae dove, far faster than anything that size had any right to be.

Mara summoned her trident and swam up, trying to get a better vantage point, but there was no time. The blue of her magic lit up the water, array forming a barrier between the Movorae and her targets.

The creature crashed into the array so hard she bounced off it, cracks threading their way through the shield. She shook her head, mouth opening far too wide to show far too many razor-sharp teeth, and she *screamed*.

The shocks traveled through the water, causing a paralysis to grab hold at the base of her spine, but Mara knew their tricks and was ready for it. She grabbed a spell crystal from the group hanging from her trident and crushed it, causing a bloom of warmth to combat the icy paralysis.

The Movorae was already moving again, and Mara kicked off to intercept it, casting another shield. But the creature was wary now and twisted quick as lightning to the side. She gave another shriek, beginning to swim in a large circle above their heads, spiraling closer and closer.

She was searching.

Mara bit her lip, descending a little farther to buy herself more time. The Veren still seemed to be suffering from the paralysis, which was extremely bad. This Movorae was much more savvy than the ones she had fought before, and faster. She needed to draw it away from the Veren, but how?

Movement from above as the Movorae stilled, then dove – straight for Mara.

Ghostly pale-blue eyes locked onto her, inches from her face.

How? Her illusion was still intact–

And then–

Everything stood still, hung on a moment. Feelings whispered against Mara's mind, not unlike how the wargs of Tarvishte communicated, but more alien.

The Movorae didn't see Mara, it saw Hades *in* Mara.

And the Movorae understood.

And she accepted.

A vision of a cave, far below but not far enough, hope/query/maybe–

A blur of orange and gold crashed into the Movorae, breaking whatever it was that had connected them for one brief moment.

"No!" Mara shouted, realizing with horror that Kaikani was now in the thing's hands, long bone claws restraining her as that mouth opened–

Mara surged forward, array blooming to life in her hand–

And *shoved* water down the Movorae's throat and into its lungs.

The creature made a confused sound of distress, choking and gasping as it clawed at its throat, leaving bloody gashes. Mara grabbed Kaikani and darted away as the tail began thrashing. Her pale eyes were wide, and then...

Nothing.

Mara realized she was shaking with adrenaline as she positioned herself between Kaikani and the corpse.

Orange-and-gold arms wrapped around her from behind. "If we could avoid doing that in the near future..." she whispered breathlessly.

Mara nodded jerkily. "Yeah, yeah, sounds good."

They floated for a moment. "What did you do?" Kaikani finally asked.

"I drowned her," Mara admitted.

Silence.

"Thank you," Kaikani finally said.

Below them, the other Veren were finally overcoming their paralysis. Kaikani sighed. "I should go... talk to them. I'll be back." Her arms tightened around Mara for another moment before she swam down to join the group.

Mara was still trying to reconcile what had happened in the moments before. *:No other Movorae has ever... recognized me like that.:* Mara shuddered.

:She was so old that hunger had less of a hold on her than on the others you've faced. They live in and among death; is it any surprise she would recognize me for what I am? She was as much a creature of this world as an Avari, or a Veren. It wasn't faith in me that she had, not really, but an instinctual knowing. She saw you as something of a harbinger of her own death.:

And something about that was just sad. Mara mentally cursed the warriors that had disturbed her; there could have been another way.

:She wanted to remember,: Hades added.

:Remember? Remember what?: Mara asked, confused.

There was a brief pause. *:There was a time when the Movorae lived in the shallows and Mid-waters, and hunted on land. She was not old enough to be one of those, but... she wanted to remember.:*

Did that mean the Movorae were *older* than the Veren? Or simply that they used to cohabitate better? Or worse? All these questions were making her head spin. Mara thought back to the brief contact she'd had with the creature, trying to untangle it. "They pass down memory to each other," she realized.

"What?" Kaikani had swum back up to her. The warriors were beginning to head back.

"When they're born, they have their mother's... memories..." She trailed off, recalling an image of a cave, and a query. "Come with me."

Mara led them to a well-hidden cave several miles away. The entrance was hidden by kelp, but she fought to keep the picture the Movorae had shown her in her mind until she saw something that matched.

"I think you all were right – the swarm surfaced because it was disturbed by the Empire's detonations," she explained to Kaikani. "But as for why they didn't attack anyone until they were attacked, what they were doing..." She squeezed herself into the opening. It was a tight fit, and she moved to the side once she was through so Kaikani could follow.

She heard Kaikani gasp as she surveyed the large cavern. Bioluminescent fungus growing on the walls gave everything an eerie green glow, dark shadows cast by the rocks and plants swaying in the water. Nestled among the kelp and coral were thousands of round bulbs, milky white in color, about five inches in diameter.

"She was laying eggs, and the swarm was merely protecting her while she did so. Once she was done, the others fed and returned to the depths. The only reason they came to the Mid-waters was because of the Empire's digging. She would have stayed until they hatched," Mara explained softly.

"There's... gods, what are we going to do?" Kaikani was horrified. "We can't let this many Movorae hatch here. Do they usually spawn this many eggs? How is that sustainable?"

"They won't all live," Mara said grimly, listening to Hades' whispers in her mind as she swam closer to one of the eggs to examine it. "Without an adult to supply food, the hatchlings will turn on each other until there's only one, maybe two left. And even if the mother had lived, she would have let them cull their number down significantly, maybe to about ten. Only the strong and the vicious survive."

"Out of thousands of eggs, only one or two?" Now Kaikani was horrified for a different reason.

Mara nodded. "They are even born among death." Though it made sense that to a Veren, who cherished every small child, the thought of having so many that were expected to die would be appalling.

Once again she was struck by the fact that out of all the creatures in the oceans, only the Veren and the Movorae had both lungs and gills. Perhaps they had evolved from a shared ancestor, but took two very different paths to where they were today – the Movorae one of violence and hunger, and the Veren one of peace and community.

She shook her head. Kaikani wouldn't want to hear that theory. "But Hades says we don't need to be concerned; the survivors will return to the depths shortly after hatching. As long as there's nothing in their way, we won't see them again."

Kaikani hesitated. "You want to let them live?"

"I won't kill thousands of lives because of actions that might be taken in the future," Mara said sternly. "I will keep an eye on the nest, ensure nothing disturbs it, but the fry will live or die on their own terms."

Kaikani bit her lip. "But the Movorae–"

"Have just as much a right to exist in this world as anything else," she interrupted. "I am a priest of the Goddess of Death; I cannot take sides in this."

"But you take sides all the time," Kaikani protested, confused.

Mara shook her head. "I intervene when doing so will save lives." She gestured helplessly at the eggs. "Which is what I am doing now."

"And when they grow up?" the Veren challenged. "When they return to murder more Veren?"

"If they come to the Mid-waters, it is to hunt," Mara corrected gently. "That is the circle of life and death. I will try to drive them back to the depths first, but I will always fall on the side of saving more lives."

She saw the understanding dawn in Kaikani's eyes. "That's why you didn't want help. You were trying to save them."

Mara smiled sadly. "I've never succeeded." She looked back down at the eggs. "But I think I understand them better after today. The Old One gave me a valuable gift. I will try harder next time."

They floated in silence for several long minutes.

"This is what it means, to follow Hades," Kaikani said finally. "You make these decisions all the time." It was not a question.

She nodded anyway.

"And... you make those decisions alone."

Mara waved her hand back and forth. "Kinda, but kinda not. I always have Hades, after all, though she won't make a decision for me."

Kaikani drifted over to her and pressed their foreheads together. "And if I were your Dedicated... you would not be so alone?"

Mara blinked, then hope rose in her chest. She grinned. "That's true. A Dedicated supports their priest, after all."

Kaikani nodded decisively. "Then that is settled. I don't want you to be alone. You are supposed to have me, even if we are separated."

"It will be easier to communicate once you are Dedicated, too," Mara chirped. "Oh, you'll really do it? Really?"

Kaikani smiled, weaving their fingers together. "Yes."

Mara wrapped her arms around her tightly, squealing with joy.

Perhaps her wish had come true after all.

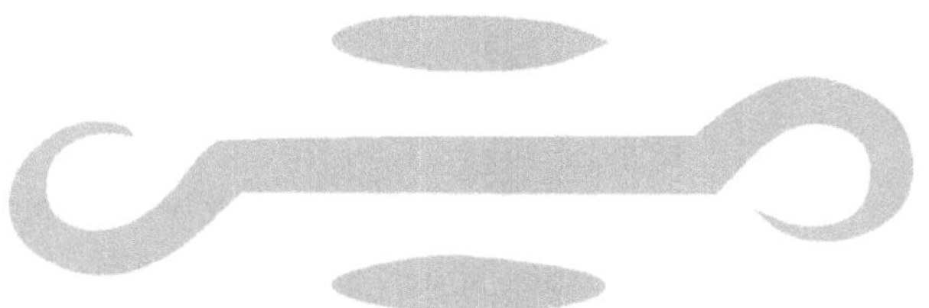

Lavender

Takeshi knew that after a certain point the promotions were far more trouble than they were worth. But what could he do? He couldn't turn them down. On what grounds would he even do so? Because he wanted to stay in the shadows? That was what all shinobi wanted. Because he didn't want the responsibility? No one would care. Because he wanted to remain an active field agent? There wasn't much "activity" these days anyway.

So he accepted one promotion after the other, and found himself wondering whether or not to be grateful as Captain of the Imperial Guard that there was nowhere else for him to go.

Then they asked him to marry the princess.

Takeshi stared at the scroll in his hands, snow-white paper with gold edges, bound with a piece of lavender ribbon, as he fought for something appropriate to say. He settled on, "Is this the best course of action?"

"Of course it is." The Empress sat behind her desk, hands folded gracefully in front of her. The sliding doors to her private garden were open, letting in a soft breeze and the delicate scent of flowers. "Our most beloved and gentle princess to marry our most powerful and popular shinobi. A gardener and a warrior. It is the kind of romance poets write about."

There was certainly no poetry in it for him, but there was no graceful way to say that. And popular? By what metric? Just because he was in the public eye the most?

Having been the most visible part of her mother's guard for the last two years, he was familiar with the princess. He liked her, but then, the whole country did. Her gentle, kind nature made her a favorite with civilians and nobles alike, but Takeshi knew that beneath that exterior there was a strong, opinionated individual. She was one of the strongest believers that there was a way for magic and tech to coexist, and one of its greatest sponsors. Though she suffered a genetic condition that resulted in terrible migraines, she refused to let that define or stop her, insisting on carrying out her role as heir. Takeshi admired her for that, and for her beliefs, but that led him to his most immediate concern.

"Has the princess been informed?" he asked carefully.

The Empress's sharp, dark eyes studied him. "Not yet, though she will be soon."

He almost pointed out that Hotaru would not be amicable to this, but swallowed the words. Her mother already knew that, and it was a moot point anyway – they would do as they were told. How they felt about the matter was inconsequential.

Dark-red lips turned down ever so slightly into a frown. "You don't seem as happy as I would have thought."

"My apologies; it is... merely a surprise." Which was perfectly true. "I'm still taking it in."

"Ah, yes. Of course you will need some time to adjust to your change in station." She smiled again, eyes softening. "At least as Captain of the Imperial Guard you have already been exposed to many of the important aspects of governing merely by being present, but we may have to work in some extra... lessons, of a sort."

He'd had to attend court hearings with the Empress and found them exhausting. He resigned himself to actually paying attention to the proceedings in the future. "Yes, Empress."

The thought of the amount of bureaucracy he was going to have to deal with was soul-crushing.

"Besides, at least you are not much older than her."

The seven-year age gap hadn't even had a chance to cross his mind yet, but as far as arranged marriages went it could be much worse. "Of course not, Empress."

"I was almost twenty years younger than my husband when I married. You will be a far better fit for Hotaru."

"I appreciate your faith in me, Empress," he said, inclining his head. The Empress's husband had passed away fifteen years ago, and from what he could tell she hadn't missed him for even a single day. Then again, Takeshi wasn't actually sure what the Emperor had brought to the marriage other than a gene pool. He barely even remembered the man.

An arranged marriage for the princess made sense. If he were being honest, it was more of a surprise that they had waited until she was twenty-six to set one up. Perhaps the Empress had hoped for a love match for her daughter? Or maybe Hotaru herself had fought it. The gentle princess had a spine of steel when it suited her, illness or no.

The Empress stood, the tiny chips of onyx on her figure-hugging black lace dress catching the light as she strode to the veranda, gesturing for him to follow. "We will introduce the concept to the ministers tomorrow, and I'd like to start planning an official announcement for next year. Please work with Hotaru to lay the groundwork for that in advance."

"Yes, Empress." So she wanted it to look plausibly like a love match. That meant switching himself to Hotaru's guard so he could spend more time with her and assigning the Empress to someone else. Satomi and Yugao, perhaps.

It would be all over the shinobi gossip circles within an hour as they tried to puzzle out the reason for the switch, especially considering how closely he was known for sticking to tradition. Some would guess correctly, some would guess incorrectly, the two sides would debate. Then they'd start digging. He repressed a sigh at the thought of the attempted interrogations he was going to have to endure by those who thought they were being subtle. Honestly, for a group of people whose job was information gathering, their attempts to do it within their own ranks showed far less finesse than what he knew they were capable of. At least they would keep their gossip among themselves.

Though... most would be downright mystified at the thought of him falling for the princess, considering she wasn't exactly his type. That couldn't be helped, unfortunately. At least he did not currently have a partner to break up with. Small mercies. His life was already about to get far more complicated; he did not need that sort of complexity added on top.

He considered the scroll in his hand as the Empress looked out over her garden. Maybe this had been the plan all along. Captain of the Imperial Guard was a mostly symbolic post. Perhaps it had been different when there were wars to fight and real intrigue to untangle, but his position now mostly involved watching over the Imperial family and doing paperwork for his subordinates. But him holding such a high rank did mean there would be no scandal regarding her marrying far below her station, and it would dissuade any courtiers who had had their own ambitions from objecting. Additionally, the princess's magic was known to be weak, so it made sense they would look for a match that was a strong mage. And there was no one more loyal to the throne than a shinobi, so in that sense he was a safe choice.

And being shinobi, he could be ordered to do it, which also simplified matters considerably. It wasn't as though he could back out.

Though, speaking of rank... "Should we discuss possible replacements for my current position, or do you think I should continue to hold it after the marriage?"

She was silent for a long time, gaze distant. He was beginning to think she wouldn't answer him when she finally said, "Yes. Let us consider the viable options."

Dinner had barely started, and Takeshi was already extremely uncomfortable. He wished he could just fade back into the shadows and ignore everything going on around him, but as one of the people this dinner was supposed to be celebrating he had to actually join the dinner – something he was usually spared – and remain visible. His flashy formal uniform worked to make sure of that as well, the red, gold, and black terrible for stealth. He reached out for a moment with his magic and was answered with four acknowledgements from the rafters. He strangled down his jealousy and desire to join them in the dark.

At the head of the table sat the Empress, in a dark-green kimono with black and pink geometric designs. It appeared to be a concession to the formality of the occasion, though its tight fit and the way it opened on the side spoke to the Rose Empire's influence on her fashion choices even when she was supposed to be wearing formal clothing. For all that the Empress despised the Rose Empire's control over Ni Fon, she did enjoy their fashion and foods, and even their music, leading to some... interesting cultural blends.

Akimitsu, the sixteen-year-old prince, sat to the right of his mother, and Hotaru sat to her left. Akimitsu could be shrewd when he wanted to be, but Takeshi had found that the boy preferred to avoid his duties whenever possible unless something caught his interest. Normally that was games and female courtiers, but he was also an avid trainer of hunting dogs and he sometimes latched onto different aspects of law.

Hotaru was dressed in a proper kimono, lavender in color with a black, gold, and light-blue floral motif. She appeared to be having a good day as far as the migraines went, as she had not required the aid of a maid to come to dinner. A fresh peach blossom had been added to her hair, and Takeshi wondered if it came from her garden. She took her duty as the heir very seriously, but her love for flower-arranging and her garden was well-known.

Takeshi was sitting next to the princess, and the remaining seats were occupied by the five most influential ministers. Takeshi had been present when they were informed of the new development earlier that day. No one had objected, of course, but there had been surprise that it was a shinobi chosen and not a noble. The Empress had merely indicated it was part of a grand plan, and that had been that. It was to be kept quiet until the appropriate time – not even the shinobi were to know the truth.

Takeshi rather had doubts that the shinobi could be kept in the dark for an entire year, but he kept them to himself.

Now they were celebrating in a sort of informal-but-formal way. All of the traditional ceremonies would be held after the engagement was officially announced and would have far more pomp and circumstance than this small gathering. It was silly in Takeshi's opinion to have these semi-formal events before the formal announcement, but since the Empress wanted it to look like a love match perhaps this was her way of allowing them to technically begin courting before the official formal meetings and ceremonies could occur. Or maybe it was something else entirely, perhaps having to do with the political reasons for delaying the announcement. Takeshi didn't know, and he wasn't sure it mattered as long as it ended with him marrying the princess.

Soft conversation floated around the table as the first course was served, and he glanced at Hotaru out of the corner of his eye. She was staring down at her plate with its small appetizer of salmon, cream cheese, and toast. She did not share her mother's taste for foreign cuisine.

Takeshi wondered if the whole meal would carry influence from the Rose Empire instead of traditional Nifoni foods, and felt a sense of mild disappointment himself. A seasonal menu would have been more appropriate for the occasion. Still, he pulled down his mask and ate the small appetizer.

"Captain Shuurai."

He blinked at the sound of Hotaru's soft voice and shifted to look at her, inclining his head. "Princess."

She smiled, gray eyes kind. She had not touched her food yet. "Your presence at dinner is welcome, but unexpected."

Takeshi's stomach sank at the question hanging in the air, unspoken. Had no one told Hotaru? When the Empress had told him Hotaru would be informed, he had not thought it would be during the celebratory dinner.

He cleared his throat, considering what to say. They weren't supposed to discuss it openly, even with those who knew... and he was not certain now that either of the Empress's children had been informed. Surely the Empress would have told Hotaru before Akimitsu? And though the shinobi in the rafters would have a hard time hearing the conversation over the sounds of the shamisen being played on the stage off to the side, he knew at least two of those present could read lips. He rested his elbows on the table and folded his hands in front of his mouth. "I'll be taking over your guard personally, princess, starting within the week."

Her eyebrows rose slightly, and he could see her sharp mind making the connections to why that would mean he was at dinner – and why he was sitting next to her instead of Akimitsu. "On whose authority?"

"Does the Captain of the Imperial Guard need someone to tell them how to arrange guard shifts?" the Empress asked, dabbing at her mouth with a napkin.

Takeshi tried again. "I believe this dinner is supposed to be something of a family affair."

Hotaru's eyebrows furrowed before her head snapped in her mother's direction, expression darkening.

"We will discuss the particulars at a later date," the Empress said airily. "For now, we will celebrate." A hint of steel entered her tone.

Hotaru's lips thinned, and Takeshi's stomach sank even further. He glanced at Akimitsu, but the boy was in a conversation with one of the ministers and wasn't paying attention to his sister and mother. Disagreements between the two women were unfortunately common.

"I see," the princess said, tone clipped. "Will I be consulted in any future particulars?"

"When it is appropriate," the Empress responded coolly.

Takeshi made a silent vow to ensure the princess knew what he knew going forward. At least taking over the main shift of her guard rotation would make that a fairly easy task. It was her wedding; even if most of it was determined by tradition there was no reason for her to be blindsided by any of it.

He glanced around, but the rest of the guests were all involved in their own little conversations. There was no way to know what, if anything, his subordinates had gotten from that conversation. Hopefully they had deemed the argument nothing of note.

The first course was cleared away, and Takeshi felt another surge of disappointment at the thick onion soup placed in front of him. He took a sip. While the food wasn't what he would have chosen, at least it was of excellent quality.

Hotaru did not so much as touch her spoon.

"I heard there was some progress made with the Hashi Integration Technique this past week?" he tried after a moment.

She did not look at him, continuing to stare at her plate as though it were beneath her to try it. "Some."

He took another spoonful of soup, gathering his thoughts. Hotaru could usually go on for hours about the attempts made to get magic and tech to work together. A one-word answer meant she was not interested in speaking to him, which... he could understand at the moment. This would be a far more awkward dinner than he had hoped, but if she wished for silence, he could at least grant that from himself.

"Which part of the equation failed?" the Empress asked, waving a hand at the musician, who switched to a different song.

Unfortunately, Takeshi could do nothing about the Empress asking Hotaru questions. He took another sip of soup.

"The same part that always does – both." A thread of annoyance entered her voice. "Which you might know if you had read any of the reports. Trying to get magic and tech to bridge and balance is more than simply mashing them together. It will take a certain... elegance, to ensure they don't clash."

Oh, that was a criticism of the dinner, and possibly her mother's dress. Takeshi kept his face perfectly blank, not looking directly at either of them. He regretted bringing the topic up.

"If your understanding of the matter was so comprehensive, surely you would have succeeded by now."

"Better to take one's time and ensure things are done correctly than to settle for something subpar."

"And yet, having any results at all indicates that one is not chasing clouds and wasting one's time."

Takeshi wasn't sure why the Empress seemed to oppose Hotaru's involvement in trying to get magic and tech to cooperate. The Empress clearly had a taste for things from the Rose, and was herself a vocal proponent of the need to integrate the two systems. It was just Hotaru's part in it she did not seem to approve of. Perhaps because of Hotaru's illness, she thought the princess should not exert herself so? Takeshi was not sure. It did not make sense.

Akimitsu was glancing at his mother and sister now. Takeshi caught his eye, ever so slightly inclining his head in their direction. The prince's mouth pressed into a thin line, a look of exasperation briefly crossing his features before he could control it.

"Perhaps–"

"Mother, have you come to any decision about the Sasaki issue?" Akimitsu interrupted his sister before the situation could escalate further. "Minister Kimura and I were discussing it, and it seems to me..."

Takeshi thankfully tuned out Akimitsu's distraction, chancing a brief glance at Hotaru. She was sitting with her hands folded tightly in her lap, and though her face was calm, her eyes sparked with anger.

He repressed a sigh; this was not an auspicious beginning to their marriage. He considered his options for how to smooth things over between them. They were going to spend the rest of their lives together, and he would prefer not to start off on the wrong foot. A gift of some sort, to show his commitment to her? The floral pattern on the princess's kimono caught his eye. The princess liked to garden and design floral arrangements; he was sure he could work with that.

He let himself contemplate different possibilities as the soup was cleared away and replaced by servings of sole that had been cooked in butter. Tiredly, he resigned himself to not having any Nifoni-styled dishes. Perhaps he could grab something from the kitchens later.

He couldn't help but notice Hotaru did not eat for the rest of the night.

Takeshi was tired. He hadn't slept well the past few days, the disastrous dinner weighing on his thoughts, more so the closer he got to switching himself to Hotaru's guard. His morning meditations had brought him no clarity on the matter, the normally comforting activity failing to bring any sort of peace.

But switching himself to Hotaru's guard had to be done.

He'd brought his peace offering with him as he approached the princess's rooms. All he could hope for was that they might find some sort of understanding. He did not want her to view him as the enemy in this.

He paused just before entering the room, Miyu and Ume sliding past him. A quick hand sign indicated that their shift had passed without issue, and he nodded permission for them to return to the barracks, ignoring Ume's blatant attempt to linger and Miyu's questioning eyes.

One battle at a time.

He closed his eyes for just a moment before letting himself in, uncertain how he would be received.

She was sitting on a low couch, holding a steaming cup of tea. Her long black hair and clothes had been redone in a more casual style for an evening to be spent in her own rooms, but she had bags under her eyes that her makeup could not hide and there was an opened blister pack of pills on the table in front of her. A blanket was tucked around her lap.

She looked up as he entered. "My apologies, Captain Shuurai."

He blinked, taking a few steps farther into the room. He hadn't actually expected to be acknowledged immediately. "Good evening, princess. For what?"

She met his eyes evenly. "For my behavior at dinner the other night. It was inappropriate of me to treat you so."

"I too should apologize," he admitted, coming to stand on the other side of the table. Carefully, he placed the small potted flower on the table. "I had assumed you were aware of the situation."

She eyed the plant curiously. "I should have been. That's not your fault. I must assume this whole thing is my mother's idea." A hint of venom entered her voice.

"To my knowledge, that is so," he agreed.

Hotaru looked away, biting her lip. "Did she ask you, or were you ordered?"

Takeshi hesitated. They were the same thing to him, but Hotaru clearly saw some important distinction. "I was... offered a scroll."

The princess barked out a sharp, bitter laugh. "Oh, I'm a mission. I see."

He could see how, put in those terms, it might be hurtful. Still, he wasn't sure how to fix that, since it was technically true. Instead, he knelt on the floor across the table from her and gestured towards the flower. "I had hoped we might start over."

She shook her head once but placed her tea cup on the table so she could pick up the small pot. "An orchid?"

"They are notoriously difficult to cultivate. I thought you might enjoy the challenge."

She hummed thoughtfully, one finger gently brushing across the lavender petals. "This particular species is known to be exceptionally temperamental. That was kind of you. And thoughtful. Thank you." A pause. "The color?"

He hesitated. "To match that of your magic, princess."

She glanced at him, expression unreadable. "I will admit I am surprised a shinobi of your caliber might deign to acknowledge my magic."

"You have magic," he hastened to reassure her, a little annoyed by those who thought that some mages weren't powerful enough to be acknowledged as such. He glanced in the direction of her courtyard. "Though you might not be among the most powerful, it takes a great amount of control to weave magic the way you do. And magic is magic – it is a shame not to use it if one has it."

"The true crime of the Rose Empire," she mused. "But that is neither here nor there. I can't help but notice you've taken over the evening shift."

He was glad the mask over the lower half of his face helped hide his expression as he cringed. "My apologies again if it feels too forward, but I was hoping we could discuss how to present ourselves in the coming months, and thought we would have more time to do so in the evening. I do plan on taking the day shift the majority of the time."

"Ah, that makes sense." She closed her eyes for a moment and sighed. "In plain language, Captain – what is your full understanding of the situation?"

It was a fair question, especially after that dinner. "Four days ago, the Empress... strongly suggested that I agree to marry you. News of the engagement is to be withheld for a year; I'm uncertain as to the full reasons why, but I suspect it is at least in part because she wishes it to appear as though we are a love match."

"So you switched yourself to my guard, a move that many will read as interest in me." Her mouth twisted, and the sharp look in her eyes reminded him of her mother. "Which also conveniently gives us the opportunity to coordinate."

He inclined his head. "Yes, princess. The only people who know about the engagement now are those who were present at dinner that night, though I will admit I am unsure if your brother knows."

She snorted. "My brother almost certainly does not know, and that's probably for the best. He's terrible at keeping secrets."

That was true, but at least he tried to keep the peace in the family. "In the meantime, we are also considering who should succeed me as Captain of the Imperial Guard, and I will endeavor to learn what I can about governing, though I also suspect my role is meant more to support your decisions than to promote any of my own." Actually, his role was probably – much like the previous Emperor – to supply a gene pool, but he didn't think she'd like hearing that, no matter how realistic it was.

He held no illusions any real power would ever be his.

Hotaru frowned. "Captain, you are one of the most highly regarded shinobi in our country. Your insights into matters of importance will surely be of value, and I will be interested in hearing them. Please do not silence yourself simply because you feel you should."

He hesitated. "If you would like, princess."

"I would, thank you," she said, giving him an exasperated look. "But moving on – why do you think my mother chose now?"

"I must admit I have no theories as to the timing," he said with a shrug. "I will say traditionally the heir is married in their early twenties, if not late teens, so it does seem odd. Have you any thoughts?"

"Part of me wonders…" She trailed off as her gaze became distant.

He waited, but she did not complete her thought.

They sat in silence for a few minutes.

"I apologize for the abrupt change in subject," she said, looking back down at the orchid in her hands, "but there is at least one other matter of which you should be made aware sooner rather than later." Her voice took on a note of disinterest.

He hummed. "Yes?"

"I'm afraid I'm not interested in men," she admitted after a moment, continuing to study the plant intently.

Ah. "I'm afraid I can't say the same," he replied evenly.

Gray eyes swung to him sharply, and then, finally, she started to smile. "My, what a pair we make. That will cause problems for later."

They could always drug themselves, and alcohol existed, but Takeshi didn't think now was the time for that suggestion. "Not insurmountable ones. An heir will be expected within the first few years." Not that the thought was pleasant, but duty was duty.

He'd never imagined himself a father before. He'd never even considered getting *married* before. The thought was… odd, distant. Difficult for him to conceptualize. He'd always considered his part in training young shinobi the closest he would ever get to fatherhood, and he had not been disappointed by that. It made the thought of a child of his own even stranger – no Imperial heir would be trained as shinobi. The best he could hope for on that front was the opportunity to supplement any magical training the child might receive.

Perhaps that was something he might also offer to Hotaru, if she were amicable? And perhaps she could show him some of the patterns she used. One was never done learning magic.

He wondered if her mother knew about her preferences, then dismissed the thought – she probably did, but sexual preference was considered irrelevant for this sort of union. He thought back, but couldn't think of a single instance where Hotaru had shown interest in another person, male or female. Had she hidden it on purpose, or was she just not that interested? Either way, it made sense for her to balk at the idea of being married to a man, though he couldn't imagine she had believed she could avoid it completely. She was the heir. It was expected.

It was less expected for him, but still. He shoved the thought of a child away for now; he would have to meditate on that later. Now he should focus on Hotaru and working out their situation in the present. The future could wait.

Her mouth twisted for a second before her expression smoothed back out. "Ah, yes. An heir. I'm sure being pregnant won't affect my already fragile health in any negative capacity." The words were bitter.

"You are the princess. The best possible care Ni Fon has to offer will be yours," he pointed out gently. "And you will not be alone," he added after a moment, placing a closed fist on his chest.

She blinked at him, then smiled a little sadly. "No, I suppose not. Though I think it would probably be best to name Akimitsu my heir, we wouldn't be bothering with this farce if that were an acceptable solution. I am sorry, Captain. Truly I am."

He blinked. "What for?"

"You've been dragged into this mess, trapped in a marriage with me. Neither of us will be able to seek partners of our choosing, and what freedom you did have before will be gone. I should have expected this, but it's entirely unfair to you."

Losing freedoms had been happening in small increments for a while now with each promotion, and as shinobi he hadn't exactly started with a large number anyway. "I am shinobi, princess. I live to serve."

She cringed and opened her mouth, but then paused, seemingly thinking better of it. She shook her head and tried again. "If we are to be married, then please – when we are alone, just call me Hotaru."

"If you would like, princess. Hotaru." He corrected himself quickly; that would take some time to make the mental adjustment needed. "You may call me Takeshi," he added.

She smiled at him wryly, then placed the orchid delicately back on the table. "Would you mind helping me up?"

He rolled to his feet gracefully, coming around the table as she folded the blanket and laid it on the couch beside her. He offered her his hand and pulled her to her feet, a little disturbed by how light she was.

She adjusted the pale-gray robe she was wearing over her kimono and picked the orchid back up. "Let's get him settled in the greenhouse," she said, a fond note entering her voice.

That did not require a response, and Takeshi followed her to the sliding doors. Half of her courtyard was enclosed in glass, a concession to her frail health that she used as a greenhouse. The sun had just barely set, and the purple dusk was lit on the other side of the glass by fireflies.

Hotaru made a soft sound of pleasure, pausing to watch the small, blinking lights for a moment before turning to a shelf with several other potted flowers. "He will get the sun he needs here," she said fondly, placing it on the shelf. Then she touched the wood, and a beautiful lavender pattern bloomed to life under the pot. When the glow of her magic faded, the pattern remained etched into the shelf.

Takeshi itched to study the pattern. The princess's patterns were often noted to be inefficient by some of the other shinobi, but he saw the beauty in her forms. He wondered what specifically this one would do. How would it help the flower acclimate to the greenhouse? Which glyphs were used? What type of bridge had she utilized?

"Do you know when he was last watered?" she asked, frowning at the plant.

"I do not." He hadn't even thought to ask. "I can check in the morning."

She shook her head. "That's not necessary; he just feels a little dry. I would have thought... where *did* you find this kind of orchid?" She swung to face him. "They are extremely uncommon."

"I asked Tano Ayaka," he admitted. The daughter of the minister of agriculture, Ayaka was an avid gardener with connections. "She supplied it from her private collection."

Hotaru stared at him.

He shrugged. "It *is* supposed to look like a love match."

She sighed, shaking her head. "You're not wrong. I'm sorry; I'm being difficult."

And they were back to apologies. They would move past that at some point; he had to believe that. "You've had a difficult situation thrust upon you," he hastened to reassure her. "I do not believe you are being unreasonable, given the amount of time you've been aware of your mother's order."

She turned back to the fireflies, staring at them silently for a long minute. "Would you think me selfish, if I told you I would rather not do my duty in this? That I would do anything to get out of it?"

Takeshi considered that. She was a princess, not a shinobi. He could not hold her to their standard of obedience. "There are many times when we do not want to do the things we have to. That's not a failing; that's just being Human. The important thing is that we do our duty despite that." He paused, then decided to be honest. "And I had hoped that we might come to be friends, in time. While parts of it will be... duty, not all of it has to be. We do not need to be miserable." He hoped.

She turned to look at him, the fireflies flickering behind her, giving her an ethereal quality. "Are you not my mother's creature?"

Oh. He… should have seen that coming. He swallowed his instinctual answer, closed his eyes, and took a real moment to give the question the appropriate thought. And in the end… there was only one correct answer, wasn't there? "As shinobi, I am loyal to Ni Fon first," he started slowly, tasting the words as they came out. "Not to any one individual. And though your mother may rule, you are the heir. If I am to marry you, then I would choose to be your ally, to support you in any way I can." And hadn't he already promised himself he would help her?

Her gaze was unreadable. "And if she asks you to spy on me?"

Takeshi tilted his head in confusion. "I am uncertain why that would ever be necessary."

"You must have noticed we don't agree on most topics."

That was true, but spying? And while the Empress outranked him in every way, and would until her death, something in him strongly objected to the thought of spying on the person he was marrying.

That was too much. He may never have wanted to be married, but he'd be damned if he didn't do it correctly.

But how to convince Hotaru of that?

He knelt on the ground before her, pulling his sheathed katana from his side and offering it above his head. "Princess Hotaru, I am devoted to you. This I swear on the blade given to me as the symbol of my loyalty to the throne. If ever you should doubt, give me the order, and–"

"*No!*" She dropped to the ground in front of him, pushing the katana back towards him. He was surprised by the tears in her eyes. "Never swear that oath again, Takeshi. *Please.* It is terrible enough you have had to swear it once before."

He blinked at her, uncertain how to respond.

She covered her face with her hands for a moment before wiping her tears away. "All right. All right, I believe you." She took a deep breath, then turned determined gray eyes on him. "Together, then?" Despite the steel that had entered her tone, her lip trembled.

Takeshi nodded. If she would not let him swear it aloud, he would swear it to himself.

"Together."

Silver

The gaggle of Avari children "oohed" and "aahed" as Ebryn flashed the watch for them to see.

"And that is how you take something off someone's wrist without them noticing," he declared, pocketing the watch. "Some of you are getting too old to continue relying on being cute. Keep working on those skills."

One of the older girls with lime-colored hair giggled. "What if we rely on someone else with skills?" Her ears twitched playfully.

Ebryn's lips pursed. "You know that's a bad idea, Brina. What's the first rule?"

"Always look out for yourself first!" a number of voices chorused. The group was huddled under a decrepit awning in an attempt to avoid the cold October drizzle that had been on and off all day.

"Right." He nodded, flicking the tail of his short red ponytail over his shoulder. "You never know when you won't be able to rely on someone. People leave all the time. You'll only ever be able to rely on yourself."

"Oh, please don't tell me you're teaching the kids that."

Ebryn's ears sank in annoyance as Aether put his arm on Ebryn's shoulder, leaning with all his weight and almost unbalancing them both. "Someone has to."

The kids weren't even trying to hide their laughter; Aether was one of their favorite people. "Ebby is really good at stealin' things!" a little boy with a missing front tooth said.

"Which is why I rely on him to do that for me!" The golden-eyed Avari flashed a bright grin, pulling Ebryn tight to his side. "Don't let him tell you otherwise."

Ebryn rolled his eyes, but Aether wasn't really wrong. He did rely on Ebryn for theft. "That doesn't make it smart," he said in token protest, trying to salvage something of the lesson. "It's better to have the skill and not use it than not have the skill and need to use it." He strongly emphasized the last few words, glaring at Aether.

Aether grinned unabashedly, flipping his long braid around his neck like a periwinkle scarf and taking a moment to stretch. "Knowing who to rely on to do what is way more important, in my opinion. And besides, the number one rule *should* be 'stay away from Truth Seekers at all costs.'"

The red-haired Avari sighed as the kids laughed again. He'd lost them for today. "All right then, shoo. Go do whatever. But don't forget to report to school tomorrow morning – you want that free food!"

The brats all scrambled to leave, shouting their goodbyes to both Ebryn and Aether as they scattered into the crumbling architecture of the Blackfields district. They'd be at it again tomorrow, or whenever Ebryn could corral them all for another lesson in "surviving Lyndiniam."

"I remember getting free meals," Aether mused. "Would be nice to sit and do nothing for a few hours and get paid in food. I don't think I appreciated it enough when I was that age." He held out his hand.

Ebryn shrugged, tossing him the watch. "It's not supposed to be sitting and doing *nothing*," he pointed out. "And we haven't been able to get food that way for, like, four years." He shifted to take advantage of what little cover the awning afforded as the drizzle turned to more of a light rain. "We should head back soon."

"Learning is doing nothing. And yeah, fifteen is a little young to cut us off, if you consider the rich Humans continue going to school until they're like... twenty-three or something." Aether laughed, inspecting the prize. "Huh. This might actually be real silver."

Ebryn would never understand how someone as smart as Aether could despise learning so much. Then again, Aether always just seemed to know things, no learning necessary. "Looked expensive. And no, learning is not 'doing nothing.' Well, some of it is, but the reading and writing bit is useful." He shivered as a sharp gust of wind blew past.

"It sure is expensive, good eye. I'll sell it tomorrow." Long ears twitched happily. "Somehow, I'm pretty sure those schools are a trap." He gestured for Ebryn to follow as he began to stroll towards their home.

"A trap?" Ebryn blinked, then hurried to catch up. "What?"

"Not sure, but they wouldn't give us free food for actually nothing. And I'm not sure I believe their 'we want everyone to read and write' crap." Aether shook his head. "Nah. Somehow, they are getting something else out of it, I just don't know what."

Ebryn thought about it, then shrugged as he tugged his vest closed a little tighter around him. "It does seem odd, but I've got no clue what other motive they could have. And free food is too important to ignore."

Aether's lips thinned. "That's what bothers me."

As they passed through Deckett Square, commonly nicknamed "Decrepit Square" due to the four statues in various states of decay, one at each corner, an unfortunately familiar voice called out. "Hey, Ebryn! Hero of the Crystal Lights, savior of the Avari, slayer of demons, god-chosen warrior, wielder of the Crystal Light Blade!"

"Oh for fu–"

"Now now, no need to get so upset about it," Aether interrupted, though he shot a calculating look at the navy-haired Avari who'd called out.

"He adds more titles *every time*," Ebryn grit out as Milo strolled over to them, a stupid grin on his face.

"And his loyal sidekick!" Milo's ears twitched as he crossed his arms over his chest. "You gunning to be Sukra, Aether?"

"Maybe. She was pretty kick-ass, and she got to go down in the history books with Ebryn," Aether said with a grin of his own as Ebryn sputtered. "Unlike some. Make better choices, Milo."

Milo's brow furrowed. "What?"

"I don't know. What were we talking about?" Aether tilted his head to the side. "Did you need something?"

The other Avari blinked. "I–"

"Excellent, we're in a hurry, so we'll have to catch up later. See ya later, Milo." Aether took off at a jog, Ebryn following close behind.

The red-haired Avari threw a subtle glance over his shoulder as they rounded the corner just in time to see Milo's scowling face disappear behind them. He let a smile form as he replayed the conversation in his mind. "That one was new."

"What was new?" Aether asked as they darted up a pile of crates to a roof.

"Aiming at you, with the Sukra comment." Aether didn't even look anything like an Aradian. Honestly, his hair was *blue*.

"Eh, it's whatever." They scaled up to a higher roof. "See, he has *no* chance of being famous or being remembered, and you do, so..."

Ebryn grimaced. "Kinda doubt that, considering" – he gestured around them at the crumbling architecture they were scaling – "everything. The only demons left in the world are Human ones. And maybe some Avari."

Aether laughed awkwardly as they came to a halt on a small ledge. "That's a little harsh."

"I don't care. My point is that there's not a whole lot for me to become famous doing, certainly not in the way Stormlight did. Don't," he warned, seeing Aether's face light up as he opened his mouth. "You know there's nothing I can do against the Empire. I'm not going to magically make everything better for Avari somehow. Not even *he* could do that. He was a swordsman."

Aether shrugged with a lopsided grin. "You could always go stab the Emperor."

Ebryn rolled his eyes skyward, praying for patience. "I really, *really* doubt that would do anything." He frowned. The clouds were getting darker; it was going to pour later. "Bad enough that I look like him; did they really have to name me after him too?"

Aether glanced away. He always tried to avoid the topic of Ebryn's parents. In fact, most Avari in Blackfields avoided mentioning anyone's parents. It wasn't that everyone was an orphan, but enough were that it was better safe than sorry.

That was fine. Ebryn was on a roll; he could continue without thinking too much about that particular pair of people who had first done everything possible to ensure his life would be difficult and then left him. "The Blade hasn't even been around for, like, centuries; what would I fight with? A normal sword? Where would I even get one in this century?"

"The Truth Seekers have 'em," Aether pointed out mildly. "I think Ni Fon makes some too. And probably other places, now that I think about it."

"Yeah, sure, let's start this amazing adventure by stealing from Truth Seekers. Always a great idea." He felt a shiver go down his spine at the mention of the Empire's elite troops. Always blindfolded, they were creepy, and Ebryn had always done his best to stay far, far away from them. "That sounds like a great way to die early." His ears twitched down.

"You could always use something else? A knife?" A grin suddenly twisted his friend's features. "Maybe a fork? You can kill him over dinner."

"A fork? A *fork*?" Sometimes the way Aether thought stunned him. "Oh, yes, I can just see it now: 'Ebryn of Blackfields, wielder of the Divine Cutlery.' Truly a worthy successor to Ebryn Stormlight, wielder of the Crystal Light Blade. How the hell would I even be in a situation where I was having dinner with him?"

Aether just shrugged. "Anything can be used as a weapon if you want it to be one badly enough. And I don't think the weapon is really the important thing. You're pretty special without a sword; I don't really think you need one." He glanced back the way they'd come. "Why don't we go fence that watch now, actually?"

Ebryn blinked, derailed from his train of thought. "What? Why?" He shivered again as another cold wind threaded through the buildings.

Aether started to say something, but then shook his head. "Just 'cause I feel like it. Besides, I think it's going to be cold tonight, and with this we can invest in a few warmer blankets."

"Colder than it has been?" Ebryn asked sarcastically, but followed as Aether started down a nearby ladder. "It's already been far colder than normal."

"Well, a watch doesn't help us, but blankets will."

"Fair." Ebryn was not against having more blankets. "We might want to see if we can find any more of that fluffy stuff to plug up those holes in the side wall, too. That'll help keep the cold out."

Aether nodded in agreement and jumped to the next roof over. "Yeah, definitely. And new coats?"

"Hell yeah." They squeezed through a tight gap between a pair of large pipes, picking their way around the debris on the other side. This roof was far worse for wear than the last time they had come this way. "And a few canned goods probably wouldn't hurt either?" he tried.

Aether hummed. "You know I don't like–"

Ebryn yanked him back, both boys falling onto the roof behind them as the section Aether had been walking on suddenly gave way, crumbling into the building below. They stared wide-eyed at the new hole.

"Holy shit," Aether said after a moment. "That was... close."

Ebryn willed his heart to stop pounding. "Way, *way* closer than I ever want to be again. Are you okay?"

"Yeah, I'm good. Let's just sit for a sec." His hand was on his chest, resting where Ebryn knew the key lay.

"Blackfields is getting worse and worse," Ebryn said grimly, peering down into the building. Luckily, whatever this was didn't seem to be in use at the moment. Possibly because of how decrepit it was. Broken glass and pieces of wooden furniture littered the floor along with the roofing.

"Well, there's no way to maintain any of it," Aether said, a worried look on his face. "The stop-gap measures we use aren't enough, not by a long shot, and all these buildings were built before lester became a common building material, so it's all just... dissolving over time."

"Eventually there won't be a Blackfields," Ebryn concluded grimly. "And then where will we be?"

"I don't know," Aether murmured, but golden eyes flicked in Ebryn's direction before returning to the hole. "Come on; let's go get rid of this watch before more of the environment tries to kill us."

Luckily, it was not difficult to trade the watch for money. Ferodin was an old friend of Aether's and was even able to give them the money on a prepaid card – they'd be able to buy things legitimately for a little while.

Well, Aether would be able to. Ebryn tried to avoid doing anything but stealing outside of Blackfields. Sure, not every Avari in Lyndiniam lived in the slums, but he always felt like he stuck out with his red hair and silver eyes. He looked too much like a person who didn't exist anymore. Aether tried to reassure him the Humans didn't really seem to notice or care about Avari colors, but Ebryn couldn't shake the feeling of everyone staring at him when he was out and about in the other districts. It was bad enough the other Avari liked to call it out whenever they felt like it; he was sure he would do something... regretful if a Human did it.

So he just avoided putting himself in that situation entirely. Casually brushing against Humans to steal their shit was fine. Purposefully getting into a conversation with them was not.

To that end, he waited outside the coffee shop with the blankets while Aether ducked in to grab them a treat, keeping his eyes on the silvery lester that made up the sidewalk. The temperature continued to drop as he waited, and he wondered if the rain would switch to snow overnight, blanketing the city in lonely isolation, or if it would remain freezing rain and make everyone miserable. Luckily, it didn't take long for the periwinkle-haired Avari to come back out with two cups and a brown paper bag.

Ebryn adjusted his hold on the bags and took his cup, ignoring the stares of a pair of Human girls at one of the little café tables as the heat bit into his palm. "This better be mostly sugar." He wished Humans would just mind their own business.

"Of course! Sugar is good for you," Aether reassured him as they turned for home. "And we could use it after that scare from earlier. Got some muffins in here for us, too. Chocolate, with chocolate chips." He shook the paper bag.

"Great." They *did* deserve something nice, all things considered. Ebryn found his thoughts circling back to the close call from earlier and shuddered. Blackfields had always been dangerous, there was no denying that, but every year it got worse and worse. More and more Avari were injured, killed, or just went missing. Eventually, something would have to give, wouldn't it? It wasn't sustainable. But what would give first – the government, the Avari, or the crumbling buildings they called home?

What would the end be? Without Blackfields, what would become of the Avari who lived there? Sure, the Humans probably wanted them to disappear, but that wasn't actually possible. So what would happen?

What else could be taken from them?

It made Ebryn's head hurt to think about.

"Hey."

He startled out of his thoughts, blinking at Aether. "Sorry, what?"

Aether shook his head. "I keep thinking about it too. But... I just wanted to say thank you, for earlier."

"Oh, yeah, of course. I wasn't going to let you just fall into a hole." He tried to brush it off. "Who would brave the cafés to get me coffee?"

A fond grin stole across Aether's face. "I'm sure you would figure it out. But really – that was pretty amazing. You were pulling me back before I had even realized there was a problem."

Ebryn frowned, thinking back. "You need to pay more attention to where you're walking, then. Never mind the roofs, there are some places in the streets I'm wary of these days." He considered the well-kept glass-and-lester buildings they were passing, windows reflecting the setting sun.

"I was paying attention," Aether protested, ears twitching. "And I didn't notice. I have no idea how you did. And your reflexes... it was crazy, how fast you were! So, see? You are pretty great." His smile gained a mischievous edge. "Some might even say–"

"No, do *not* say it," Ebryn groaned, stomach and ears sinking.

"–heroic!" Aether finished cheerfully.

Ebryn, hands full with the shopping bags and his cup of coffee, shoved Aether with his shoulder.

The other Avari laughed. "Hey, be careful! I'm carrying our muffins."

Ebryn glared at the paper bag. Was it worth it? No, it wasn't. He wanted that muffin. "Then don't say stupid things."

"It's not stupid! I mean it! Hey, no, don't–" Aether jumped away as Ebryn's eyes narrowed. "I'm *complimenting* you!"

"Only technically." He took a sip of his coffee – it had plenty of sugar, wonderful – and glanced around, but no one seemed to be paying attention. The streets weren't terribly busy as the weather continued to worsen, and it was mostly Avari in this area anyway. Already, the pavement in some areas was dull concrete instead of lester. They'd have to look out for icy patches.

They subsided into silence again as they walked, each lost in their own thoughts as they drank their coffee. Ebryn mourned that the coffee never seemed to last as long as he wanted it to.

It didn't take long to reach the little hole in the wall they called their own. It had probably been an office at some point, but now it acted as an apartment building for a number of Avari. Large sections of it were caved in, but a few years back Aether and Ebryn had claimed a corner room on the second floor that was mostly intact. They went up the stairs, careful to skip the third and seventh steps, and turned left down the hallway. Aether moved the board that blocked off their little nook for Ebryn to go through and replaced it behind them. The small hallway was littered with traps Ebryn had painstakingly set up; though there was a door into the living area proper, the lock was long gone, and you could never be too careful.

Home.

Ebryn dropped the bags on the pile of blankets that made up the bed and got to work making it far more comfortable with the new blankets while Aether secured the entrance as best he could. Ebryn made a mental note to replace some of the traps in their little hallway; they didn't want their new stuff taken by anyone nosing about.

Later, after everything had been placed and the muffins had been devoured, they settled down to bed. Aether had been right; the old building creaked with the moaning wind as the temperature dropped, but their new nest was comfortable and warm.

"Hey, Ebryn?"

"Mm?" He snuggled under the blankets, determined to sleep comfortably.

"If the name bothers you so much, why don't you change it?"

Ebryn stifled a sigh. It was something he had thought about a lot. "Because it wouldn't matter."

He could almost feel Aether frowning at him in the dark. "What do you mean?"

"People would still call me Ebryn," he explained, tone flat. "It's too late, if there ever even was a chance to do something about it. Maybe my colors damn me no matter what. But, like… if I change my name to, oh, Grentin, do you really think Milo is going to call me that? Or Pryia? Navin?"

Aether was silent for several minutes, before quietly responding, "I would call you it. The kids would call you it. The people who matter would respect it."

Ebryn doubted the kids would ever call him anything but Ebryn. Or Ebby. "There's no point," he reiterated.

"Like, maybe Grentin is a bad choice, but we could workshop it!"

"No."

"Pavin is a good name. Or Frand."

Ebryn draped an arm over his eyes. "For the love of the Three, please stop."

"Maybe something with an 'S'? Or a 'J', that's a good letter."

"Aether," Ebryn ground out. "Drop it."

"It would be a declaration, if nothing else," Aether pointed out. "People who never knew you as Ebryn wouldn't think anything of it. Set a foundation, you know? You always have to be looking towards the future."

Ebryn peeked out from under his arm as the wind groaned through the building, low and haunting. He could just barely see Aether on his back next to him in the dark, holding up his key and looking at it. It was an old, mostly worn brass key that looked like it had once belonged to someone's house, but where or whose neither of them knew. Aether had had it for years, always kept it on a string around his neck. He clung to it like it was a magical talisman of his own.

Ebryn blinked both eyes open and said fondly, "I don't think that particular key is ever going to do much of anything anymore." An old argument.

Aether whacked him. "That's not the point, and you know it! It's *symbolic*. One day... one day we'll have a door we can lock." A beat. "We're going to make it one day!"

Ebryn closed his eyes again. "Mmhm."

"And it's fine if you don't want to be *Ebryn*, is my point." Aether continued. "You can be whoever you want. It'll be a new beginning!"

Ebryn wanted it to be true, but he didn't have Aether's optimism. He just wanted somewhere safe, where they could live in obscurity and not have to worry about food every day. They didn't need anyone else – they had each other. Maybe they should try to leave the city, see if life was better elsewhere. Maybe they could find a way to live in a little house in the middle of nowhere where no one could bother them.

No. Best to stick to what they knew. Safer that way, too.

Still, it was nice to dream.

They woke to the sound of a large crash.

"That was close," Ebryn said grimly as they shot up from the nest of blankets. The room was still dim, but bits of dawn were seeping in through the cracks in the walls. The morning air was chilly, and he shivered.

"Why is everything 'close' recently?" Aether complained, staring in the direction of the sound. His hand fidgeted above his key.

Ebryn shrugged.

Aether sighed. "All right then, let's see if there's anything we can do."

"There's definitely stuff we can do; the better question is 'should we do it?'" Ebryn mused, keeping an eye on Aether for his reaction.

"Oh for the love of– *yes*, we are going to help; the question was rhetorical!" Aether stomped a foot and flicked his braid over his shoulder, scowling at Ebryn.

He ducked his head to hide his smile. Aether was very easy to rile up in the mornings.

Ebryn's stomach growled as they left their building, earning him an amused glance from Aether. The rain had stopped overnight, but everything still glistened wetly. He allowed a fleeting wish for breakfast before reining those thoughts in. Any food would have to wait for later, no matter how much the air smelled... like...

"That's not just me smelling that, right?" Aether asked, eyebrows furrowed as he sniffed at the air.

"No... it's..." Ebryn trailed off, and they both came to the same realization together.

Fire.

They broke into a sprint. Other Avari were running as well, some towards and some away.

They rounded a corner to see that one of the smaller buildings was on fire and had partially caved in. A few Avari were sitting or lying nearby, covered with soot. Some were coughing, others were still. A number of people were already at the scene and were trying to put the fire out, but Ebryn could hear the sirens in the distance.

Even the government took fire seriously in Blackfields.

Knowing there wasn't anything they could do until the fire was out, Ebryn and Aether scaled a building across the street and waited on the roof, watching the other building burn. Ebryn tried not to look at the Avari who had been saved, though he could hear the crying of several from his perch.

Aether was surveying the scene, lips pressed together tightly. As the water trucks arrived, he turned to Ebryn. "Why don't you go and acquire some bandages and shit? Maybe that cream that's good for burns if you think you can manage it?"

Ebryn considered. There was a clinic on the edge of Greenmeadow with a shop that was small enough not to be too busy but large enough that it should carry what they needed. He wouldn't be able to take a lot working on his own, but anything was better than nothing. "I'll see about disinfectant, too."

"Great. Once those guys leave" – Aether indicated the water trucks, which were now hosing down the building – "I'll see about trying to organize everyone into groups. We'll need some people to scavenge and see if anything is salvageable, some to help the injured, food..." He considered the scene down below. "Yeah, I'll probably send you back out with five or six others to see about trying to feed everyone."

"Wait 'till tomorrow to–"

He was interrupted by the scream of metal giving out, and they watched in horror as one of the adjacent buildings began to shift sideways.

"Oh, that's... that's really bad," Aether said, horror in his voice.

Ebryn frowned as the water trucks began to pull back. They wouldn't let themselves get caught in a building collapse. "It's not just that one." He pointed to the building on the other side. It was swaying too. "The whole block might come down at this rate."

People down below were screaming as they tried to get clear, and Ebryn noticed a gaggle of short figures with brightly colored hair escape the building on the right – some colors he recognized.

Not all of them were moving on their own.

He bumped his shoulder into Aether's as he stood, indicating the kids with a tilt of his head.

"Hm? Oh." Aether scrambled to his feet as Ebryn swung down to street level. "Hey, wait for me!"

Ebryn was already jogging to the group, who were huddled together across the street from the building they had dropped from. "Hey," he called as he got closer, and was rewarded with several dirty, tear-streaked faces turning in his direction. "Come on, you need to go somewhere else." He eyed the buildings with concern; the sounds of twisting metal continued to grow in frequency as they swayed back and forth.

One of the littles threw himself at Ebryn's legs as Aether caught up. "Ebby!" the little boy sobbed, and Ebryn awkwardly patted his dirty blue hair. "Brina's still in there!"

Silver eyes met gold as Ebryn and Aether shared a grim look.

"She pushed us all out of the den," one of the other children explained, voice hiccupping. "But then a beam dropped down and separated us. She told us to go without her."

The building rocked again, and from inside, the terrified scream of a young girl.

Ebryn bit off a curse.

"Get the kids somewhere safe," Aether said firmly, taking a step towards the building. "I'll see if I can–"

"No!" Ebryn interrupted, a sick feeling forming in the pit of his stomach as his ears flattened. Aether couldn't go in there; the whole thing looked like it could come down at any moment. "That's not–"

He was interrupted by another scream from inside the building.

Ebryn shook his head at the determined look on Aether's face. There was only one way Aether wouldn't go into that building. "I'll go. You get the kids to safety."

Aether stared at him. "What?"

He couldn't shake the feeling of dread, but he didn't see any other way. "I'm faster than you, and better at navigating dangerous places. You should start rounding some of the others up into setting up a first-aid station. Maybe in..." he glanced down the street, trying to decide, and noticed the perfect spot. "Over there, where the blue-and-white-striped awning is? There's a large empty space in there that would be perfect for taking care of the injured." He was talking fast, aware time was running out. He untangled himself from the little boy. "I'll be back in a minute!"

And then he was off, darting across the rapidly emptying street as other Avari rushed out of harm's way, trying to escape the doom that was coming.

Ebryn went in.

Immediately he wondered why the hell the kids had waited so long to flee. Smoke from the fire next door rolled thick through the building, and he mentally noted that the fire might have actually hopped to this building without the water trucks suppressing it. Crouching down, he called out, "Brina!" before covering his mouth and nose with his arm. If she didn't answer–

"Here!"

The call was weak and was followed by coughing, but it gave Ebryn a direction. It was difficult to see, but she hadn't sounded too far. Definitely on this floor. He had maybe minutes; maybe less. Even through the smoke he could see the pillars move in an unnatural way, and he could hear the building groan as it tried to hold on.

It needed to hold on just long enough.

He jumped to the left as a piece of the ceiling came down, and scurried in the direction of Brina's voice. It was beginning to get difficult to breathe, but he could hear her crying now, and he held onto that as a lifeline. A moment later he almost crashed into concrete, crumbled and in pieces with rebar sticking out, but there, on the other side, he saw a flash of lime green through the smoke.

Brina.

"Hey!" he snapped, aware they had no time as the entire floor began to shift under their feet. The way the concrete had fallen... "Can you climb over?"

"Ebryn?" came the whimper from the other side. "I... my ankle..." She broke off into pained wheezing.

Okay then. "Can you come here? Closer, at least?" The pillar was only at about chest height for him; if he could grab her he could pull her over.

Her small figure stumbled through the haze, collapsing on the floor against the other side of the pillar. He reached over and down, but she was just out of reach, even if he strained. "Brina, I need you to work with me here!"

She coughed again and forced herself up. Ebryn wanted to scream at her to move faster, but he knew that wouldn't help.

His hands met skin.

He gripped her tightly and pulled with all his might, ignoring her shriek as the rebar cut a gash in her arm. Better injured than dead.

He could hear another building coming down somewhere close by. The one on the other side? It didn't matter; they were out of time as the floor shifted beneath them again, almost knocking Ebryn off his feet. He regained his balance and picked Brina up, hurtling towards the exit as the ceiling began to cave in above them.

He dashed out into the hazy sunlight and didn't stop running, well aware he needed as much distance as he could get between them and the destruction. He could hear the building coming down behind them, could feel the air being expelled from the demolished structure as the dust and debris almost overtook them.

But then they were clear.

He held Brina tight as he took a moment to catch his breath, refusing to turn around. If he didn't see it, he didn't have to confront what had just almost happened. He just needed a minute to gather himself. It was okay. He had made it.

He had even saved Brina!

The little girl was still wheezing in his arms, but they were safe. It would be okay now.

Ebryn wiped soot and dust from his face, blinking as he finally took in his surroundings. Avari were rushing about, but he noticed with some confusion that they were... hauling debris out of... yet another building?

He noticed Milo leaning against a nearby wall, sweating and breathing heavily. "Hey," he called, dragging himself over. "What's going on?" He scanned for periwinkle hair. Where was the awning he remembered directing Aether to?

Milo turned to look at him and went pale, ears flattening. "Ebryn! Where have you been?"

"Getting Brina," Ebryn answered tiredly, as the girl coughed against his shoulder. "Where are we putting the injured?"

Milo cringed. "That building, but..." He looked down at the ground. "As we were getting everyone set in there, the ceiling caved in."

Ebryn stared at him. "What the hell?" Was the whole district going to collapse today?

"Yeah, it's... uh... it's pretty bad." The other Avari shifted, still not looking at him. "Um, Ebryn... maybe..." Milo trailed off into incoherent mumbling.

Ebryn decided to ignore him. People were clearing the rubble of the new catastrophe, then. Though... how many people had been in the building when the ceiling gave out? Milo had said the injured had been in there. That wasn't good.

He caught a glimpse of the inside–

Oh, yeah. It was bad.

Where was Aether? Usually he was trying to run these things.

Aether... had been going to set this up.

Ebryn felt his blood run cold.

He caught a flash of blue hair, and looked over to where the group of kids were gathered in a little circle out of the way. He started to hurry over, but paused as Brina tugged at his arm.

"Ebby…" she gasped, and he was alarmed to see how pale she was beneath the soot. "I… I can't…"

She was struggling to breathe, he realized. He looked around, beginning to panic, and was relieved to see a flash of emerald hair. "Pryia!" he called.

Maybe it was the desperation in his voice, but the pink-eyed Avari came over immediately, ears trembling with unease. "Ebryn? There's–"

"It's Brina," he said quickly, turning so Pryia could see her face. Pryia was good at helping people. "She's having trouble… breathing…" He trailed off with horror as the little girl's eyes fluttered shut as she gasped for air.

He saw the look on Pryia's face, and he knew.

"Bring her over here," Pryia suggested gently, drawing them both off to the side. Ebryn looked around desperately; where was Aether? Aether would know how to deal with this.

He couldn't… he couldn't do this alone.

He tried to stroke Brina's back comfortingly as the girl gasped, trying to get more air.

Pryia eyed Ebryn carefully for a moment, then took Brina's face in her hands, resting her forehead against the little girl's. "It's okay," he heard her whisper. "It'll be over in a moment. We are with you."

Brina wheezed once more, then went still.

Ebryn felt tears threaten to spill over as he put the body down gently on the ground.

He hadn't saved her.

He tried to force the emotions clogging his throat back and managed to choke out, "Where's Aether?"

Pryia closed Brina's eyes gently, then took a deep breath and straightened up. In a steady voice she said, "We lost nine people when the ceiling collapsed. Aether was one of them."

He stared at her. Those words didn't make sense. "What?"

Pink eyes met silver. "He's gone, Ebryn. I'm sorry."

Gone? Aether couldn't be gone. Not when he *needed* Aether.

That building should have been safe. He'd told Aether to...

He found himself standing in the building, other Avari trying to move the pieces of ceiling and whatever had been on the floor above that had smashed into the people below. He looked around, trying to find–

There.

Periwinkle hair among the rubble.

Then he was on his knees, trying to get this debris out of the way–

"Ebryn!" Pryia's hand was on his arm.

He shook her off without looking.

"Ebryn... he's gone. They're... they're all gone. There's nothing you can do anymore."

But of course he was gone. Everyone left eventually. Ebryn knew that. Hadn't he been telling the kids just... yesterday? When he'd told them to look out for themselves first and foremost?

If Brina had listened, maybe she'd still be alive.

If he and Aether had just walked away, Aether would be alive.

There was so much blood. From the cuts caused by the debris. And from the... Aether wasn't supposed to get hurt. Ebryn had always managed to sa– to pull him away.

Dull brass glinted against a chest that wasn't moving, that wasn't shaped right anymore. Ebryn reached forward and tugged gently. The cord it was on snapped, and he stared at the key in his palm.

A bell started ringing outside. Warning.

"There's been too much death here. The Seekers are coming; we need to go!"

Seekers... Aether had always said that the one thing they needed to do above all else was avoid Seekers.

He gripped the key tightly in his fist, and he left.

Days passed, and so did nights.

It was raining again, a cold drizzle against a gray October sky, blanketing a gray city, but Ebryn just felt numb. People who were gone didn't return, no matter how much one might wish. So, there was no point in wishing. He was on his own now.

Ebryn drifted through Lyndiniam, munching on a stolen pastry. What was he going to do without...?

He should have known better. Hell, he *had* known better, he'd just chosen to ignore the truth. And now... now he was going to have to figure out... everything.

Because he was alone.

There was no one to rely on, and there never should have been. Everyone left eventually. There was no denying that. He'd ignored his own lesson. Now he was going to pay for it.

Winter would be long and miserable. Actually, so would spring, probably. And summer. Fall too, come to think of it.

He glanced over the Humans traveling the sidewalk with him, but he couldn't bring himself to case them seriously. His mind was not interested in doing much of anything right now. He just wanted to be sad.

But he couldn't afford to be sad. He had to keep working because otherwise he wouldn't be eating, and that would only make everything worse. He still needed a coat of some sort for the upcoming season too; he'd have to manage a decent score soon.

His ears sank as he shuffled along, trying to savor what taste of butter and cream from the pastry he had left, ignoring the pain in his throat when he swallowed. It felt like knives.

"Watch it!"

Ebryn sidestepped reflexively out of the woman's way, but found himself staring after her as she breezed by him. That dress was *stupidly* fancy, some sort of white silk and gemstone monstrosity. What the hell?

His eyebrows scrunched together as he watched her. She was going into a large building, matte stone facade instead of the usual shimmery lester and glass.

The Silver Ring Casino.

Now that he was paying attention, something different was happening. There were a number of Humans dressed in fancy clothes heading in. All of them screamed wealth.

Oh, right. The annual autumn party for the obnoxiously rich.

Ebryn shook his head, ears sinking even lower as he passed by. He was so far from that life he might as well be in Dalmara. Or maybe the Emerald Shore.

But what he wouldn't give to have even a small fraction of that much money. Even just a little would go a long way.

Maybe things could be easier again. And this time, he'd have done it on his own. No reliance on others who could be gone at any moment. Just him.

He didn't need anyone. And no one needed him.

He tightly gripped the worn key hanging from his neck, and in the back of his mind, a plan began to form.

White

S he was herself, and then...

She was still herself, but different. Less, but the same. Too much magic in too small a space; contained, but willingly. Ander's work was holding.

How strange. Was this what mortals felt like all the time? Confined to one small space? This was not her first time in a physical form, but it was her first time in one not of her own making. This one did not allow her to breathe *through* it the way the ones she'd created out of magic had. It was... uncomfortable.

"Lady?"

Hades opened her eyes.

Everything was... dimmer than she was used to. The plain white ceiling above her did not have lines of colorful magic running through it, and even the color of the ceiling itself seemed less than what it should be. She turned her head slowly to the side, new muscles protesting at the movement, and saw Ander leaning against a desk, arms crossed. She could feel him – he was patiently waiting for her to settle into this new body – but he looked so very different to her, dull and muted.

Except for the green of his eyes. That was correct, and it soothed her to see. She blinked – sometimes mortals did that to clear their vision – but nothing changed. Still, only Ander's eyes looked right.

Sounds were also... not what she expected. She could still hear the World Sound, but it was distant, a whisper instead of a song. She could not hear Ander's heartbeat, even though he was only a few feet away from where she lay on the metal table. This realization saddened her, but then...

She reached *down*, into the core of herself that had always been and always would be. Life came back to her vision, and the World Song sang. And there were her beloved priests, here and there, scattered across the world with her shards beside them. There were several Valkyrie nearby, watching in interest, and the wargs had amassed themselves near her temple. Thousands of lives in the city around her, and then millions as she spiraled out, then billions. She could not be truly contained. She was the second to have existed, and though she would wear this body for a time, it could not change what she was.

Ander frowned. "Whatever you are doing, stop," he said sharply, pushing himself forward from the desk and coming over to her, taking her chin in his hand and forcing her eyes to meet his. "You are going to burn out your retinas, and it's going to be obnoxious to fix that."

Obediently she let her senses fade back to those of a mortal, secure in the knowledge she could still reach for her own if she wished to. An odd feeling danced across her skin, and she realized – cold. She could not feel the warmth from the distant stars in this body. For a moment, it made her feel horribly alone, but...

She gathered herself and sat up slowly. She brought her new arms up, pausing for just a moment to inspect them – smooth, pale skin that had never seen sun or weather – then brought them around Ander's body in an awkward hug. He was warm, magic humming just beneath the surface. She laid her head on his chest, and... yes, there. His heartbeat.

She snuggled in contentment.

He stared down at her, and she could feel his uncertainty. "Is this necessary?" he asked after a moment.

She hummed in agreement, blinking in surprise at the feeling of her vocal cords vibrating in her throat. That was strange. What would speaking be like? Or singing?

She took a moment to take stock of the body. It was breathing the mortal way without her input, though she found she could control it if she thought about it. There was an unfamiliar feeling in her chest she realized was her own heart beating. Her mouth was wet, and she swallowed instinctively. She could wiggle her fingers and toes after thinking about it for a moment, flex different muscles, though it was far more difficult than simply *moving* as she could in a body of her own creation. Unfortunate, that the world could not support such a construct at this time. But Ander had done an incredible job creating this container for her.

It made her feel closer to Alexia, in a way.

Well, almost. Hades wiggled her ears. Alexia had been Human, not Avari.

But still. Hades smiled, feeling a warmth in her chest. There was the gentle hum of Ander's magic deep in this body as well, magic he'd used to create it. She held it close, pleased with the feeling. The body was magic in the same way all mortals were, just not in the way *she* normally was.

And in the end, some discomfort was to be expected. She wasn't doing this for herself, she was doing it for *them*. Abomination was growing in the world; she could feel it. The people of the world needed help. And she was willing to do what she could, even if her siblings would think this completely insane.

"You seem to be moving slowly. Are you doing that on purpose, or is something wrong?" Ander asked finally. "It would be nice to be able to examine you."

Reluctantly, she let go. She opened her mouth to speak, but only a croak came out. She frowned.

Fingers glowing green found her throat, and she could feel the array as her vocal cords were prodded by magic. "They're just new," Ander reassured her. "Sometimes it takes a moment to get them going again if you've been silent for too long. Try again."

There was a thick feeling in her throat, and she coughed weakly, trying to get rid of it. "I..." The sound was rough, and not at all what she associated with herself, but Ander nodded encouragingly and she tried again. "I feel... strange." She paused, but it was getting easier. "New. Everything... is new." The sounds she made were evening out to what she had expected. "This is fascinating."

"Does anything hurt?" Ander was studying her intently.

She shook her head slowly. "No. I'm just... getting used to it, I think."

"Okay. Would you like to try standing, or do you need more time to acclimate?"

She considered the question, wiggling her toes again. Slowly, she pulled her knees up to her chest, trying to analyze the movement. "Everything in this body takes so much more... *work*. Is that normal?"

Her priest's head tilted slightly to the side. "I'm unsure which benchmark you usually would use, but moving for mortals is not an overly difficult action most of the time. It can be, especially after long periods of disuse or injury. While I did my best to stimulate the muscles before you inhabited the body, a short adjustment period is to be expected. I anticipate it will get easier over time. But nothing hurts?"

She didn't think so, comparing how she felt now to how some of her priests had felt in moments of injury. "No. It is uncomfortable to be in such a small space, but nothing... hurts."

"Excellent." He took a step back and gestured in the air, the green of his magic sketching an array between them, circles of glyphs spinning lazily as he studied her through them. She stayed still; that was a much more thorough scan than he normally performed, but then he had made this body completely from scratch. It made sense he would want as much data on how it was functioning as possible. She let her eyes fall on the glass prism on the desk behind him as she waited, but she could not see it break the light apart in this body.

After a moment he dismissed the array. "Very well then. Everything seems to be working as expected from my end, though if you think something feels wrong, please let me know. I know we went over everything you will need to do to care for the avatar already, but now that you are inhabiting it, we should start some of the more practical applications."

"Like eating?" She felt her ears shift up with her excitement at the prospect. She had consumed food and drink when she had taken a mortal form before, but she was interested to see how different it would feel and taste in this body.

He nodded. "Yes, that is certainly on the list, considering that body runs on food, *not* magic. It will tell you if you forget."

Yes, her priests had been hungry before. She thought she would recognize the feeling if it came. She intended to try all manner of foods while she had the chance. And though Ander was somewhat notorious for cutting back on both food and sleep himself, she chose not to point that out.

Carefully, she rotated herself to the side and let her legs hang down over the edge of the table. There was a brush of something soft against her back, and she realized it was her hair. She pulled some of it over her shoulder, marveling at the feeling beneath her hands, the white color familiar and comforting.

There had been a time when the shape and look of her form would not have mattered to her, but she had mirrored this one for so long that it would be sacrilege – and a violation of her oath – to take another. She found herself stroking the silky strands.

Ander came closer, and she could feel his concern that she would try to stand without help.

"So many new sensations," she mused.

"Do you not feel things? Either as a god, or when you took a mortal form in the past?" He was curious. She loved that about him – his desire to know, to understand.

She considered the question, uncertain how to answer in a way that would make sense to one who had only ever experienced such a body. "I do, but it is not the same. The emphasis is different, is on magic. The physicality of everything is so much... less important. It feels more immediate in this body, demanding my attention."

He hummed softly in agreement. "I suppose it makes sense since you aren't really a physical being, though you are able to interact with those that are."

"Magic is... everything. Physicality is just what is... laid on top of it, I suppose." She'd never really thought about it before. She just was, had always been. Trying to label it meant nothing in the long run, but then, mortals did so love their labels. She could not fault them for trying to understand it in their terms.

"Interesting."

She could feel his mind turning the concept over, studying it from different angles, and it made her smile, fighting back the desire to go and lean against him and hear his heartbeat again. She turned her attention back to her new body instead. It had a surprising amount of weight to it, which she had not expected, but which was becoming familiar to her the longer she inhabited it. She had a feeling it would make walking... interesting.

A Valkyrie fluttered closer, and Hades smiled. Though she could not see it without her true sight, she was pleased that she could still hear and feel the little spirit's presence as it settled on her shoulder. It was curious, and concerned – why was she making herself less? Was she being trapped again?

She sent a gentle wave of reassurance. This was temporary. And not all of herself was contained – shards of herself were still out there, connected at a single thought. The order of things would not be affected by this experiment.

Pleased, the Valkyrie drifted off.

She closed her eyes as a wave of exhaustion washed over her. That she knew, though the physical sensations that went with it were unfamiliar.

"It may take some time to build your strength up to where it should be," Ander admitted. "The body is new, and it needs rest."

"I remember," she said, frowning in disappointment. "I just started using it, though."

"It will get easier the longer you inhabit it." He guided her back to lying on the table. "Rest for a few hours. We will try again later."

She didn't want to, but it was becoming difficult to keep her eyes open. Strange, that the avatar was able to tell her what to do! "If you think it is best." She felt a soft blanket being draped over her.

"I do," he said dryly.

She could not sleep the way mortals did. Instead, she drifted for a bit, still tethered to the body but closer to her normal state of being, basking in the feel of magic and many mortal minds all around her. Lives came into existence, and lives ended, a cycle that had persisted since the beginning. She reveled in the order of it.

And somewhere out there, that order was threatened. A stain on existence itself, growing in strength. Crackles of Abomination disrupting the World Sound, popping up in too many places. She could sense its presence, and yet its very nature confused her, made it difficult to actually locate. The form it had taken was not like the summoning of demons it had favored since the cataclysm. This was something new, something... she had just barely been able to glimpse at the moment of Ebryn's second death, but it had a feeling of being incomplete.

This battle would be very, very difficult.

But she was determined to see it through.

Alexia's sacrifice would not be in vain.

Hades sat up.

The body felt refreshed, and she realized it too had cycles – just much shorter ones than she was used to. That was fine. She could work with that.

The room was dark. Ander had been called away to the hospital for an emergency consultation and was focused on that for the moment.

:Stay in my office,: he sent curtly at the touch of her mind against his. *:This won't take too much longer.:*

She considered watching him work, but the feel of a large furry body against hers drew her attention. Three wargs had found their way into Ander's office in his absence. Two were curled up under the table. The third was pressed right up against her, radiating warmth. She knew them, in the way she knew all wargs, and they knew her. All three tails began to wag.

"Hello!" Pleased and amused, she wondered how they had gotten in. While he would never dream of forbidding the wargs access to the Temple, Ander hated wargs in his office and went to great efforts to keep them out.

The dark-gray one lying with her licked her face, greeting her back, and she marveled at the feel of that rough, slimy tongue on her skin. The black one put his paws up on the table behind her to sniff at her neck.

The gold one sat with her head resting on the table, more patient than her brothers. Was the Lady okay? She had sat up without noticing them, but sometimes pups woke up disoriented, and this body was like a pup body, wasn't it?

It was certainly *new*, the black warg agreed, continuing to sniff intently. It smelled like pups did. But it was not the right size for two-feet pups. Those were small!

"Ander made this body for me, yes," Hades agreed, reaching down to pet the gold warg's head. "I suppose it is similar to a pup. I haven't even left this table yet."

Immediately all three scrambled to gather on the other side of the room.

The gray one snorted. They taught pups to walk every spring; they could help the Lady!

Yes, they would not let her fall, the gold one agreed.

Hades felt her ears twitch as she carefully swung herself around on the table so she was sitting with her legs over the side.

The black warg gave a supportive tail wag. The Lady should put the blanket aside; it looked like she could get caught in it.

Hades looked down at the faded green blanket Ander had covered her with. It did seem wrapped around her in a somewhat hazardous way now that she'd moved. Carefully she pulled at it until it was free, then she attempted to fold it. Unfortunately, while her control of this body was getting much better, folding the blanket as neatly as she would have liked did seem to require more coordination than what she had at the moment. She placed it in a partially folded, partially balled-up bundle next to her on the table and turned her attention back to the wargs, who were watching her intently.

She considered her situation. Her feet were not touching the floor, so she was going to have to drop the extra foot or so without damaging the body. She inched herself forward, stretching down with her feet to minimize the gap, and tried to prepare to support herself with her arms.

Her arms were not ready, giving in like a fledgling presented with fresh blood as soon as the table was no longer supporting her weight.

Like a flash, the gold warg moved beneath the Lady so she did not fall. It was okay, she had new legs. And new arms. New limbs needed a little time before they could be relied on!

Her gray brother sneezed. This was why pups were usually close to the ground. The Lady had long legs; that would make this more difficult than it needed to be. And she only had two of them.

Hades chuckled awkwardly, practically sitting on the gold warg with her arms twisted up behind her, palms still on the table. There was a sting in the bottom of her feet traveling up to her knees from when she'd hit the ground, which Ander would surely not approve of, but it was fading quickly. Nothing seemed to be damaged thanks to the warg's quick reflexes.

Hades frowned, ears sinking. Standing was proving to be a challenge, never mind walking.

But she had decided she was going to do this. She could not share the secrets of the dead, but... there was some wiggle room for her, personally, to act on those secrets as long as she did not share them with the living.

And an Avari had died thinking of Ebryn almost a year and a half ago in Lyndiniam.

But as she half-lay on the warg, trying to figure out how to rebalance herself without damaging this surprisingly fragile and heavy body, she found herself wondering how she was going to convince them to let her take it into the Empire if walking was this difficult for her. She brought one hand down to tangle in the warg's fur as she wobbled again.

Ebryn had never seemed so far away.

The black warg woofed softly. The Lady could do it!

The gray one agreed. She just needed a minute to gather herself and try again.

And the Lady was not as heavy as she seemed to think she was, the gold one reassured her. She could carry the Lady easily if necessary.

Hades smiled, taking the comfort and support her sacred creatures offered her. There really were no better beings in existence than her wargs. Firilae had outdone herself with them.

Then she focused and pushed herself up and onto her legs.

Her weight pitched too far to the left and she stumbled, reaching out for balance, but she managed to catch herself without the wargs' help. They gave tail wags of encouragement, mouths open in wolfish grins, and she slowly rightened herself until she was standing in a natural position.

"Excellent," she whispered, taking a moment to catch her breath. Step one down, a million more to go. She could feel her heart beating quickly and wondered why.

The gold warg stood just out of her reach. Walking for two-feet was really more like controlled falling.

Hades nodded. That made sense. She was more concerned about whether her legs would support her, though the longer she stood, the better she felt about it. Rather than learning, it felt more like her body needed to *remember* what to do, even though it had never done it before. She wondered if that was something Ander had done, or if it was a result of her having done these things in other bodies before.

That was a question for Ander later. Now, she had to walk.

She hummed a song to herself, one from a children's cartoon from a world long gone about putting one foot in front of the other, letting the tune strengthen and guide her. The hum of the World Sound shifted to match her as it usually did, and she smiled. Then she took a small step forward.

Her legs held.

She took another, wobbling just a bit when her weight transferred entirely to one leg, but she recovered quickly. It felt... okay. She took another step, continuing to hum, and was pleased to find it getting easier.

The wargs howled in triumph, answered by numerous other warg voices from somewhere outside Ander's office.

Hades laughed, managing the last few steps to where the brothers were waiting with only one small wobble. She reached down to scratch their ears in thanks for their support as their sister joined them.

The black one licked her. Would the Lady like to see the others? Everyone was very curious. Well, not everyone. Some thought this was just a way for the two-feet to see her, and since the wargs already saw her, there was no reason for excitement. But many were curious!

And she would be with them! Surely tall-white priest could not object to that! The gray warg circled around behind her, brushing up against her but careful not to push and strain her newfound balance.

She grinned, delighted. "I would *love* to see the others!"

They all turned their attention to the door, and Hades carefully made her way over. She reached out and touched the handle, feeling the cool, smooth metal in her palm. The door opened easily.

The wargs flowed past her into the entrance hallway of her temple. The stairwell to her priests' apartments was just a few steps away, and she shuddered at the thought of having to master stairs so soon after walking. Those could wait. To her left, the hallway opened up into the main sanctuary, and the cool breeze caressed her bare skin, likely from the courtyard on the other side. Ander usually left the back door open for the wargs.

She turned her attention to the right, where the main door to the Temple was slightly propped open. The wargs were already ahead of her, pushing open the heavy door with no trouble. Bright sunlight streamed in, and she found herself squinting, struggling as her eyes tried to adjust to the light. No wonder her children disliked the sun; this was terrible. She had never had to deal with all of these little inconveniences in any of the bodies she'd made for herself. She stepped forward over the threshold as the wargs prodded her forward.

"*No!*"

A dark shape materialized in front of her, and unbridled joy rose in her chest. "Vlad!" She hurled herself at her son, wrapping her arms around him.

And if it was more of a fall off the front steps of the Temple, then probably only the wargs noticed.

Her most precious son caught her and scooped her up, draping his cape over her as he brought her back inside. "Mother..." he trailed off, sounding pained.

"Isn't this so exciting? It's been ages since we've been together." She pressed herself against his chest; though he lacked a heartbeat she could still feel the magic in him. She sighed in contentment.

He said nothing, turning to carry her up the stairs to the apartments.

She frowned. Was he not happy to see her? She could not read him like she could her priests, but... it had been millennia since she'd held him in her arms. Surely he wanted to see her again without the aid of a mirror? They could touch like this; that was amazing! "What's wrong?" She glanced over his shoulder at the three warg siblings now following them up the stairs.

They were also puzzled at the Lady's son's reaction. Why could she not go outside? All the others were waiting!

Vlad shifted to open the door at the top of the stairs with one hand and sighed as the wargs slid in around him.

Hades' eyes were drawn by Ander's fish tank, the blue water and colored fish looking almost as bright as she had expected them to. She could feel the echoes of Mara's magic in the tank, and she smiled at the expression of love. She had the best priests!

Vlad put her down on one of the couches next to the fish, leaving her with his cloak. She was surprised to see him covering his eyes with one hand as he took a step back. "Mother... did Ander not give you clothing?"

She blinked, looking down at herself.

Oops.

Mortals did tend to get a little caught up on that. She should have remembered.

But then, usually the water elementals took care of her clothing so she didn't *have* to think about it. She focused herself a smidge, searching the surrounding area, and realized that the elementals were chittering angrily at her too. Hmm. She'd have to get used to dressing herself again; they could not dress a physical form the way they did her normal one. It would be hard to even take advice from them.

The gold warg huffed. Two-feet cared too much about all the wrong things.

The black one agreed. The Lady was the Lady. Why did the coverings matter so much? There were times in the summer when some two-feet wore about the same amount.

The gray one jumped onto the couch and lay on top of her lap, his bulk hiding the entirety of her front. Problem solved.

Hades reached up to scratch behind his ears thankfully, pulling the cloak around her shoulders and resting her chin on the warg's back as Vlad just slowly shook his head at them, lowering his hand. "I'm not sure what Ander's plans for clothing are," she admitted. "I could ask Mara or Daiyu if they have anything here I could borrow."

"I have to believe that a man who plans things as meticulously as he does did, in fact, prepare clothing for you. Unfortunately, we will have to wait for him to get back to determine what that plan is." He took a seat across from her, red eyes betraying his exasperation.

"I am glad you came, though!" She laughed with delight. "I have been getting used to this avatar. It is different from the bodies I have created before. Did Ander ask you to come and help?"

"I'm here for a few reasons," he said, leaning forward to rest his elbows on his knees, hands steepled in front of his face. "For one, Ander did contact me when it became clear he would be otherwise engaged for longer than anticipated and asked that I ensure you do not do anything... unwise in the new body."

She was absolutely certain Ander had not phrased it like that.

"For two, almost every warg in the city is outside the Temple at the moment. I had to wade through a sea of fur to get here. Even if Ander hadn't told me, I would have been able to guess something unusual was happening here. And for three, they *all* howled at once shortly before you made it outside."

Oh, right. That had probably been unnerving for those on palace grounds.

"They can't all see you at once," he continued. "That would be complete chaos. We might never see you again. We will have to arrange meet-and-greets or something."

She blinked. "Are you suggesting the wargs would kidnap me?"

"It's happened before," he said dryly.

"Well, yes, but to save people from *bad* situations, not... this." Her situation was certainly new and strange, but it wasn't bad. She did not need the wargs to rescue her.

The black warg settled on her feet. The Lady did not need rescuing from her own temple. But if it turned out she *did* need rescuing, wargs would be happy to oblige.

She rubbed her foot against his stomach, a quiet thank you. Her wargs were truly the best of all creatures. "Besides, they do not want to meet me – they want to sniff me."

Vlad just sighed.

She tilted her head to the side. "You seem tired."

"A lot is happening right now," he said with a shrug. "The Gini are being difficult about trade treaties for perhaps the six hundredth time this decade. Dalmara is requesting more political support against the Empire. Two members of the Black Watch have gone missing south of the Wall. The Empire is ever scheming, we just don't know what at the moment – is it connected to the recent grand marriage announcement out of Ni Fon? Who knows. Abomination is definitely somewhere, but no one seems to know where. Is *that* connected to the Empire's scheming? No one knows that, either. Then there's the whole you situation." He gestured at her. "Though don't misunderstand – it is wonderful to have you here with us again. Almost like old times, hmm?"

Though he smiled at her, she could feel his grief for those they had lost long ago. "I am always glad to walk among mortals, but I have missed being close to you, and to the others. I... will go visit the Towers, at some point. Give my love to your siblings."

He closed his eyes, hiding the red welling in them. "Yes, they will like that."

They sat in silence.

Nine days later, Hades found herself wandering the palace late at night. She ghosted through the hallways, purposefully avoiding the people who were up and about. Though she was overjoyed to meet so many face to face, the part of her that normally existed alone was tired, and so she sought solitude.

She found herself on one of the high balconies overlooking Tarvishte. She looked down over the city and could feel the worship coming from here and there. So much less than she'd had in the past, but more than in other eras, and she was always thankful for *any* belief in her.

She smiled as her eyes caught on the soft lavender fabric of her nightgown, itself a relic from times long past. Vlad had kept a chest of her clothing from four thousand years ago, a bit of nostalgia that came in handy when it was revealed Ander had not made any arrangements for clothes. Vlad was having a new wardrobe made, but these would do for now. The pale color reminded her of her own magic in this body, faded and distant unless she risked straining the avatar.

She found her eyes drifting up to where the moon hung full in the sky. She reached out to it, but this body could not touch it, could not stop the sudden chill in the air. Even as she watched, white light bled to red and the sky itself darkened – a blood moon in all its glory. She closed her eyes. Perhaps it had been foolish to believe this avatar would go unnoticed.

He did nothing to hide his presence from her.

"Beloved. What have you let them do to you?" The deep voice crept around her, and though her eyes were closed she could feel shadows gathering. Something stroked her hair.

"I am no beloved of yours, brother," she murmured, a reflexive response after so many ages. She did not wish to entertain him, but...

...he was like her.

"But you are. Always do your domains rule over mine." Kaldor, dark god of the moon and night, laughed softly, and she felt his arms come around her, his sharp chin digging into her shoulder.

"That is not a basis for love," she reminded him. "And why should it matter to you how I choose to spend my time?"

"Oh beloved, do you think we all keep our heads in the sand?" His grip on her tightened. "It is happening again."

She repressed a sigh. "Then you do know why I am doing this."

His head shook against hers. "Why you allow them to mute your beauty into this ugly mortal form? I absolutely do not. Guide them from a position of divinity. This is unnecessary."

She could feel the inky blackness of his magic hover around her, and allowed a fraction of her own power to bleed through. "I see your fear, brother."

Silence.

"You were always so much braver than the rest of us," he finally murmured into her hair. "I see it, even if our siblings do not."

She knew that. "You could help."

He laughed again, but for all its dark menace she could hear the regret beneath. "No I cannot, beloved. What would you have me do? Drop a crystal of my magic somewhere for a new champion of yours to claim? There's not enough magic in the world for that any longer, or you would not have to resort to such measures." Nails raked down her arms roughly. "It is ironic that our salvation *must* come from mortals."

She hummed thoughtfully. Kaldor never lied to her, but that did not mean he was correct. "Must it? Or do we choose to stand back and let them bear the brunt of it?"

"Ah, you are in that sort of mood, I see. Do not be like that, grave sister." She could hear the pout in his voice. "Remember that you are eternal, and they are fleeting. Do not sacrifice yourself for them."

"I do what I do for all. Even for you, Kaldor." She felt a smile twitch at her lips.

He hummed. "Even for Tadurin?"

The smile fell, but... "Yes. Even for him."

His grip around her tightened.

She allowed it for another moment. "You should go. This place is not for you."

His finger found her chin and turned her head, but she kept her eyes firmly closed. "Would you not look upon me, even if only briefly?" A note of hope.

And a thread of fear.

She wished she could roll her eyes. "You only think you want that. You'll regret it as soon as I do."

"But it is what I want *now*, and is that not what matters?" She felt him flow around her to stand in front.

Kaldor would forever be Kaldor. There was no changing that. She gathered herself, even the fragments of her that were elsewhere, and opened her eyes – giving him for one brief moment her complete attention.

The red eyes of the shadowy figure widened in distress, and he tried to flee.

Cruelly, she pinned him in place with a thought. "But while you are here... leave my children alone, Kaldor." She watched him writhe for a moment, then released him. Maybe that would make the warning stick.

His laugh echoed through the night even as he fled, his power fading from her senses as the moon's glow returned to white above.

"Oh, beloved – you know I'll never make you a promise I can't keep."

And then she was alone again.

Well, not fully. "Thank you for not interfering."

"I'm not sure what I could have done." Ander strolled out onto the balcony with his hands in his pockets and looking entirely un-bothered, but she could feel his distress beneath the surface.

The three warg siblings darted in front of him, flowing around her and offering their support. Unlike Ander, they were angry.

Wargs hated Kaldor.

She ran her hands over their fur, allowing their raging belief in her to give her strength. "I would greatly prefer for you to never attempt to challenge one of my siblings. Let me deal with them instead; that is the best course of action."

But we could have tried to bite the shadow-stalker, the gold warg growled.

How dare he stalk in the Lady's territory, the gray one agreed, teeth snapping at nothing in frustration.

The black warg shook himself. How dare he stalk the Lady at all.

She should eat him, the gray one suggested. That would solve the problem.

She smiled. "Nothing is forever."

Ander raised an eyebrow.

She just shook her head, turning to look back up at the moon. "He knows, though."

"Is that bad?"

She considered the question for a moment. "My siblings do not like to acknowledge that which they can ignore. That he would come to me now..." She trailed off.

"Means it's grown enough that he had to acknowledge it?" Ander hazarded, tilting his head to the side.

"Yes."

They stood in silence as the wargs finally settled around her.

"We are running out of time," he said finally.

She nodded. "We are."

The world was ending again.

But all wasn't lost just yet.

Abomination needed to be reminded that everything had an end.

Glossary

Abomination: A malevolent force that has haunted the world since the beginning of time. Taking different forms, it returns again and again, seeking to destroy all life and magic.

Agale: The main province of the Rose Empire. Was originally the country of Agale, but in the time of Queen Saran over a thousand years ago it joined together with Elbe, Hispa, and Gallia to form the Rose Empire.

Ahulowaki: The main Veren city, located underwater near Crescent Island and Marcrae.

Aradian: A race formed by the Faleri. Aradians hail from the eastern desert continent of Falin. They generally have darker or tan skin, pink, orange, or red hair, and eyes that look like flames flickering behind glass. They live for three hundred years, and all are able to magically create fire. They have a matriarchal, warrior culture.

Array: The term used by northern mages to describe the arrangement of glyphs and bridging lines that is used to cast spells.

Avari: A race formed by the Three Goddesses. They have long, pointed ears, brightly colored hair and eyes, and are strongly inclined towards magical ability.

Avhad: The title of the matriarch of a House of Dalmara.

Blackfields: A poor district in Lyndiniam where many of the city's Avari live.

Black Watch, the: A peace-keeping force in Romanii comprised entirely of Vampires.

Bridging Lines: A part of spell crafting; bridging lines connect and balance glyphs in an array so that the spell is able to be cast.

Cartago-Mir: A province of the Rose Empire, south of Agale and on the Patoran continent.

Chatori: The god of tricks, chaos, twilight and stars. One of the Distant Trinity.

Court: The term for a family of Vampires, related by blood turning.

Crescent Island: The eastern-most island in the Nyphoren Islands.

Crystal Lights, the: Powerful magical artifacts created by the elemental deities long ago.

Crystal Light Blade: The sword created by Hades specifically for Ebryn Stormlight after he collected the crystal lights from the various elemental deities. It is meant to destroy Abomination, but will not work for anyone other than Ebryn.

Crystallus Canis: A violet-colored spell crystal in the shape of a running hound; these are gifted by Hades to her priests as a way of marking them as hers. Can be used to store magic for later use.

Dalmara: The main country on the continent of Falin, comprised mostly of Aradians.

Dedicated: The term for those who dedicate themselves to one of Hades's priests.

Demons: The expression of Abomination Ebryn Stormlight fought a thousand years ago with the Aradian Sukra. They are very difficult to kill, but have a weakness to fire.

Distant Trinity, the: Common term for the three gods associated with the celestial bodies. Comprised of Kaldor, Chatori, and Vin.

Edo: The capital of Ni Fon.

Elbe: The easternmost province of the Rose Empire. Was originally the country of Elbe, and chose to join with Agale, Hispa, and Gallia to form the Rose Empire.

Emerald Shores: The southernmost province of the Rose Empire; situated on the continent of Vien.

Espon: The continent named for the Espera. Where the Rose Empire is based, as well as Romanii.

Faleri, the: The elemental twin deities of fire. Their names are Falare and Falera.

Firilae: Goddess of magic, soul, emotion, and trickery. See also: The Three Goddesses.

Fledgling: The name for a new Vampire who is still bound to the Sire.

Gallia: A province of the Rose Empire situated on the western coast of Espon. Was originally the separate countries of Hispa and Gallia, but were combined early on in the Empire's history.

Gini: A race formed by the Espera, the Gini are few in number a live primarily in the norther mountains of Espon. They have six wings, feathered ears, and talons for feet. They value education, learning, art, and divination – many of them are Graeae, and able to see the future.

Glyph: The basic symbols used to create spells. There are over fifty of them, and the way they are combined is what creates the spell's effect.

Hades: The goddess of death, destruction, healing, and rebirth. She is primarily worshiped in Romanii, as she created the Vampires and they see her as their mother. She is also very active in attempting to destroy Abomination. Called "The Silent Goddess" in Ni Fon.

Hemjer: The Aradian word for "priest".

House of Dawn: A House of Dalmara, of which Sukra is a member.

Human: One of the oldest races on Gaia, and the most numerous. Currently ruling the Rose Empire.

Hunt / Hunter: An Aradian tradition in which one is called to perform a great deed and return home with trophy and story. Necessary to gain the official rank of "Warrior", there are a number of positions in Aradian culture that require one to have completed a hunt.

Inherents: A type of magical ability that a person can be born with. Some examples include Master of Blades, Voice magic, and Shadow Walkers.

Kaldor: The god of the dark, night, the moon, and evil. One of the Distant Trinity.

Karnstejn: A town in Romanii in the Carpas Mountains. Where Mircalla's estate is located.

Kilpe: A blue vine with white flowers, grows mostly in underwater caves and moist environments.

Lanarae: Goddess of healing, war, fighting, the body and physicality. See also: The Three Goddesses.

Learned Magic: The type of magic that allows a caster to cast spells; learned magic is so named because one must learn how to use the glyphs and bridging lines in order to successfully cast spells. A caster must still have enough magical ability in order to activate the array. It is the most common magical ability.

Lester: A type of building material popular in the Empire; it can be white, gray, or black and tends to have a sheen to it. It is stronger than concrete and has a longer life-expectancy.

Lokanu: The term for a Veren seer.

Lorn: A large species of lizard made of rock. Commonly found on the Falin continent, they are highly aggressive.

Luminpearls: A type of pearl used by the Veren for lighting due to it's fluorescent nature.

Lyndiniam: The capital of the Rose Empire and Agale.

Maji: The Aradian word for "mage", can also be an official title.

Marcrae: An island in the north-east of the Nyphoren Islands.

Master of Blades: A type of inherent magic most common in Aradians, this ability allows its user to pick up various combat styles by fighting against them.

Memph-Aisan: The capital of Dalmara.

Mer: The name for those who have the inherent magic to be able to breathe underwater.

Montu-Ra: The Aradian name for Lanarae.

Mother-sister: The Aradian term for a sister who shares a mother, but not necessarily a father.

Movorae: A species with skeletal, human-like upper bodies and extremely long eel-like tails. They seem to grow longer the more they age. Usually they live in very deep waters, but occasionally come up to prey on the Veren.

Navodar: A town in Romanii.

Ni Fon: One of the provinces of the Rose Empire, Ni Fon is located across the Shae Sea from the heart of the Empire. Ni Fon was brought into the Empire only about two hundred years ago, and they have no interest in remaining a province. They call their duchess Empress, and they actively seek to break free from the Empire. They are also interested in trying to make magic and tech work together.

Night Children: An older, more formal term for Vampires.

Norik: A town in northern Agale. The Crystal Light Blade was housed in a museum here until three hundred years ago, when it was stolen.

Noror: A country to the east of the Rose Empire.

Nyphoren, the: The elemental twin deities of water, the ocean, and storms. Their names are Nyphora and Nyphore. Created the Veren.

Nyphoren Islands, the: A province of the Rose Empire located in the center of the Shae Sea. They were brought into the Empire almost seven hundred years ago. Originally the home of the Veren, who now live mostly in the deep ocean nearby.

Omega Energy: A spike of energy identified by Alexia's team that happens at the moment of death. Preventing it from reaching a life form can prevent death. Omega-type B is a weaker form of it.

Palace of Dusk: Located in Tarvishte, the seat of power of Romanii. The palace itself has been so steeped in magic over the centuries that it has become somewhat aware, and attempts to help people find their way.

Pattern: The term for an array used by Nifoni mages.

Reaping, the: A last-ditch attempt by Hades to clear the world of Abomination. Done with great sacrifice, the world was forever changed because of it.

Romanii: A country in the north of Espon. Ruled by Vampires, when they saw what the Rose Empire was becoming five hundred years ago, they cut themselves off by creating the Warcross Wall.

(Rose) Empire, the: Created a thousand years ago when the countries of Agale, Hispa, Gallia, and Elbe came together under the rule of Queen Saran shortly after Ebryn Stormlight ended the threat of Abomination. Originally under Avari rule, it is now ruled by Humans, and consists of seven provinces: Agale, Gallia, Elbe, the Nyphoren Islands, Ni Fon, Cartago-Mir, and Emerald Shores. Each province is ruled by a duke or duchess, who wield the true power of the Empire.

Rose Queen, the: A common way of referring to the young Queen Saran of Agale, who ruled in Ebryn's time and is responsible for the formation of the Rose Empire.

Rot, the: An affliction that affected the world shortly before the Cataclysm, killing all manner of life. A form of Abomination.

Shinobi: A specialized force of mages utilized by Ni Fon. Shinobi candidates are chosen early, and are raised to be shinobi, known for their loyalty to the ruling power of Ni Fon. Wear a mask over the bottom half of their face. Often specialize in stealth.

Sire: The Vampire term for one who has made a fledgling. Referred to by their fledgling as Master or Mistress.

Solar Agis: A spell cast around Vampire cities to protect against the sun; it is complex and difficult to cast.

Soulforging: A type of magic used by Vampires and priests of Hades. Allows the user to manifest their soul in the form of a crystal, which can then be manipulated into powerful weapons or armor.

Spell Crystal: A way to store spells for future use. Anyone can activate a spell crystal, one does not have to be a mage. A common use is to create a crystal that can warm the bed at night.

Suncoral: a bioluminescent coral that is only lit during the day.

Tadurin: The god of life, chaos, and creation. In theory, equal in power and status to Hades.

Tarvishte: The capital city of Romanii. On the northern coast.

Temple of Night Rising: Temple to the goddess Hades in Tarvishte.

Three Goddesses, the: Common term for the three sister goddesses, often shortened to just "The Three". Comprised of Lanarae, Selenae, and Firilae. Responsible for the creation of the Avari. They have many names across the globe.

Truth Seekers: Specialized, highly trained troops in the Rose Empire. They all wear a blindfold, and use advanced tech. Feared throughout the Empire.

Turning: The term for becoming a Vampire.

Valkyrie: Special death spirits that aid Hades.

Vampire: A member of any race who has died and been bitten by another Vampire to transfer Hades' gift, gaining immortality. Vampires require blood to live, and will burn in the sun until they are well over a thousand years old. Struggle to cross large bodies of water.

Vaslu: Town in Romanii.

Veren: A race formed by the Nyphoren, the Veren are fairly isolationist and live in the coral reefs and underwater caves below the Nyphoren Islands. They tend to be talented in illusion magic and astrology.

Warg: Large, wolf-like creatures sacred to the goddess Hades. Are far more intelligent than normal dogs or wolves.

Warcross Wall, the: A magical barrier that separates Romanii and the Rose Empire. Was created about five hundred years ago in a ritual where nine Romanii mages sacrificed themselves to bring it into being. Each mage became one of the towers along the Wall.

Weave: The Nifoni term for casting spells; also occasionally refers to the spells themselves.

Weiba Port: Port city on the south-west of the Falin continent.

Acknowledgments

Book number three! Even if it is "just" a short story collection... I'm still very excited, especially since these short stories are some of my favorite things I written yet, and as such, I am incredibly grateful to everyone who helped me bring them to all of you.

Thank you:

To Jessy Jacobs, Lydia Troiano, Ashley McKhann, and Bill Millette, who let me feed on their feedback and put up with me asking weird questions at weird times. To Andrew LaFontaine, whose enjoyment excites me and inspires me to write more. To my brother John Sauco, who hates Jamirh but is willing to help me figure out stuff anyway. To Sarah LaFontaine, who keeps coming back to my house for some reason. To the Writing Forge authors for understanding how weird publishing is and being a constant forum of discussion, ideas, and support.

To my editorial team, Breyonna Jordan, Naomi Munts, and Jane Spencer. I apologize for my inability to know the difference between lay and lie, and appreciate your willingness to keep fixing it.

And finally, to my parents, from whom I inherited my love of reading and fantasy, and without whose support this never could have been written.

About the Author

Liz Sauco is an author from Rhode Island who enjoys a host of nerdy pastimes, such as crocheting cute animal plushies and playing video games. After graduation from the University of Rhode Island with a degree in Classics, she spent several years teaching Latin to high school students while working on her first manuscript. You can find her on Facebook, Discord, and Tiktok, and read her blog at lizsauco.com.

Free Short Story

Want to stay up to date on the latest news?

Join my newsletter, and receive a free short story "Another Beginning", set twenty years before *Lost Blades*. Be among the first to get news about new releases, giveaways, events, and promotions!

Want more from the world of Gaia?

Can't get enough? Want to really dive deep into the lore? Check out Campfire, where you can get character profiles, art, maps, timelines, location info, bonus short stories, and more for all of my stories!

But... maybe you are interested in being *spoiled*? Ream is a new subscription platform - like Patreon, but for authors - and having one allows me to spoil readers with tons of extra content! Sneak peeks, art works-in-progress, name in the acknowledgements of books, polls, direct access to me, and more are all offered at different tiers. You can even give me a follow for free to get a monthly update!

Also By Liz Sauco

Colors of Magic is a companion to the Blades of the Goddess series

Blades of the Goddess is a high fantasy, character-driven adventure following Jamirh – a street thief on the run from crimes he both did and did not commit – and Takeshi – a ninja trying to help his country break free from the Empire – and how they both get pulled into an ancient battle between magic, life, and a force that seeks to end existence itself.

Lost Blades
Preview

"Hey! Look at me!"

A voice cut through the surrounding haze where nothing else had. He tried to focus on it.

"Come on. You can do it."

He was trying, but he couldn't focus on the voice long enough to figure out where the sound was coming from.

"Damn; they hit you pretty badly, huh?"

He couldn't even lift his head from where it rested on his chest, a position he wasn't entirely sure how he had gotten into. He thought he heard a sigh.

"Look at me."

A musical ring, almost like bells echoing, entered the voice, and he felt compelled to lift his head until he met violet eyes.

"Ah, that's it."

Immediately his head cleared and most of the pain faded, allowing him to focus on where he was.

He appeared to be in a cage, with dark metal bars and harsh lighting. It was just big enough for him, a small lumpy cot, and a waste disposal unit. The room holding the cage was gray and bare; it had only one door, with a sophisticated electronic lock, and no windows.

Wonderful. He was in jail.

There were seven other cages in the room, but only the one across from him was occupied. An Avari woman with long white hair tied up in a ponytail and curious violet eyes had somehow hooked her legs through the bars that crossed the top of her cage and was hanging upside down, long ears twitching happily. Her all-black clothing fit tightly to her body; it looked nothing like any of the local fashions. There were no guards in sight.

Then again, he was in the middle of a security station in the heart of the Empire. Of course they would have only the latest technology to keep lawbreakers in their nice cozy cages. No extra guards were required; every move they made was most likely being monitored and watched carefully for any hint of escape. Probably by more tech programmed to look for such things so no one would have to do such a dull and boring job.

She waved at him.

He stared at the woman blankly, unsure what to make of her. She was looking at him intently, but the effect was somewhat diminished by her position.

She looked ridiculous.

Then she smiled, ears perking up happily as she saw that she had his attention. "Welcome back to the land of the living," she said cheerfully. "It seems like they really don't like you, the way they just threw you in there like a sack of bricks. Are you feeling any better now?"

He ignored her, feeling his own ears drop slightly in annoyance, and brought a hand up to rub his eyes. He was not feeling quite up to speaking yet, and especially not with some weird person hanging upside down in a jail cell.

He felt a sudden spike of panic, and his hand darted down to his ankle. He touched metal and sucked in a breath in relief; his key was still tied there.

The woman seemed to take his movement as an affirmative and began to swing herself from side to side silently for a few minutes as he tried to get the last of his headache to go away. "So... what are you in here for?" she asked finally, interest clear in her voice.

He raised his eyebrows and sighed, shaking his head and letting his gaze sweep over the room again, not that there was much to look at. He didn't feel up to dealing with eccentric strangers right now. He shivered as a cold draft worked its way by him; his coat was gone. His new, warm, comfy, gray coat. It was probably considered evidence for the stolen chips, he figured glumly. Or they had wanted to make him suffer a little. Either option was a possibility.

He sighed and picked himself up off the floor to sit on the cot. It felt even lumpier than it looked, but it was better than the floor. At least everything was dry and looked clean – that was even an improvement over his normal living arrangements, where filth was practically a method of interior decorating, and the weather affected the inside of structures only marginally less than the outside. Even the fabric covering the cot was of a higher quality than he was used to.

"Well?"

He looked over at his chatty neighbor in annoyance, realizing that she was still waiting for an answer. Part of him wondered absently if she just didn't like silence. "Do you really want to know?" His voice was a little rough, but at least it didn't waver or slur. Better than he had hoped for after such a hit to the head. For that matter, he was surprised that his short ponytail was still mostly in place, just a few ruby-colored strands escaping their tie.

Her eyes widened, violet meeting silver, and she nodded earnestly at him.

He sighed again and cast his thoughts back to earlier in the day, before everything had gone to hell.

www.ingramcontent.com/pod-product-compliance
Lightning Source LLC
Chambersburg PA
CBHW022014310726
48972CB00006B/1650